A MESSAGE FROM CHICKEN HOUSE

Vi blew my socks off in her first whirlwind adventure (ouch, those piranhas!) and now my favourite junior undercover agent is back – making a hash of spy school, fending off threats to world peace (again), and trying to make sense of those pesky parents. Fabulous author Maz Evans is funny and thoughtful with the best puns *in the world*!

BARRY CUNNINGHAM
Publisher
Chicken House

Maz Evans

VI SPY

NEVER SAY WHATEVER AGAIN

Chicken House

2 Palmer Street, Frome, Somerset BA11 1DS
www.chickenhousebooks.com

Text © Mary Evans 2022
Illustrations © Jez Tuya 2022

First published in Great Britain in 2022
Chicken House
2 Palmer Street
Frome, Somerset BA11 1DS
United Kingdom
www.chickenhousebooks.com

Chicken House/Scholastic Ireland, 89E Lagan Road, Dublin Industrial Estate,
Glasnevin, Dublin D11 HP5F, Republic of Ireland

Cover and interior design by Steve Wells and Helen Crawford-White
Cover and interior illustrations by Jez Tuya
Typeset by Dorchester Typesetting Group Ltd
Printed and bound in Great Britain by CPI Group (UK) Ltd, Croydon, CR0 4YY

FSC
www.fsc.org

MIX
Paper from
responsible sources
FSC® C020471

1 3 5 7 9 10 8 6 4 2

British Library Cataloguing in Publication data available.

PB ISBN 978-1-911490-74-6
eISBN 978-1-913696-44-3

For Johnny B.
My top agent.
My techie.
My love.
21221

And for Dilly. The original Missy Fit.

xxx

Also by
MAZ EVANS:

Who Let the Gods Out?
Simply the Quest
Beyond the Odyssey
Against All Gods

Vi Spy - Licence to Chill

You smell lovely . . .

CHAPTER 1

'Agent Day . . . Agent Day . . . VI! You have . . . five minutes and twenty-three seconds! That ship is going to blow, repeat, the ship is gonna blow! Transmitting route to hostage containment facility and optimum exit strategy for immediate evacuation! You have to get those children out of there!'

Vi listened to her technician, Tamina, plead through her earpiece as Doomsday Dan jumped on a jet-ski and blasted across the ocean. The notorious super-villain now had the codes to the nation's nuclear arsenal. He could destroy the whole world. Doomsday Dan had to be stopped. And Valentine Day was the agent to do it.

'Agent Day!' Tamina barked in her ear. 'Have requested urgent back-up for pursuit of target! Three ally agents within two kilometres! Your mission objective is to save the hostages! There are twenty children locked in the cargo bay, transmitting coordinates! Do you copy? Agent Day! Do you copy?!'

Vi could hear the urgency in Tamina's voice. Her techie was brilliant at running the numbers, analysing the threat, finding an exit strategy.

But she wasn't in the field. Vi was. And she was going to catch Doomsday Dan.

'Negative,' she announced into her mic, running towards a jet-ski at the end of the jetty. 'Engaging in pursuit. Target within range. Mission parameters unchanged – detain villain and save hostages. We need a win.'

'You can't win if you're dead!' Tamina shouted. 'Repeat, support incoming from ally agents! Your mission is to save the children!'

'I know my mission,' Vi growled, leaping deftly aboard the jet-ski. She could see Doomsday Dan just ahead – Vi could do this. Vi wanted to do this. And after her last few disastrous missions, Vi needed to do this.

'Abort, abort, abort!' Tamina screamed in her ear. 'Agent Day, you are not authorized for pursuit! New mission objective is to save the hostages!

DO YOU COPY?'

Vi winced. Her techie was loud when she was excited. Vi ripped her earpiece out and threw it in the water.

'No, I don't copy,' she said, revving up her jet-ski. 'Valentine Day leads . . .'

Vi smiled. She'd been waiting to use that line.

She yanked back her jet-ski handle and it roared off underneath her, skipping across the choppy waves, the warship shrinking in her rear-view mirror. Vi bent over the handlebars and gritted her teeth. She was going to stop Dooms-day Dan. *And* she was going to save the hostages. Vi was going to save the world. All by herself.

She watched her target grow on the horizon. She was gaining on Dan. Vi reached for her Eye-Spy watch on her left wrist and set it to one o'clock: *tranquillize*. She needed to bring this one back alive – Doomsday Dan knew a lot that could help SPIDER foil future threats to world safety. With her right hand steadying the jet-ski, she held up her Eye-Spy on her left, framing her target between the cross hairs on the watch face.

OUT OF RANGE.

Her display flashed the inconvenient warning.

Vi cursed – she had to get closer. Yanking back on the handle, she drove her jet-ski harder, her legs clinging to it as the surging waves threatened to unseat her. The warship was just a speck behind her now. She was further out than she realized. Vi needed to be quick if she was going to save those kids.

She raised her Eye-Spy again, her heart lurching as a big wave lashed her jet-ski and threatened her balance. The cross hairs found their mark . . .

TARGET IN RANGE.

'Yes!' hissed Vi, holding her jet-ski as firmly as she could with her legs. Now all she had to do was squeeze the button on the side of her Eye-Spy and—

VROOOOOOOM!

With a tidal wave of a turn, Doomsday Dan suddenly jerked his jet-ski around. The splash was so immense it took a second for Vi to see what was happening. But as the wave subsided, the situation became worryingly clear.

Doomsday Dan was heading straight for Vi.

Vi tried to line up her target in the cross hairs again. But this villain was no fool. Dan swerved his jet-ski from side to side, making it impossible to get a lock on his position. Vi could feel her heart rate rising as Doomsday Dan got nearer and the warship further away. She looked at her watch. There were less than two minutes. She was running out of time.

'It's OK,' she reassured herself, bitterly regretting leaving Tamina on the jetty. She could really use one of her techie's cool exit strategies right now. 'I've got this.'

She raised her Eye-Spy and fired a wild shot, guided more by false hope than true aim. Doomsday Dan dodged it with ease, now close enough for Vi to hear his laughter ripple across the water. He reached inside his jacket. Her heart was racing. It hadn't occurred to her he might be armed – what if he . . .

But it wasn't a gun he produced.

It was a detonator.

'VALENTINE DAY!' he shouted, circling her. She fired another hopeful shot, which was just as unsuccessful as the first – and apparently just as funny.

'Come quietly!' she called, trying to keep the tremble out of her voice. 'And you won't be harmed!'

The roar of laughter was matched only by the roar of the jet-ski as Doomsday Dan gleefully whizzed past her.

'You should have saved those poor children,' he gloated.

'I WILL save those poor children,' said Vi unconvincingly, trying not to glance at the diminishing numbers on her watch. She had under a minute. How was she going to get out of this and back to those kids?

'I don't know about you,' said the villain. 'But I can't bear dragging these things out. Watching a timer tick down to zero, it's just so . . . clichéd.'

Vi's panicking mind randomly turned to her father, Robert. He loved a ticking clock. She could do with him being here now. He used to be a super-villain. He'd know what to do.

'So let's not,' said Doomsday Dan. 'Let's just give it a quick three . . . two . . . one . . .' He slammed his thumb down on the detonator.

'NOOOOOOOOO!' screamed Vi.

She turned to face the warship, although the sickening explosion told her everything. The debris from the ship flew across the ocean. Those poor children. She'd failed them. She'd failed her mission. She'd failed herself.

Again.

The villain circled her like a maniacal shark.

'Oooops!' he cackled, reaching into his jacket.

Vi could feel anger burning in her stomach. She was going to avenge those children. She was going to get those codes. She was going to save the world ...

Doomsday Dan produced a large gun from his jacket and aimed it straight at her.

Vi felt her breath catch.

She was going to die.

'Better luck next time, Valentine Day,' grinned the villain. 'But for now, your mission is over ...'

Vi closed her eyes. She knew all too well what was coming.

BANG!

Vi recoiled as the device around her upper body smacked her hard in the chest. If these simulation vests were anything to go by, she hoped she never actually did take a bullet. It didn't matter how many times she got virtually shot – and there had been many over the past year – it always really, really hurt.

She yanked off her virtual reality mask and tried to gather some breath in her winded body. The screen in front of her flickered off its ocean view and returned to green for the next Recruit's simulation. The actor playing Doomsday Dan grabbed a coffee.

Vi dismounted the Multi-Vec, the mock 'jet-ski' she'd been riding, and couldn't resist giving it a swift kick. The same piece of equipment, a kind of high-tech gym horse that served as whatever you needed in a simulated mission, had failed her in every single assessment. In her last one, the Multi-Vec had been a car she'd driven to pursue a jewel thief – she'd ended up driving it into the River Thames. The one before, it had been a motorbike she rode to foil a plot to bomb the Welsh Parliament building – she'd ridden it off a cliff near Penarth. She'd hoped that making the Multi-Vec a jet-ski would bring her better luck. But she was wrong. Vi was wrong a lot these days. And it didn't get any easier each time.

She looked over at Tamina in the tech booth, who gave her a wave and a cheeky grin. At least

Tam wasn't disappointed in her. But Vi knew someone who would be . . .

'Agent Day. Agent Shalli. Please report to Ms Direction for debriefing,' came a stern voice over the intercom.

Vi groaned. She'd been 'debriefed' too many times this year to feel more positive. Vi had been so excited about getting into Rimmington Hall, it had never occurred to her that she'd be anything but brilliant when she got there. After all, she came from a long line of successful spies, she'd already proven herself against a super-villain when she defeated Umbra last year, she . . . she just thought she'd be really good at this.

But no matter how hard she tried to prove she was the best, something kept going wrong. She should be a natural. So why was she finding this so hard?

Vi trudged out of the virtual reality simulator and along the corridor towards Ms Direction's imposing wooden office door. Tamina was already outside, tying her long, dark brown hair back from her smiling light brown face. Her mischievous blue eyes turned to Vi and she grinned.

'Hey,' Vi began to the friend she'd made on her

first day at Rimmington Hall. The friend who, now they had nearly finished their first year, was still her only friend at Rimmington Hall. 'Look, I know you disagreed with me back there, but you have to understand that . . .'

'You're in field and I'm not,' said Tamina breezily, offering Vi a sugared almond. 'Don't stress. You know I couldn't care less. If we get kicked out, you're doing me a favour.'

'I know,' said Vi quietly, declining the sweet. She wished she didn't care either. But unlike her friend, Vi was desperate to stay at Rimmington Hall. Spying was her destiny.

Wasn't it?

'Enter!' came the clear instruction from inside. Vi felt her innards wobble. This was not going to be fun.

They both held their faces up to the facial recognition scanner.

'*Agent Shalli, Tamina. Agent Day, Valentine,*' it intoned. '*Access granted.*'

The large mahogany door clicked open to reveal Ms Direction's beautiful old-fashioned office. Around the sumptuously carpeted room, portraits of previous head teachers of Rimmington Hall adorned the wood-panelled walls, with Ms Direction's own picture suspended above her large oak desk. The portrait wasn't a recent one — Ms Direction's brown face had a few more lines and her black hair a few more streaks of grey than her painting these days. But her determined brown eyes had lost none of their intensity. An intensity Vi tried to avoid by looking around the office, although she already knew every inch. In the past year, she'd spent plenty of time inside it.

Vi reached for a chair.

'Agent Day,' Ms Direction said in her clipped tone. 'You have not been invited to sit.'

Vi silently reprimanded herself. She always forgot that. She looked over at Tamina and mirrored her correct pose, feet slightly apart, hands crossed behind her back.

'Agent Shalli,' Ms Direction began, lifting her eyes from the screen on her desk and turning them to Tamina. 'How do you feel your mock assessment went?'

Tamina took a slow breath. Vi figured she was trying to find words that weren't too rude.

'Agent Day faced a tough call,' she began. 'She's the field agent and in her estimation, there was enough time to achieve both mission objectives, so she—'

'Your loyalty is admirable,' Ms Direction interrupted, 'if misguided. You analysed the data well and correctly reassessed a rapidly evolving situation. Were it not for the outcome, you would be on target for an A-plus . . .'

'. . . but given how epically we tanked, you have no choice but to fail me and throw me out of Rimmington Hall. I get it,' said Tamina casually. 'No biggie.'

'But, given the results,' Ms Direction spoke over her, 'the best I can award you is a C-minus. We both know you are capable of better, Agent Shalli. I look forward to you demonstrating it next week.'

'Thank you, Ms Direction,' said Tamina, looking miserable at her pass grade. Vi doubted she was about to be so lucky.

'And, Agent Day,' said Ms Direction, turning her cool gaze on Vi. 'How do you explain the absolute failure of your mission?'

'I made a call,' said Vi, trying to sound confident. 'I decided—'

'—against the sound advice of your technician,

who has boundless data at her disposal and whose job it is to change the parameters accordingly? Remember: surveillance, then action.'

'Well . . . yes . . . but with respect, Tamina – Agent Shalli – isn't the one in the field.'

'More's the pity,' sighed Ms Direction, turning her eyes back to the screen before turning the monitor towards them. 'Agent Bhatt has just freed all twenty hostages while his colleagues apprehended Doomsday Dan. *He* listened to his technician, Agent Sprout.'

Vi rolled her eyes. Oh, good. Another win for Russell. Like he needed it.

'The fact remains, Agent Day,' Ms Direction said, 'that your place at Rimmington Hall depends on you passing your end-of-year assessment next Friday.'

Vi shuffled her feet. She was painfully aware of that. After all, she'd failed all the others. This was her last chance. But she wasn't going without a fight.

'I understand that, Ms Direction,' she said. 'But while I've not totally aced these tests, I do have proven experience in the field. I mean, I saved the world from Umbra and the Neurotrol last year . . .'

'And where is Umbra now?' Ms Direction asked, removing her glasses.

'I . . . we . . . no one knows,' Vi muttered in frustration. Since their showdown at Norton Power Station, Umbra had retreated to the shadows. No one had heard anything from the super-villain for nearly a year. 'But if I could spend less time doing assessments and more time doing actual field work, then I know I could—'

'Your performance today demonstrates precisely why you are not ready for the field, Agent Day,' said Ms Direction at an uncomfortable volume. 'And until you learn to listen and work as part of a team, you will never be ready. Failing your assessment will cost your place at Rimmington Hall. Failing a mission will cost innocent people their lives. Thus our school motto – *non est optio deficere.*'

'Failure is not an option,' sighed Vi. If failure wasn't an option at Rimmington Hall, why did she keep picking it? No. Valentine Day was going to be a great spy. Whatever her assessments said . . .

That was it! She didn't need some stupid school assessment to prove herself – they were for kids. No, Vi needed a real mission in the real world. That was the true test of a great spy. If she aced that, there was no way Rimmington Hall could fail her.

'Your grade is an F,' said Ms Direction, failing her immediately. 'You are certainly consistent, Agent Day. I'll see you both in the Great Hall for assembly later. Agents dismissed.'

Vi wanted to say more, but a warning glance from Tamina made her think better of it. They walked out of the office, just as Russell and Adi Bhatt came towards it, saluting each other with a high five.

'Hey, Vi,' grinned Russell. 'How did you do?'

'Great,' smiled Vi falsely. 'Ms Direction had a ... really strong response to my performance.'

'Nice one,' said Russell, as Ms Direction commanded him to enter. 'See you in assembly.'

'Whatever,' grumbled Vi, watching her nearly-stepbrother practically skip into the office. Russell Sprout had spent a lot of time in Ms Direction's office that year too. The head teacher must have been running out of commendations to give him. Vi trudged off down the corridor.

'Cheer up,' smiled Tamina. 'It's only a mock, it doesn't count – unfortunately. Maybe if I fail the end-of-year assessment I can actually get out of here. Even if my dad would put me on eBay. That's if he could figure out how to use it. Philosophy professors are great at the mysteries of the human condition. Less good at the mysteries of the internet.'

Vi grunted. Her mum would probably buy her an actual jet-ski if Vi got a C−. It would be by far the best grade she'd achieved at Rimmington Hall. Mum would go mad at Vi for failing again − Easter Day had been a top student during her time at the spy school, as Vi's teachers never tired of reminding her. But thankfully, Vi's mum was super-preoccupied with her wedding to Russell's dad tomorrow. Vi could get away with it. For now.

'What have you got next?' Tamina asked.

'PE,' Vi groaned. What on earth climbing ropes and ladders had to do with being a spy, she didn't know. But she sucked at that too.

'I've got advanced analytics,' Tamina sighed. 'Save you a seat in assembly?'

'Can't wait,' grumbled Vi, the sound of an exploding warship still ringing in her ears.

CHAPTER 2

Fridays always ended the same way at Rimmington Hall, with an end-of-week assembly before the students were returned to their families for the weekend in blacked-out vehicles. Because Rimmington Hall was . . . well, actually, Vi still didn't really know where it was, so secret was its location. She knew it always looked like a stately home on the outside and sometimes felt like a prison on the inside. All students boarded during the week. The school said this was for security reasons. But Vi had come to suspect that being forced to spend the week eating 'healthy' school food was in fact preparation to withstand torture.

Vi was running late after she'd been forced to do a totally pointless extra rope climb in PE by her totally pointless teacher, Mr Repp. The Great

Hall – a grand, high-ceilinged, wood-beamed space – was therefore already full of her schoolmates by the time she arrived. Tamina was waving at the front, where the first years, the Recruits, always sat. Behind them were the second-year Cadets, then the third-, fourth- and fifth-year Junior Agents. If you were still at Rimmington Hall at the end of year five, you applied to spy agencies to train for the field. You specialized as a field agent or a technician – Vi had known immediately that the field was for her, just as Russell and Tamina instinctively knew that they were techies. Vi couldn't help but notice how few Junior Agents there were compared to Recruits – not half as many. Rimmington Hall only kept the best. With a silent pledge, Vi vowed she would be one of the students who made it to the back of that hall.

Vi made her way down the plushly carpeted aisle towards her friend. She passed under the gaze of the portraits of previous students of note, smiling as she always did at young Easter's picture as Head Girl. Vi always knew that spying was tough, but after a year of Rimmington Hall, Vi had a whole new appreciation for how hard her mum must have worked to become a super-spy. Easter had recently returned to SPIDER, the agency for whom she used to work, and Vi was glad. Easter Day, AKA Agent Lynx, had defeated Umbra before. With the super-villain on the loose, SPIDER would need her. Besides, with Vi away all week, her mum needed something else to focus on. And reviving her career was massively preferable to Easter expanding her experimental fusion cuisine.

Vi reached the row where Tamina had saved two seats.

'I thought Russell might need somewhere to sit,' she said, looking around the hall and offering Vi another sugared almond.

'I think Russell's just fine,' said Vi, taking one – Tamina always had the best snacks – and gesturing to where Russell was already sitting, surrounded by laughing friends as usual. It turned out that at spy school, Russell's top techie skills had won him an army of friends and he was one of the most popular Recruits in their year. In fact, other than their weekly trips home, Vi barely saw Russell any more – she had a growing suspicion that he was embarrassed by their connection. Much as she didn't like it, she couldn't really blame him – she'd been exactly the same at their last school, where he'd been the geeky outcast and his dad, George, had been their teacher.

'What goes around comes around,' her nan, Independence Day, always told her. Vi's had certainly come around at Rimmington Hall. And it had knocked her flat on her butt.

'Urgh, I'm just not getting the hits,' moaned Tamina, looking at her phone. 'Have you seen my new fundraising page?'

Tamina was an ardent environmentalist and she always had some campaign on the go. She pulled her latest project up on her phone and Vi squinted at the picture of something that looked like a slimy pencil with legs.

'It's an olm,' Tamina explained. 'It's a blind Slovenian amphibian that lives in deep underwater caves.'

'I can see why,' said Vi, squinting at the ugly worm. Tamina loved an obscure species. Apparently she'd once raised £3.56 to save the dodo, before she discovered it had died out in 1681.

'It's under threat!' said Tamina passionately. 'This is why I need to get out of here and study something useful if I'm going to help! I don't care what my dad says, I don't give a stuff about being the first spy in my family! The damage we're doing to our oceans is poisoning so many natural habitats! The olm are being hunted to the point of extinction!'

'Who'd want to hunt an olm?' Vi asked. 'That has to be one of the least attractive creatures I've ever seen. And I live with Russell . . .'

'There's nothing wrong with being different,' Tamina pronounced. 'And there's nothing wrong with Russell. I admire anything that stands out from the crowd.'

Vi smiled as Tamina looked over at Russell, who'd apparently just said the most hilarious thing his friends had ever heard. Tamina was one of the few kids Vi knew who genuinely didn't care what anyone else thought. And surely the only one who had a not-so-secret crush on Russell Sprout.

'That olm's more likely to be attacked by a crowd,' Vi muttered. 'But you've already raised 73p, so that's good.'

'I put it in myself,' said Tamina sheepishly. 'I thought it might encourage more donations.'

'Well, put me down for 73p too,' said Vi. 'Save the olm!'

'What's an olm?' trilled a high voice behind them. 'It sounds like something you'd use to clean the toilet!'

Tamina rolled her eyes to the predictable chorus of giggles as Vi turned around to face Jenny Stellar, the top Recruit in their year. Jenny was the latest in a long dynasty of Stellar spies, all of whom had excelled at Rimmington Hall and many of whom were smugly grinning down from the portraits on the wall. Like her ancestors, Jenny's perfect red hair framed her perfect white face atop her perfect . . . everything. She was pretty, she was popular and everyone followed her like sheep. Everyone, except Vi and Tamina.

'It's a blind Slovenian cave dweller,' Tamina declared. 'From the genus: Mind Your Own Business.'

'Gracious! Well, it's not the saddest thing I've seen in here today,' Jenny smiled. When Vi first joined Rimmington Hall, she'd thought Jenny was really nice – until Tamina pointed out that there was always something unkind lurking just beneath every sentence Agent Stellar uttered.

'She's like a triatoma – a "kissing bug",' Tamina had explained. 'Painless at the time, but hours later, you realize you've been stung.'

'Aw – a fundraiser,' simpered Jenny. 'That's so . . . adorable.'

'At least we're doing something good for the planet,' said Tamina, who truly hated Jenny's guts. 'Look at all that plastic you're carrying. Have you any idea what that does in landfill?'

'This is the latest line of BRAT stationery,' Jenny sang, waving a scented plastic pencil case that was filled with a miniature pinball machine. BRAT stationery was huge at Rimmington Hall, just as it was in every other school in the country. 'It's what all the coolest kids are using. No wonder you haven't heard of it . . . But as for our environment, you could improve it by . . . just leaving?'

'You could improve it by . . . just shutting your mouth?' Tamina mimicked. 'All that hot air you release ain't helping global warming.'

Vi laughed. And made a mental note not to show Tam her new BRAT slap band.

Jenny looked more than ready for something else to come out of her mouth, but was interrupted by

Ms Direction calling for attention on the stage.

'Agents,' she said. 'Good afternoon.'

'*Non est optio deficere*,' the hall chanted back. Vi rolled her eyes and settled into her chair. Failure might not be optional at Rimmington Hall, but she wished these assemblies were. She was desperate to get home for the weekend – Easter had been planning her rearranged wedding to George for a year and Vi was actually looking forward to this one.

'A few administrative matters to start,' Ms Direction announced. 'Dr Scott?'

Vi's psychology professor stepped forward, removing the pipe he never actually smoked from his mouth. He adjusted the gold, round glasses that sat like windows on his black, bald head. Dr Scott dressed like someone from an old novel, always in a tweed suit with a different-coloured bow tie. He took a deep breath and waggled his pipe at his audience.

'I knew from the lingering scent of pampas grass, carried on a gentle north-easterly breeze, that I was dealing with someone of Slovakian descent on their grandmother's side, who was wearing blue underpants and a suspicious smile,' he began. 'Only someone born on a Wednesday with a mild gluten intolerance would think to behave thus, leading me to the conclusion that they once owned a pet gerbil. Probably called Hilda.'

He returned the pipe to his mouth with a satisfied nod.

'Dr Scott?' Ms Direction prompted. 'Your announcement?'

'Ah, yes,' Dr Scott said quickly. 'Please don't pee on the floor in the gents. It's unsanitary. And gross.'

Vi smiled. At least spy school had more interesting admin than her last school.

'Thank you, Dr Scott,' Ms Direction continued. 'Secondly, due to the unfortunate incident in the auditorium last week – which reminds me, will Bomb Defusal Club please restrict their activities to the designated areas? – we will have to limit tickets to one per student for your graduation ceremonies here in the Great Hall next week. Please let our office manager, Mr Poyntment, know the name of your one guest when you return after the weekend.'

Vi groaned inwardly. One ticket? Both of her parents were planning to come. And now she had to choose one. There were some problems that only kids whose parents weren't together understood. 'Together' parents would decide who would go, the kid would have nothing to do with it and life would carry on. 'Not Together' parents like Vi's would make her choose a parent and then start lobbing grenades. Actually, that might just be Vi's parents. But who should she pick? The mum who had always been there for her? Or the dad who had missed out on so much already? Things had been fairly chill between her parents for the past few months. But this was sure to heat them right back up again.

'And now to today's main event,' Ms Direction continued. 'Our Recruits will be sitting their first end-of-year assessment next week in order to retain their place at Rimmington Hall. As is our tradition, field agents will choose their technicians according to their ranking in today's mock.'

'I hope you choose me,' whispered Tamina. 'I love working with you.'

'Says the girl who wants to get kicked out,' Vi whispered back, wiggling her eyebrows. 'You know I'm your best chance of getting out of here.'

'Maybe,' grinned Tamina. 'But it would be a

really fun exit strategy . . .'

Vi squirmed in her seat. She'd been dreading this conversation.

'Thing is, Tam,' she whispered awkwardly, 'I kinda promised Russell that I'd be his partner when we first got here. He was worried about being really unpopular and made me swear to work with him, or he'd tell my mum what I really think of her jerk haggis surprise.'

'I don't think you need to worry,' said Tamina, looking over at Russell whispering excitedly with his mates.

'You haven't tried my mum's cooking,' scoffed Vi.

'No – I mean about Russell's popularity,' said Tamina. 'But I understand. Blood is thicker than water.'

'Although not as thick as me,' Vi sulked. 'I've got zero chance in this assessment, with or without you.'

'And so,' said Ms Direction, shooting Vi and Tamina a warning look, 'I invite the top-scoring Recruit to come up here and select her technician. Agent Stellar – please come to the stage.'

Jenny stood up, pretended to be shocked, then

worked her way down the row, banging into the back of both Vi and Tamina's heads as she passed. She glided to the stage, flicking her already-perfect hair perfectly into its perfect place as she went.

'*Trip, trip, trip*,' Tamina chanted under her breath as Vi stifled a snort.

'Agent Stellar,' Ms Direction smiled. 'You have the privilege of first choice of technician for your assessment. It is an important decision and you will require their agreement. So use it wisely.'

'Oh, gosh,' simpered Jenny, putting her perfectly manicured fingers to her mouth. 'This is just so . . . unexpected. I haven't had a chance to give it a moment's thought. If only I'd had time to extensively research each techie's grades and analyse our personal compatibility.'

Tamina made a slightly too loud retching noise, earning her a look from Jenny.

'But, of course,' Jenny said sweetly, 'there are some techies that it's easy not to choose. I need a techie who's going to save *my* life, not a blind Slovenian cave dweller's!'

The hall erupted in laughter as Tamina silently fumed. Vi watched as Jenny did a half-decent job of looking embarrassed while lapping up the attention.

'The name, Agent Stellar?' Ms Direction prompted with a sigh.

'Oh, well, if I have to choose someone, I'm going to say . . .' Jenny squeezed her eyes and fists shut and jiggled around.

'Get on with it,' Tamina said slightly too loudly again.

'I'm going to choose . . . RUSSELL SPROUT!' Jenny squealed, pointing at Vi's nearly-stepbrother.

Vi looked over at Russell, who was being roundly congratulated for this great honour. He looked simultaneously like he'd won the lottery and forgotten to put his trousers on.

'Agent Sprout?' Ms Direction asked Russell as he stood. 'Do you accept this mission?'

'Oh, this is going to be hilarious!' Vi whispered gleefully. 'Russell's working with me! He's going to turn Jenny down in front of the whole school! This will be so humiliating for—'

'YES!' shouted Russell, now the colour of a squished triatoma. 'I accept!'

'Wh-what?' Vi spluttered. Russell had made this huge deal last year about them being a family and sticking together. But the moment Jenny Stellar clicked her fingers, he was going running?

The hall cheered as Russell bumbled on to the stage to greet his partner.

'Are you OK?' Tamina asked Vi, her eyes searing into Vi's.

'*Pfffft* – whatever,' said Vi, doing her best impression of not caring.

'Well . . . I'd still love to work with you,' grinned Tamina. 'If you'll have me.'

Vi tried to ignore the enthusiastic cheers in the hall as Jenny and Russell beamed from the stage. She turned to her loyal friend and smiled.

'Agent Shalli? It will be my proud honour to get you kicked out of Rimmington Hall.'

CHAPTER 3

'**Y**ou are *so* lucky,' moaned Vi in the back of the blacked-out car. She and Russell were on their way to Autumn Leaves, the retirement home that housed both Vi's nan and the Silver Service division of retired agents to which she belonged. Russell had been looking at his phone the entire journey, and Vi was bored and wanted someone to talk to.

'How do you figure that?' said Russell, answering the hundredth message since they'd left Rimmington Hall. 'Ha! Have you seen this thing on the class WhatsApp group? It's sick . . .'

Vi nodded as if she knew about it, or even that there *was* a class WhatsApp group.

'I mean this end-of-year graduation thing,' Vi said, trying to start the conversation up again. 'I can only choose one parent. You only have one parent to choose from . . .'

'I have *two* parents,' said Russell firmly, finally putting down the phone. 'My mum is just . . . she's just busy with her new business, that's all. Events don't organize themselves . . .'

Vi winced at the big foot she'd just put in it. Russell's mum, Genevieve, was less a parent, more a part-timer. Russell barely heard from her, and when he did it was only to make promises she was bound to break. Lately he'd heard nothing at all from his mother, her new business being the latest in a long line of excuses not to spend time with her son. It was so sad to watch. Whatever faults her parents had – and there were loads – Easter and Robert always put Vi first. Russell didn't even seem to make his mother's to-do list.

Although after he'd just ditched her for the assessment, she was not as sorry as she could be.

'Anyway – won't Dad and Easter be on their honeymoon?' Russell pointed out.

'Good point!' said Vi brightly. Of course! Easter and George would be away – her mum had probably forgotten all about it. So that meant her dad could come without any drama. Problem solved. Phew.

'Ha!' said Russell, laughing at his phone. 'Jenny just sent me this epic link . . .'

'I'll probably fail the assessment anyway,' Vi said loudly. 'I mean, it's all about your choice of techie.'

'Tamina's an excellent techie,' said Russell. 'One of the best.'

'One of them,' said Vi pointedly. But if Russell was getting her hint, he wasn't showing it. Vi let it drop. It wasn't worth spoiling the wedding weekend. And after the way she'd treated him at her last school, her moral high ground was a speed bump.

The car pulled up outside Autumn Leaves, where they were spending the night before their parents' wedding. But as they got out of their black car, another was in front of the retirement home. And it wasn't from Rimmington Hall.

'Oh, no. A funeral,' said Russell quietly as the Autumn Leaves residents formed a guard of honour to wave the funeral car away. As it passed, Vi read the floral tribute on top of the coffin.

'Wendy,' she said. 'Oh – Agent Pirate – she was so lovely.'

'And an awesome technician,' said Russell, who, like Vi, had spent a lot of time around the Silver Service over the past year and become very fond of them all. 'That's so sad.'

'Not many spies die peacefully in their sleep,' said a familiar voice behind them. 'But like all great techies, Pirate planned the perfect exit strategy.'

'Nan!' cried Vi, giving her grandmother a big hug, which Russell was quickly invited into.

'Hello, you scamps,' spluttered Nan, suddenly seized by a coughing fit. 'Good to see you.'

The two children backed away as Indy caught her breath.

'Are you OK, Indy?' Russell asked with concern. 'Can I get you some . . . water or . . . something?'

'It's Friday evening,' Nan twinkled. 'You can get me something a lot stronger than that. Come on, you pair. Let's go inside.'

They made their way through the main hallway of Autumn Leaves and into the light, bright recreation room favoured by the elderly residents a) because the light was perfect for dominoes, b) because it was the HQ for their top-secret over-seventies spy operation and c) because it was nearest to the downstairs toilets. With no carers nearby, the room was in spy mode, the wide-screen TV doubling as a computer screen – the place where Wendy had always sat. Vi immediately recognized the cheery pensioner replacing her at the main computer console.

'Hi, Reg!' she grinned. 'How are you doing?'

'I am super, thank you, Valentine – and, hello, Russell,' waved Reg. 'Do you know, I was only talking about you two the other day with Desmond and Felicity.'

'Are they enjoying their cruise?' Russell asked.

'Oh, yes, they're having a marvellous time,' said Reg, pulling a postcard out of his cardigan pocket. 'They just left Tibet – bit of a shorter stop than they'd hoped.'

'That's the trouble with these cruises,' said Indy. 'No sooner are you somewhere, they whisk you off to the next stop.'

'Well, there's that,' said Reg. 'And Felicity caused a bit of a stir at the silent monastery they visited . . .'

Vi smiled as she thought of inventor Desmond and his explosives expert wife, Felicity, who couldn't hear very well – but then again, nor could anyone when Felicity was around.

'Speaking of Tibet,' said Reg, 'my second cousin Derek – you know, Indy, the one with the dodgy pancreas and a bungalow in Luton – went open water swimming last week. At his age! Can you believe it?'

'What's that got to do with Tibet?' Indy asked.

'Oh – he has a jug made in Tibet on his French dresser!' said Reg. 'Small world!'

Indy coughed into her handkerchief. Vi thought she heard a rude word.

'Any updates on Umbra?' Vi asked Reg. 'Anything at all?' Vi had been relying on the Silver Service to keep their hearing aids to the ground since she battled Umbra for the mind-controlling Neurotrol device the year before. She knew it was only a matter of time before Umbra made a move. But so far the evil overlord had been quieter than Felicity's Tibetan monastery.

'Well, it's funny you should ask,' said Reg, turning back to the giant screen. 'There's not been so much as a whisper on the CobWeb. But then this very week, we noted some activity from an old IP address – which reminds me, I've ever such a funny story about my great-niece Beryl in the postal serv-ice – the things she finds in that sorting office . . .'

'Focus, Agent Huntsman!' snapped Indy. 'What did you find?'

'Well, I'm not entirely sure,' said Reg, typing into his keyboard. 'It's a search. For this . . .'

He pulled the page on the screen.

'What's . . . what's a NIDUS?' asked Vi, reading the strange word in the search bar.

'Not a clue,' said Reg, throwing up his hands. 'A bit like my old neighbour's murder mystery night. I must tell you about their new water feature . . .'

'A nidus is where something breeds,' said Russell, pushing his glasses up his freckled nose. 'Like a . . . like a nest.'

'That's weird,' said Vi, trying not to be impressed by the encyclopedic geeky knowledge that Russell had inherited from his father. 'What does Umbra want with a nest?'

'We'll keep an eye on it,' Nan promised. 'Umbra might be quiet. But he—'

'Or she,' Vi pointed out.

'Or they,' Reg chipped in.

'Or she or they – hasn't gone away,' Indy sighed. 'And if Umbra really is hiding at SPIDER, we all need to be on our guard.'

Vi felt the familiar tug of worry in her guts. Her dad had been informed by his government sources that Umbra was most likely posing as one of three SPIDER agents – Walter Toppington, AKA The Cardinal; Isaac Payne, AKA The Wolf, or her own godmother, Honey B, AKA Agent Unicorn. One of them was her mother's mortal enemy, and yet she was working alongside all three of them every day. Should she tell Easter?

'You *cannot* tell your mother,' said Indy, freakishly reading Vi's mind like she so often did. 'It's for her own safety.'

'How can it be safe for her to be with Umbra every day?' Vi insisted.

'Because she doesn't know she is,' Nan insisted. 'And that's her best defence. Besides, you know your mother. When it comes to secrets, she's about as secure as Doris's bloomers . . .'

'Do you mind?' huffed Doris, quietly hitching up her undies as she waited for her turn at dominoes.

'It's for the best,' said Nan, holding Vi's hand. 'And mind you don't say anything to your father about Easter being back at SPIDER either. The less he knows, the better too. We don't want him wading in and ruining everything. The man is a complete idiot.'

Vi sighed. Nan was probably right. Not about her dad, but about keeping Easter's new job from him. Over the past year, Vi had learnt that the less her divorced parents knew about each other, the better. She'd learnt that the hard way when she'd mentioned to her dad about Easter's night braces and he spent the next two months calling her 'train-tracks'. Besides, her mum's job was supposed to be top secret. It still felt wrong, though.

'Come along, you tinkers,' said Nan. 'Let's get you up to the guest room – it's Fajita Friday and there'll be a stampede at dinner.'

She stopped and coughed into her hankie again.

'Nan – are you OK?' Vi asked. 'Have you got a cold?'

'Don't be daft,' scoffed Nan. 'I'm as strong as an ox. I'm spry as a sprite. I'm—'

A huge roar cut her off. The residents – at least those who could hear – jumped in their armchairs and reached for their weapons, from knitting needles to ninja stars.

'What in the name of . . .' Nan muttered as the double doors to the rec room flew open and a flame-covered mobility scooter burst inside.

Perched atop it was an old man. Everyone at Autumn Leaves was old, but he was *really* old. His long white hair hung from his otherwise bald brown head, his eye colour a mystery behind his shaded bifocals. He was mostly dressed in leather, from a waistcoat that hung off his still-broad shoulders down to the loose leather trousers that ended in black biker boots. Although as Vi took a closer look, she saw they were, in fact, black biker slippers. The intruder pulled to a skidding stop right in front of Nan.

'I don't bloomin' believe it!' Nan gasped.

'INDEPENDENCE DAY!' the rider cried. 'I always knew we'd meet again. I just assumed we'd both be dead.'

'You are yanking my . . .' gasped Indy, standing the Silver Service down with a wave of her hand. 'Rod Staff – where in the blazes have you come from?'

'You know me, Indy,' growled Rod in his gruff voice. 'My father was descended from the Navajo. My mother came from a long line of caravan enthusiasts. So I go where the wind blows me. I go where a man can be free. I go where there's perfect insulation from a nuclear blast and sufficient tinned beans to last twenty years. I live each day like it's my last. Because it probably will be.'

Rod winked at Doris, who immediately dropped her dominoes.

Vi tried not to laugh as she looked between Rod and her grandmother. There was clearly history there. Really, really ancient history . . .

Rod switched off his engine and leant over the handlebars of his souped-up mobility scooter. He looked at Indy through the top half of his glasses and smiled. Vi watched Nan get all flustered before shoving her in front of the newcomer.

'Rod – this is my granddaughter, Valentine,' she began. 'And this is her stepbrother, Russell.'

'Hi,' said Vi and Russell together. Rod winked at them and extended a leathery hand.

'You take care, kids,' he said, warmly shaking their hands. 'Don't be afraid. But the world will probably end tomorrow . . .'

'Appreciate the heads-up,' grinned Vi. She liked Rod already.

'Saints preserve us – you're still on that?' Indy shrieked. 'You've been saying the world will end tomorrow for sixty-three years!'

'My days, Indy,' growled Rod. 'You've still got that same sparkle in your eye.'

'Probably me cataracts,' Indy scowled.

'I mean it, Lotus Flower,' Rod insisted. 'You're just as beautiful as the last day I saw you.'

'You mean the day you left me?' said Indy. 'At the altar. At our wedding.'

Vi gasped. She didn't know Nan had been engaged before Grandad. And she wasn't sure Grandad had either.

'I couldn't do it, Indy,' said Rod, looking into the distance. 'Back then, every day felt like our last. Governments hovering over their nuclear buttons. The threat of war in the air. Disgusting food in bags you could boil. But with you by my side, I felt hope – like I could face the unbearable agony of being eviscerated by an extinction-level event. The day I left you felt like the end of the world. One for which I hadn't prepared an adequately reinforced fallout shelter. But I couldn't stand there in good faith and promise you tomorrow. I didn't think any of us had one. We probably still don't.'

'Well, you were out by about sixty-three years,' snapped Nan. 'Not that it matters. My Winston was a better man than you ever were. He won my heart.'

'Maybe then,' growled Rod. 'But now I have something he doesn't.'

'Like what?' Indy scoffed.

'Like a pulse,' Rod replied. 'And at our age, that makes me the winner.'

As Doris fanned herself with a stair-lift brochure, Vi waited for Indy to give it to Rod with both barrels. But before her nan could let rip, something caught Rod's eye on the screen.

'NIDUS?' he said. 'Who wants to know about NIDUS?'

'Umbra, apparently,' said Vi. 'Why, do you know it?'

'Know it?' said Rod, placing a domino on his way past Doris's table. 'I built it.'

'Hey – you can't do that!' said Maud, Doris's partner. 'That's against the rules!'

'Yeah?' growled Rod. 'Well, maybe I don't play by the rules.' He wheeled away, blowing a kiss to the whist circle.

'Crikey – there go me trumps,' whispered a blue-haired pensioner, mopping her brow with a sterile hand wipe.

'What do you mean, you built it?' asked Russell curiously. 'What is it?'

'NIDUS,' Rod stated. 'Neo Interstellar Domestic Universal Station.'

Rod paused, as if that explained everything.

'And?' Indy insisted.

'I was part of SPIDER's top-secret space programme – back when it had one,' Rod explained. 'I've been obsessed with space ever since I was a boy, and was determined one day to build my own rocket to head to the stars . . .'

'That's lovely,' said Reg. 'A boy should have a dream. Speaking of which, the man who cleans my carpets had the strangest dream about an ostrich that speaks Finnish . . .'

'It was a nightmare, actually,' Rod continued. 'After reading a Maya prophecy that the world would end on the twenty-first of December 2012, I figured I needed a Plan B. So I devoted my life to space research, hoping that when Earth was annihilated, we'd have somewhere else to live. NIDUS was to be the world's most advanced space station. It was an astonishing feat of engineering – a central control hub with concentric structures around it for people to live and work in – it looked like a space-age spider's web. It boasted the world's most advanced antenna, capable of communicating with every other antenna on Earth. And I was one of the pioneering agents who was going to live and work on it.'

'So why didn't you?' Vi asked.

'Because NIDUS never became operational,' sighed Rod.

'Why not?' Russell asked. 'It sounds awesome.'

'It was, little man,' Rod said wistfully. 'But it could never be. At first we were told it was to pioneer a new age, to use advanced telecoms to promote safety and communication on Earth. But those of us who built it soon realized that there was another, much darker agenda.'

'What?' Vi asked, the room silent, but for the sound of Doris's bloomers hitting the floor.

'NIDUS was actually a way to spy on everyone on Earth,' Rod said, shaking his head. 'That antenna could locate and track anyone and anything in the world with pinpoint accuracy. No regard for privacy. No care for personal freedoms.

When we realized what was going on, a group of us threatened to go public. SPIDER couldn't risk the scandal. NIDUS was quietly shelved. And after a substantial payout to secure my silence, so was my career.'

'Oh, no,' muttered Russell as he grabbed a piece of paper and started scribbling frantically. 'Umbra. The Neurotrol . . .'

'I had no idea,' said Indy quietly. 'I just assumed you'd been in your bunker all this time.'

'I was for a while,' said Rod. 'But there are only so many tinned beans a man can eat in a confined space before he needs to reassess his life choices. I gave my life to SPIDER. And they took it from me.'

Vi watched Indy stare at Rod. There was something different in her eyes. And it wasn't her cataracts.

'OK, so this is incredibly rough,' said Russell, holding up an astonishingly detailed schematic diagram, 'but, Rod, you said that antenna could pinpoint anyone or anything?'

'As surely as an asteroid will destroy all life on Earth. Probably tomorrow,' said Rod.

'I still don't get it — why would Umbra be

bothered about a defunct space station?' Indy asked.

'Because NIDUS can communicate with every antenna on the planet,' said Russell, 'so you can basically transmit anything you want . . .'

'To any and every living being,' Vi gasped, finally understanding what Russell was getting at. 'So then all Umbra would need for their master plan to work is . . .'

'The Neurotrol,' said Russell grimly.

Vi exhaled heavily. The Neurotrol was the mind-control device that she and her family had taken from Umbra at Norton Power Station. The only one in existence was safe in her dad's keeping. She hoped.

'So if Umbra got his—'

'Or her,' Rod added.

'Or their,' Reg chipped in.

'—hands on the Neurotrol and somehow got it to NIDUS,' Vi said, 'Umbra could control any and every mind on the planet. Just as he . . . she . . . they always wanted.'

A weighty silence followed the realization.

'Robert has to destroy it,' Indy said. 'He should have done it straight away. The man always was a complete idiot.'

'I'll sort it,' said Vi quietly. She was staying with her dad after the wedding tomorrow. She'd make sure the Neurotrol could never fall into Umbra's hands.

'Rod – how was NIDUS going to be controlled?' Russell asked. 'Presumably there was a ground station somewhere?'

'Er – anyone else who doesn't speak Geek need a translation?' Vi asked.

'A ground station – it's an Earth terminal capable of extra-planetary telecommunication with spacecraft,' Russell explained to an approving nod from Rod.

Vi stared at him blankly again.

'It's the building on Earth that makes NIDUS work in space,' Russell sighed. 'It's the control centre. It's the heart of the operation. It's . . . it's really important.'

'That's all I needed,' said Vi, turning back to Rod. 'So was there a . . . ground . . . thingie?'

'A ground station. Yes, there was. It was called Gumfoot,' Rod confirmed. 'It was to be the mission control and it housed the rocket that would shuttle crew to and from NIDUS. But I was never told where it was. No one agent knew about the whole project. That way, if any of us was captured, we could only tell our enemies a small part of the plan.'

'We need to find Gumfoot before Umbra does,' Russell said stridently. 'Then we have to shut NIDUS down.'

Vi nodded wisely, like she'd already thought of that.

'I built a Doomsday Protocol into the system,' said Rod. 'If we can find Gumfoot, we can force NIDUS to self-destruct. I don't know where it is. But I've still got some contacts. Let me see what I can find out.'

'Brilliant,' said Vi. 'And thanks for your input, Rod. With this information, we can stop Umbra's plan before it starts.'

'My pleasure,' said Rod, looking at Indy. 'But until you do, treat everyone like they're guilty. They probably are. I'm at your service. Always. Or at least until the world ends. Probably tomorrow.'

'Come on, kids,' said Indy. 'Assuming the world hasn't ended, we've got a big day tomorrow. Your parents can't wait to get married. Unlike some . . .'

Vi waved to Rod and Reg as she was bustled away by her nan to the guest rooms at Autumn Leaves. She allowed herself a small smile. By the same time tomorrow, the Neurotrol would be destroyed and Vi would have thwarted Umbra a second time.

The smile became a grin.

Take that, Rimmington Hall and your stupid assessments. A+ to Agent Day.

CHAPTER 4

After the disaster that had been their first wedding, Easter Day and George Sprout were taking no chances second time around. Their first wedding had been thwarted by Robert posing as the registrar. This time, no unwelcome guests were sneaking in.

Because this time, the ceremony was aboard a boat.

'Isn't this gorgeous?' squealed Easter, taking a sip of champagne on the deck of *The Magpie* as the luxury yacht set sail from Norton-on-Sea Marina. 'What a beautiful day!'

Her mum wasn't wrong. As Vi looked out at the sunny, blue sky and calm, clear water, today had an auspicious feel to it. Even Vi's outfit wasn't awful this time – a simple light-blue summer dress that

Easter had let Vi choose herself. She pushed all thoughts of Umbra, NIDUS, Gumfoot, the Neurotrol and Rimmington Hall out of her mind. Today was going to be a good day.

'It's wonderful to see you so relaxed,' said Nan, who had once again dyed her hair a fabulous shade of pink for the occasion. 'You just enjoy yourself, love.'

'Oh, I will – thanks to Gigi,' smiled Easter, taking another sip of her champagne.

'Gigi?' Vi asked.

'My wedding planner,' Easter replied. 'She's been an absolute superstar – and she was a bargain too! She's around somewhere, I'll introduce you . . . She's taken control of everything – apart from the buffet, of course. I wanted to do that – consider it my gift to you all. Who's going to try a Senegalese-spiced herring burger with rice and peas?'

Indy immediately started coughing again, although Vi suspected it had nothing to do with her health. Easter loved to combine their family's assorted heritages in her fusion cuisine. At Christmas, she'd given George a DNA kit to trace his ancestors, which had revealed he was descended from Vikings. This now meant that pickled fish featured prominently in Easter's Senegalese/English/Jamaican/African–American/Scottish menus.

'I'm trying to give them up,' Vi said hastily, grabbing a handful of plantain fries instead.

'OK,' said George, popping out of nowhere and looking unusually flustered. 'So I've checked with the captain – the passenger manifest matches the approved guest list and all showed at least three types of ID and their biometric wedding invitations. It is impossible to board the ship from the water as there are no access points below the waterline and it is a restricted airspace overhead, so we should be free from any parachutes.'

Vi and Russell exchanged a smirk. Poor George.

'Hey, everybody! We're . . .' came two voices in unwelcome unison. Vi rolled her eyes. Oh, no. They were here again. Who had invited—

'The . . . MYSTERY SISTERS!'

Vi turned around to see her amateur – and usually incorrect and always irritating – sleuthing cousins, Milly and Tilly.

'Pssst – we're finding clues to protect you all!'

said Milly, looking over the buffet with a magnifying glass.

'Do you have a cure for food poisoning?' whispered Indy.

'We've heard that a shady figure from the past is planning to sabotage the wedding again!' said Tilly, flicking a braid out of the smoked mackerel hummus. 'But don't worry – we're ON THE CASE!'

'I have no idea what you're on,' sighed Vi as the cousins continued with their search while George reeled off his security checks.

'... and I've made sure that all the band's instruments aren't weapons in disguise and that the flowers don't have any explosives concealed in them – although did you know that several species of flower, including the touch-me-nots, or *Impatiens capensis*, do in fact disperse their seeds by exploding? – and that the chairs aren't actually landmines, and ...'

'Oh, darling, you're so clever,' simpered Easter, giving George a kiss. 'You've thought of everything.'

'Oi!' said Indy, trying to push George and Russell away. 'You know you're not supposed to

54

see the bride before the wedding – get out of here! We don't need any bad luck today. It's daft enough you're getting married aboard *The Magpie* on the thirteenth.'

'Mum – chill,' said Easter, taking another sip of her drink. 'Don't be so superstitious. We've had all the bad luck we're going to get. This wedding's going to be great—'

MIAAAAAAAAOWWWWWW!

A black cat raced across the deck.

'Blimey!' said Nan, reaching for the table and knocking over the salt. 'So much bad luck! Quick!'

Nan picked up a pinch of salt and threw it over her left shoulder. Unfortunately, it went straight into George's right eye, temporarily blinding him and causing him to thrash about, knocking a mirror off a nearby wall, which promptly smashed all over the deck.

'WHO'S THERE?' boomed Mason Vaughn, a paranoid distant cousin. 'WHO ARE YOU? YOU'LL NEVER TAKE ME ALIVE!'

And with that, he clambered aboard the railings and jumped into the sea.

'Well, that's one less for the buffet. I'll call the

coastguard,' sighed Indy, spitting a mouthful of neep-and-tattie upside-down cake into a napkin as she shuffled away.

'Oh, no,' grumbled George. 'This wedding is doomed.'

'You are adorable,' giggled Easter, stifling a gentle hiccough as Vi took her champagne away. 'Now go and get ready in the ceremony room. Because in a few minutes, I'm going to come in there and marry the very heck out of you. Oh – and you must try my gorgeous pickled saltfish banana chips.'

George's stressed face relaxed a little as he accepted Easter's canapé and a smoochy kiss for afters. He seemed to enjoy both a great deal. Vi and Russell exchanged another look. And this time, it wasn't a smirk.

'I'll see you soon . . . Mrs Sprout,' George giggled.

'Never gonna happen,' smiled Easter. 'But I'll see you in there . . . hubby.'

The two of them exchanged soppy grins, before a gentle shove from Russell sent George on his way.

'See you in there . . . sis,' Russell smiled.

'Never gonna happen,' Vi repeated. 'See you in a bit.'

'Oh, Easter, you look . . . heavenly!'

Vi's blood froze as she heard the familiar voice of her godmother – and Umbra suspect – Honey B. She remembered Rod's advice. Treat everyone like they're guilty. She had to assume that Honey B was Umbra. It was the only way to keep them all safe. But it still felt weird. She'd known Honey since she was a baby. She was her godmother. And she always gave her sweets.

'You made it! I didn't know if you'd get security clearance!' cried Easter, throwing her arms around her best friend as Honey B secretly dropped her customary bag of giant sherbet lemons into Vi's hands. Vi loved sherbet lemons. She always sucked them into a massive point that she could pretend was a giant fang – Honey had taught her how to do that. And they'd take the taste of Mum's gross food away. Result.

'I'm not entirely sure I have got clearance,' winked Honey B. 'But what The Cardinal doesn't know can't hurt him.'

Vi tried not to let her face betray her suspicion. The Cardinal, Honey B's boss, knew everything.

Active SPIDER agents were supposed to keep a low profile. What was Honey B really doing here? Supporting a friend? Or hiding in plain sight?

'Oh, and, Vi!' Honey squealed. 'You look absolutely gorgeous!'

'Thanks, Aunty Honey,' said Vi, plastering what she hoped was a convincing smile on her face. 'You look ... nice.'

'So, how's Rimmington Hall?' asked Honey. 'I bet you're acing it.'

'Kinda,' said Vi. 'I've got my end-of-year assessment next week.'

'I know – I can't wait to come and see you in action!' Easter said. 'We've delayed our honeymoon especially so we can be there! We're going away for a minimoon for a few days, but I'll be back to cheer on my girl on Friday! And George is beside himself about it – he's not been to Rimmington Hall yet, but he's researched the complete history. Did you know that the building originally housed the secret spy division that foiled the Gunpowder Plot in 1605?'

Vi's heart lurched. So her mum hadn't forgotten. Now she had to hope that her dad had.

'Oh, cool!' said Honey. 'Did you know I built

the Rimmington Hall VR room myself from tech I'm developing at SPIDER HQ?'

'Wow,' grimaced Vi. 'So it's all your fault!'

'Aw – you're sweet,' laughed Honey, giving Vi a big hug.

Vi tried not to freeze in her arms. Honey had hugged her a million times but now it just felt . . . weird. Was it all in Vi's head? Or were her spy instincts trying to tell her something?

'Now I know you'll try some of my buffet, bestie,' said Easter, picking up a canapé. 'These curried goat mac 'n' cheese mini bites are divine, if I do say so myself.'

'Er, thanks . . . but I'm on a major diet,' said Honey, avoiding the canapé that Easter was pushing in her face.

'Come on,' Easter cajoled. 'You know you want to . . .'

'I . . . I really don't,' said Honey, wriggling around as the mini bite came closer to her lips.

'Yes, you do,' chimed Easter.

'No, I don't,' Honey laughed nervously back.

'You do,' Easter stated.

'I don't,' Honey insisted.

'Just a little taste . . .' said Easter, practically

wiping it on Honey B's lips.

'A minute on the lips, a lifetime on the hips,' Honey B sang back.

'EAT IT!' Easter commanded, bringing the boat to a shocked standstill.

Honey B looked around nervously as Vi tried not to laugh.

'I mean,' said Easter more softly, looking embarrassed. 'Just a tiny bite.'

'Oh . . . OK,' said Honey, looking like she was about to taste poison. 'Just a bite.'

She opened her lips a coin's breadth apart – and Easter shoved the whole canapé in.

'You see?' said Easter brightly.

'Mmmmm,' gagged Honey, reaching around for the nearest napkin.

Vi grabbed another handful of plantain fries and stuffed them in her mouth to hide her giggles.

'Well – I'd better get this show on the road,' said Easter, picking up her bouquet. 'I'm just going to freshen up. You coming, Vi?'

'I'll meet you outside the ceremony room,' smiled Vi. 'I haven't seen Aunty Honey for ages.'

'Sure thing,' said Easter. 'See you in a bit.'

'Mmhmmmhmmmhhhm,' smiled Honey, the offending canapé still in her mouth.

'It's OK now,' whispered Vi. 'She's gone.'

'Oh my days,' said Honey, spitting the food into the napkin. 'I paid my way through uni as a stunt-woman at a theme park, where I literally had to pretend to get beaten up every day by a man in a giant SuperBunny costume to pay my rent. Even that experience isn't half as painful as your mum's catering . . . but don't tell her I said that!'

'Your secret's safe with me,' said Vi, her eyes narrowing. 'So how are you, Aunty Honey?'

'I'm good,' she said. 'A bit stressed with work, but nothing new there.'

'Oh?' said Vi. 'What's wrong?'

'Just the usual. Walter . . . er, The Cardinal seems to think I'm completely incompetent,' she sighed. 'And I keep proving him right. I feel like he's watching me all the time – if only he'd get to know me properly . . .'

'Oh, I'm sure there's so much more to you than he realizes,' Vi said sweetly.

'Bless you, Vi,' said Honey, putting a hand on Vi's shoulder. 'I'm so happy to hear you say that.'

Vi looked deep into Honey's wide-open eyes.

There wasn't a guilty shadow in them. And Vi wasn't picking up on any tells – she could normally spot a lie a mile off. Honey B was either a really good person, or a really good liar.

'Goodness,' said Honey. 'Is that the time? I'd better take my seat. And you'd better get to your mum – she'll be worrying where you are.'

'She'll be fine,' said Vi. 'She's got me to take care of her. I'd never let anything happen to her. Ever.'

'Of course you wouldn't,' smiled Honey, squeezing Vi's shoulder. 'I'll see you later.'

'Whatever,' muttered Vi as Honey stumbled off to the ceremony room. If it was an act, it was a convincing one. Could her ditzy godmother be one of the greatest criminal masterminds ever? It seemed unlikely.

Which made her all the more suspicious.

Vi picked up her posy of flowers. Umbra would have to wait. Today, her mum needed her. She was sure that everything would be absolutely fine this time.

But then again, if living in a family of spies and super-villains had taught her anything, it was never to take anything for granted.

CHAPTER 5

As Vi approached the door to the ceremony room that would see her mother marry George Sprout, she was impressed that Easter was still keeping her cool. Since returning to SPIDER, her mum had seemed a lot calmer. Retraining to become a deadly killing machine had really brought out Easter's softer side.

'Hey, sweetie,' smiled her mum. 'How you feeling?'

'Can't wait,' beamed Vi, and she meant it. Although at first she'd not been overjoyed about her mum marrying her former teacher, over the past year, she'd got to know – and really love – George Sprout. He was a good, kind man who loved her and Easter very much. And she'd learnt more trivia than she could shake a set of encyclopedias at.

Vi looked up the aisle to where the groom was anxiously checking every last detail. He patted his pocket for the rings, then checked that all the doors and windows were locked, before embarking on a brief interrogation of his cousin Margo as to why she had changed her hairstyle since he saw her at their great-aunt's diamond wedding anniversary.

'Poor Georgie,' laughed Easter. 'I'm sure he'll calm down once that ring's on his finger.'

Vi looked at the anxious and clammy Mr Sprout. It was going to take more than a ring to calm him down. Although the after-effects of her mum's buffet might at least give him something else to worry about.

The wedding march rang out through the room. Easter took Vi's hand and gave her a huge, teary smile.

'Ready to make a new family?' she whispered.

'Ready,' Vi whispered back, her own voice cracking in the emotion of the moment.

They walked together up the aisle into the intimate, nautical room to the admiring gasps of the congregation. Vi recognized some of her family from other gatherings over the past year and some new acquaintances from Clan Sprout. She smiled at the similarity between all of Russell's relatives, who were all slight variations on a theme of white skin, brown hair, some freckles and glasses that didn't stay on their noses. Although one guest did stand out – a super-glamorous, white, blonde lady dressed in a chic designer suit, who was hidden from general view behind a wooden pillar. She gave Easter an enthusiastic thumbs up as they passed.

'That's Gigi,' Easter whispered to Vi. 'Honestly, today is all about her, she's been a star. And so cheap . . .'

'Today is all about you,' Vi corrected. 'You're always a star.'

Easter gulped back a tear and held Vi's hand tighter. They passed Indy sniffing in her chair and took their places at the front, where a lovestruck George Sprout gazed adoringly at his bride.

'Wowsers,' he gasped. 'You shine brighter than the last known supernova – which was discovered by Kepler in 1604, although remnants of more recent supernovae have been observed since.'

'Oh, George,' Easter gushed. 'You're so romantic.'

'Welcome, everybody, to this happy occasion,' began the registrar. 'We are here today aboard *The Magpie* to celebrate the marriage of Easter and George—'

'Wait a minute!' said George suddenly. 'You're not the woman we met at the registry office! You're an imposter! SECURITY!'

'Mr Sprout,' the registrar said calmly. 'As you were informed last week, your registrar is having her tonsils out. I have been through all your security checks. I can assure you, I come in peace.'

'It's all fine, George,' giggled Easter. 'Gigi took care of everything.'

'OK,' whispered George uncertainly. 'I just don't want your ... past causing us problems again.'

'Let's just focus on our future,' smiled Easter tersely, before turning to the registrar. 'Please continue.'

'Today marks a new beginning in their lives together,' the registrar went on. 'Marriage is a desire by two people—'

'Ah-ha!' George suddenly declared, pointing at a member of the congregation. 'You! I've never seen you before in my life! Whoever you are, you are not causing trouble here! SECURITY!'

'Um, Georgie,' said Easter, a slight note of irritation creeping into her voice. 'That's my cousin Violet. You went to her Thanksgiving dinner last November.'

'That's not Violet!' George insisted. 'Violet was younger, better dressed, had nicer hair. This is clearly someone impersonating Violet in a bad mask and a cheap wig! SECURITY!'

'You're thinking of my cousin Tina,' Easter whispered so loud, it was hardly a whisper. 'This is her mother.'

George shrank. 'Oh,' he said. 'Nice to see you again, Violet. Love what you've done with your hair.'

'Hrumph,' said Violet, rearranging her umbrella, which immediately opened up, smacking the row in front of her.

'Saints preserve us,' muttered Indy, making the sign of the cross.

'George,' said Easter firmly, her smile just about still in place. 'Everything is fine. Everyone who is here has been checked and double-checked. There are no imposters. No one is dressed up and my past is just there – in the past. Now, please – PLEASE – can we get married? I'm desperate to be your wife. And if my pickled shrimp fritters with haggis ice cream sit out in the sun much longer, they'll be absolutely disgusting . . .'

'Too late,' muttered Nan.

'I'm sorry,' said George, taking a deep breath. 'You're right, of course. I'm being silly. The past is in the past. Nothing and no one can spoil today. Let's just get married. Those fritters sound delicious.'

Vi smiled. If anyone had any doubt that George Sprout really loved her mother, there was the proof.

'Perhaps we'll get down to business,' whispered the registrar. 'Ease the nerves a bit . . . You are here to witness the joining in marriage of George Douglas Sprout and Easter Day. If any person present knows of any lawful impediment why these two people may not be joined in marriage, they should declare it now.'

Vi looked at Russell, who had closed his eyes and crossed his fingers. For a scientist, he was very superstitious.

But then again, it couldn't hurt.

Vi stood there with her eyes shut and fingers crossed for what seemed an age. But this time, no objection came. She heard both Easter and George breathe a huge sigh of relief.

'In which case,' the registrar smiled, 'could I please ask everyone to stand—'

'WAIT!' screamed a voice from the back of the room.

'You have *got* to be kidding me,' Vi groaned as she strained to find the objector over the standing adults.

'Er . . . does someone have something to say?' said the confused registrar. 'If so, you need to make yourself known.'

There was a gasp as the glamorous woman Vi had spotted moments ago started walking towards them. What was the wedding planner doing, objecting to the wedding?

'Gigi?' Easter asked, aghast. 'What are you . . . George – George, you have to listen to me, this is NOTHING to do with me, I swear, she's just the wedding planner, I only met her a few months ago, she's practically a stranger . . .'

But Vi wasn't listening to her mum. She was watching the horror unfold on George Sprout's face. If Gigi was a stranger to Mum, it didn't look like she was to Mr Sprout.

'Russell?' Vi whispered across the aisle. 'Do you know . . .'

But Russell Sprout wasn't answering either. His horrified face mirrored his father's – he knew this woman too.

'What the—What are you doing here?' George hissed at the intruder.

'I can't do it, George!' Gigi declared. 'I can't stand by and watch you marry another woman! I love you, George Sprout! I've always loved you! We belong together! I'm YOURS!'

Vi joined the rest of the congregation in dumbstruck shock. The wedding planner was in love with the groom?

No wonder she'd been so cheap.

'George?' said Easter in her trying-to-stay-calm voice. 'Could you explain what is going on? Are you . . . are you in love with this woman?'

'No!' shouted George. 'I mean . . . I was . . . but that was a long time ago and she left me and I met you and . . . I'll ask you again, Genevieve – what are you doing here?'

'Genevieve?' Easter roared. 'Gigi . . . you are . . . GENEVIEVE? SECURITY!'

Genevieve . . . Genevieve . . . ? Vi looked at

Russell again. But he was still rooted to the spot.

The realization flashed in Vi's mind like Kepler's Supernova.

Genevieve!

Of course!

Genevieve was Russell's—

'Mum?' Russell asked. 'What . . . why are you here?'

'Oh, Russy,' said Gigi – Genevieve – Mrs Sprout – whoever she was – rushing over to embrace her son. 'I've missed you so much.'

'Er . . . I haven't gone anywhere,' said Russell from inside her smothering hug.

'And you'll never have to again,' said Genevieve, releasing him, then immediately clamping him to her side. 'Because Mummy's back now. And this time, Mummy's here to stay.'

CHAPTER 6

'I don't understand!' George cried in the privacy of the captain's quarters. 'We've been divorced for seven years! You left me for the man who laid our patio! You're married! You have a young son! And now, today, you've decided you want me back! This is like cold fusion – it just makes no sense!'

'What can I say? It's a woman's prerogative to change her mind,' sighed Genevieve, chucking Russell under the chin and jumping up to sit on a table. Vi watched her cross her long, tanned legs. She was so glamorous. So elegant. So . . . not at all who she imagined would have married George Sprout and created Russell. There was no anorak, for a start.

'Well, you'd better change it back – double-time,' snapped Easter. 'And if you think I'm still booking you for Cousin Violet's retirement party, you can think again!'

'I'm sorry, Easter – you seem like a good woman,' said Genevieve. 'You paid a twenty per cent deposit up front and settled your outstanding invoice promptly. I respect that. And if there had been any other way to get George's attention . . .'

'Er – the phone?' George suggested.

'I needed to show you how much I love you!' pouted Genevieve. 'No phone call could do that! I needed to come here to make a big gesture! And to distribute some business cards – this game is all about word-of-mouth recommendations . . . But you were mine first. And now I want you back. I want my family back. Because my family will always come first.'

'Which one?' Vi scoffed.

'Shush,' snapped Genevieve. 'The grown-ups are talking.'

'Don't you tell my daughter to shush,' warned Easter. Vi smiled. Her mum was very cool. 'But, Valentine – shush.'

'Whatever,' Vi muttered. Her mum was also very contradictory.

'Genevieve,' George began. 'You made a choice

all those years ago. It was a terrible time for us all, but we've moved on to new, happier lives now. You're with Dwayne. And I'm with Easter.'

Genevieve jumped down from the table and sauntered slowly towards George.

'You say that now, Georgie-Porgie,' she pouted, taking George's suit lapels in her hands. 'But you know what we had was good. Very good. So very . . . very good . . .'

Easter cleared her throat.

'Just like your new patio,' she said flatly. 'And anything that is still on my fiancé's suit in the next three seconds will be returned with it to the hire shop on Monday.'

'What's the matter, Easter?' Genevieve goaded. 'Can't take the competition?'

'I'll say this once,' Easter said darkly. 'You do not want to pick a fight with me.'

Vi could feel the tension in the room rise ten notches. Her mum was right. She could kick Genevieve's butt into the middle of next week. And it looked like she really wanted to.

'What do you want?' came a quiet voice behind them.

They all turned to where Russell hadn't moved

since they were ushered out of the ceremony room.

'Isn't it obvious?' said Genevieve, rushing towards him for another smother. 'You, baby! I want you! You, me and your daddy all back together again, like the happy family we always were . . .'

'So happy you left it?' Vi couldn't help but say. This woman was unbelievable.

'Shush!' Genevieve said again.

'Don't you shush her!' Easter said again. 'Valentine! Shush!'

'Whatever,' Valentine said again.

'You've . . . I've . . . all this time, I've hardly seen you,' said Russell. 'You didn't want me. You just wanted Dwayne. And Lucas.'

'Oh, baby, no, you've got it all wrong!' Genevieve wailed. 'That wasn't me – that was Dwayne! He made me stop seeing you – he never liked you. He always said you were wet and wimpy, a bit weird. He said you reminded him of something he'd shoot in a video game—'

'OK, I get it,' Russell interrupted.

'And then when we had our Lucas . . .' Genevieve continued. 'That's one of the reasons

I've left Dwayne. Because he was making me choose. And I choose you.'

'What about Lucas?' Russell muttered.

'Lucas will be fine,' grinned Genevieve, taking Russell's face in her hands. 'He has two parents who love him very much.'

'Bit late to start being a parent now,' Vi muttered.

'Valentine!' Easter warned.

'Like your dad, you mean?' Russell muttered back.

'Russ!' George warned.

'Er . . . everybody,' Indy interrupted, peering round the door. 'Just to say, we're coming in to dock. The registrar has to get to her next wedding. What shall I tell everyone?'

Vi looked at her crestfallen mum.

'Tell them all to go home,' Easter sighed. 'But to take as much of the buffet as they want. It's a sin to let all that good food go to waste.'

'That food's a sin all right,' muttered Nan. 'Are you OK, love?'

'I'm fine, Mum,' said Easter, taking Nan's hand with a weak smile. 'Just . . . it's just one of those things.'

Nan squeezed her daughter's hand, giving Genevieve a death stare as she backed out of the door. Everyone just looked at each other for a moment, unsure what to say or do.

'So . . . where do we go from here?' Easter finally said. 'George, are you leaving me for Genevieve?'

'No!' shouted George. 'Absolutely not! Easter, I love you – you're my family now, you know that. We're like a pair of Laysan albatrosses, who incidentally mark every year of their union by dancing together.'

'Well, then, Gi— Genevieve, I think it's time you left,' said Easter, rising to her feet.

'Not without my boy,' said Genevieve, clamping Russell to her again. 'You might be able to keep me from my Georgie! But you can't keep me from my son!'

'No one's ever tried to keep you from your son,' sighed Easter.

'Except maybe you, *Gigi*,' Vi muttered.

'SHUSH!' came the simultaneous response from the two mothers.

'We have so much catching up to do, Russy,' pouted Genevieve. 'I want Russell to come home with me. Now.'

'Oh, I don't think that's a good idea,' Mr Sprout sputtered. 'You can't just waltz in here, ruin my wedding and leave with my son!'

'He's *our* son,' said Genevieve through gritted teeth. 'And you've had far more than your fair share.'

Vi could see a whole buffet of fusion emotions travelling across Russell's face. There was anger with a worried sauce. The joy was accompanied by an extra helping of fear. And the excitement was served with a side of conflict.

'Russell?' Easter asked. 'What would you like to do?'

'I . . . I . . . I guess I haven't seen Mum for a while,' he said, not looking at George. 'It would be kinda . . . nice to spend some time with her.'

Genevieve shot George a look of pure triumph. It was like an emotional bullet, puncturing George Sprout through the heart.

'Then you must go,' he said quietly. 'He needs to be back home . . . back with me tomorrow. Rimmington Hall sends the car for him Sunday night . . . oh, no, wait – we'll be on our minimoon.'

'No, we won't,' Easter sighed.

'What?' said George. 'We're not going to the Elsmere Country Manor Hotel? But it's just down the road from the country's largest miniature railway, which incidentally used enough plywood to cover four tennis courts.'

'Another time, darling,' said Easter wearily. 'Today, I just want to go home.'

'I see,' said George sadly. 'Well, Russ, you'll need some clothes . . .'

'Oh, don't worry about those drab old things – we're going shopping for all new trendy ones!' squealed Genevieve, picking at Russell's suit. 'As it happens, I've just been paid for a wedding I organized, so I'm feeling pretty flush.'

'Let's see how you feel when I post my online feedback,' promised Easter. 'We'll see you tomorrow, Russ. Have a nice time.'

'Yeah,' said George as Russ gave him a hug, still unable to meet his eye. 'Have fun, son. See you tomorrow.'

'We're going to have *so much* fun!' Genevieve giggled to Russell as they walked out. 'After shopping, let's treat ourselves to a fancy dinner and maybe a movie? Or would you prefer to play those arcade games you like? Or both?'

The string of promises echoed up the stairs and out on to the deck as the door shut behind them. Vi looked between George and her mum.

'Easter . . . I'm just . . . I'm so, so sorry,' said George tearfully.

'I know you are,' said Easter, holding out her hand. 'It's not your fault.'

George took Easter's fingers in his but said nothing more. Vi looked between them. They both looked horribly sad. Vi was relieved when there was another knock at the door.

'Vi, love,' said Nan. 'Your dad's here to collect you.'

'Great,' groaned Easter, dropping George's fingers. 'This should be fun. Come on, darling. I'll see you off.'

Vi started to walk across the cabin, but quickly ran back to give George a hug.

'Thank you,' he said shakily. 'I will make this right, Vi – I promise.'

'I know you will,' Vi smiled. 'You're like an artichoke – which incidentally is an unbloomed flower, part of the sunflower family, from the Mediterranean and the Canary Islands – you have a big heart.'

George tried to laugh as Vi let him go and followed her mum out of the door and upstairs on to the deck. There, leaning against the railings, was Robert. And he looked highly amused.

'Robert – don't,' Easter warned before he could say anything.

'I was merely going to compliment you on your wonderful spread,' Robert smirked, gesturing to the virtually untouched buffet. 'I hope you don't mind, I helped myself to a mini saltfish 'n' chips. I wanted to beat the rush.'

'Do you have everything you need?' Easter asked Vi, ignoring Robert's burn. Vi loved her dad. But he could be a complete idiot sometimes.

'Think so,' Vi replied. 'Are you and George going to be OK?'

'Of course,' Easter replied unconvincingly. 'You have a good time with your dad. Enjoy his new house. Do you like it, Robert?'

'I do,' Robert declared loudly. 'Oh, I'm so sorry, that was insensitive of me.'

Vi trod on her dad's foot, really hard.

'Try not to worry, baby,' said Easter, giving Vi a big hug. 'We'll figure it all out.'

Vi hugged her mum back and followed her dad

off *The Magpie* and on to the jetty. She wanted to believe her mum that everything would be OK, she really did.

But as she looked back and saw Easter gazing over the water alone in her wedding dress, Vi couldn't help feeling that her little family was all at sea.

CHAPTER 7

'**S**o how do you like my new wheels?' Robert asked, pointing to the parking space in front of them.

Vi looked at the empty gap.

'Have you been practising your dad jokes again?' she asked. 'Because like dad dancing, they are not a necessary part of fatherhood.'

'Well, you might not think my moves are cool,' Robert whispered, waggling his eyebrows, 'but I defy anyone not to dig this . . .'

'Dad – the only people allowed to use the word "dig" are gardeners and archaeologists and whoawheredidthatcarjustcomefrom?'

Vi's words stuck in her mouth as an iridescent sports car suddenly appeared in front of her.

'An invisible car!' she gasped. 'That is so cool!'

'Told you you'd dig it,' grinned Robert, putting on his shades and opening the door for her. 'Auguste made it for me. He'd originally intended the technology to help him drive unnoticed into buildings so he could take everyone hostage for ransom. But now he's a . . . mostly changed man. And when I needed a safe ride to my safe house . . .'

Vi hitched up her bridesmaid's dress and got into the low car, her dad taking his place next to her and switching the car back to invisibility mode. She watched a squirrel scuttle towards them across the car park looking for food. It was really cute and furry and . . .

Doink!

. . . and probably concussed after running straight into the car.

'Don't worry,' laughed Robert, flicking a switch. 'The magnetic repulsion system keeps other cars away on the road. It's perfectly safe.'

'Tell that to Mr Nutkin,' said Vi as the squirrel wobbled off.

'You see, there's no point in taking a year to build a state-of-the-art safe house if your enemies can simply follow you there,' Robert explained, revving up the engine. 'This way, I can come and go as I please, safe as I like.'

Vi felt the familiar knot of concern tighten in her stomach. By going straight and turning government informant, Robert had made a powerful enemy of Umbra, not to mention many other villains. She wasn't confident her dad could really be safe anywhere.

'I'm so excited to show you the new pad,' Robert grinned. 'I hope you like it.'

They pulled out of the car park and on to the road. Vi was excited too. Because her dad had been living in a small flat for the past year, she'd not been able to stay with him overnight before. An ex-villain's safe house. She was definitely going to dig this.

'Here we go,' said Robert an hour later as they came out of the garage, leaving the invisible car parked inside. 'It's not much. But it's home. Welcome to Casa Del Ford!'

Vi surveyed the modest brick house in front of her. She wasn't 'digging' this quite as much as she'd thought. It wasn't that she wanted her dad to be a villain any more – she was glad he'd decided to live a better life. But . . . villains did have really cool houses. She'd imagined a lair like the ones she'd seen in the movies – a sparsely furnished, ultra-modern home with every high-tech device you could think of, cleverly concealed in the side of a hill, far from prying eyes.

What she got was a three-bedroom, semi-detached house in a quiet suburban cul-de-sac. And judging by the curtain twitching, there were plenty of prying eyes.

'What do you think?' Robert said proudly.

'It's . . . nice,' said Vi, struggling to find the enthusiasm she wanted to show her dad.

'Oh. Nice,' said Robert with a twinkle in his eye. 'We'll have to see what we can do about that . . .'

'Er . . . Robbie, you've snuck past me again, hahaha! Could I have a word?'

Vi turned around to find a white man in white golfing clothes wearing a white cap standing on her father's white driveway. Her father's rolling eyes indicated exactly how welcome he was.

'Hello, Gary,' he said, his voice dripping with

insincerity. 'How nice to see you. Again.'

'Uh, yes, well – I really don't want to be "that guy",' said Gary, making speech marks in the air with his fingers, 'but if you recall, we operate an alternate weekly refuse and recycling system here. We'd normally expect to see your domestic waste out on a Thursday, hahaha!'

'Good to know,' said Robert, ushering Vi towards the house.

'It's just …' said Gary, barring his way, 'your bins weren't out on Thursday.'

'You're absolutely right,' said Robert, releasing a long breath. 'I'll make sure they are this week.'

He tried to steer around Gary, who took another step in his way. Vi couldn't help snorting. As Sir Charge, the world's second greatest criminal mastermind, Robert had probably vaporized people for less. Lucky for Gary, her dad was a new man.

'It's just . . .' Gary repeated, 'here in Nimby Close, we try to keep a fundamental respect for our surroundings. It might only be a missed bin night for you. But an overflowing refuse container places undue strain on the local infrastructure and potentially exposes us all to foxes, rodents, suburban foragers or any other number of unwelcome vermin, hahaha!'

'Hearing you loud and clear, Gary,' said Robert.

'Thanks ever so,' said Gary, finally moving out of the way. 'We don't want a repeat of the unpleasantness at number forty-six, when we won legal proceedings to evict Edna Morris for not observing the garden waste protocols. You have no idea how hard it is to get a ninety-six-year-old partially sighted woman evicted from the home she's always lived in. I wouldn't want to have to do that again. The paperwork was horrendous, hahaha!'

'As I said,' Robert growled, 'my bins will be out. On Thursday. Goodnight.'

'Will Gary be in them, hahaha?' Vi whispered as they entered the house. Her father didn't laugh back. She feared she'd just given him an idea.

They stepped inside the narrow hallway. Vi looked through to the average kitchen and average living room with their average decor and average everything.

'Perfect, isn't it?' Robert sighed happily.

'Sure,' said Vi. 'Can I see my room?'

'Of course,' said Robert enthusiastically, leading her up the small staircase. 'I've spent the week decorating it. You're going to love it.'

Robert led the way upstairs to a door that had 'Valentine' spelt out in pink unicorn letters. Vi smiled. It was a nice idea, but she hadn't been into unicorns since she was, like, seven. These days she thought they were pretty lame. But it was only a door. It wasn't like she had to look at it all the—

The thought stalled in her brain as her dad opened the door to reveal her new room. She was in the Museum of Unicorn. There were unicorns everywhere – on the wallpaper, the rug, the bedspread – even the bed was shaped like a unicorn. Every spare inch was filled with stuffed unicorns of every variety: pink ones, ballet-dancing ones, even one that was actually a pig with a horn on its head.

'What do you think?' said Robert, looking immensely pleased with himself.

'I'm . . . speechless,' said Vi honestly.

'I remembered how much you loved unicorns,' he said, surveying his handiwork proudly. 'So. Do you like the new pad?'

'It's . . . good,' said Vi, nodding her approval. After all, there was nothing wrong with it. It was . . . fine. It was smaller than her room at Mum's house. And had about seventy-five thousand more unicorns in it, but there was nothing wrong with it. It just wasn't what she'd expected. And by 'expected', she meant 'hoped for'.

Robert smiled one of his knowing smiles.

'Do you still like to read?' he asked.

'Sure,' shrugged Vi.

Robert gestured to the bookcase on the opposite wall.

'I took the liberty of filling your bookshelf with some personal favourites,' he said. He gestured to a big novel in the middle of the shelf. '*A Perfect Spy*. It's a classic. You should try it. I think you'll like what's inside.'

'OK,' sighed Vi, going to take it from the shelf. 'It'll make a change from uni— WHOA!'

As she pulled the book from the shelf, the whole wall gave way. Vi snapped her hand back – had she broken something? She leapt away, expecting the bookshelf to topple down on top of her. But rather than fall over, the bookshelf simply moved sideways, like a sliding door. In fact, as Vi watched the shelf shift to the right, she realized that's exactly what it was – a sliding door that was opening up. And when it did, it revealed a sparsely furnished, ultra-modern home with every high-tech device you could think of.

'Do come in,' smirked Robert, stepping through into the opulent room. 'I hope you liked the entrance hall. This is where I really live. Welcome to our new home.'

Vi stepped into the vast space. One side of the room was entirely glass, looking out on a dramatic valley below. They were cleverly concealed in the side of a hill.

'A bit of smoke and mirrors,' whispered Robert. 'The view is actually projected on to a screen. Otherwise we'd be looking out over Gary's back yard. And he likes to garden. In his pants.'

'Eurgh,' said Vi, shaking the image from her mind.

'I hope you'll forgive the deception,' Robert whispered, gesturing for her to join him on a massive semicircular sofa. 'Dad joke . . .'

'Whatever,' grinned Vi, looking around the ultra-cool room. Now this, she could dig.

'I'M GOING TO KILL YOU!' came a sudden roar from the other side of the room.

A bald man mountain was charging towards her. Her spy instincts immediately kicked in to defend herself. Vi grabbed the nearest thing to hand, which happened to be an interior design magazine. The man threw himself at her, disarmed her with a swipe of a huge arm and slammed the magazine down on the coffee table in front of her. She waited for him to turn around and knock her into the middle of next week. But instead he stood up slowly and brushed himself off.

'So sorry,' he said with a warm smile and posh accent. 'I've been trying to catch that spider all day – little blighter's been giving me the run-around since breakfast! How wonderful to meet you properly – we met briefly at Norton Power Station last year? My name's Michael. But all my friends call me Mick!'

'You should hear what his enemies call him,' Robert smiled. 'What was it – the Bone-Breaker of Basingstoke?'

'Don't be so silly!' Mick laughed. 'It was the Skull-Smasher of Slough. This business can be so catty . . . But it's just gorgeous to meet you.'

Vi took a longer look at the spider slayer. She was still speechless, but accepted the bulging, tattooed white arm being extended politely towards her. She shook Mick's hand.

'Er . . . nice to meet you too,' said Vi uncertainly, looking at the skull and crossbones adorning Mick's enormous bicep.

'Urgh, isn't it ghastly?' Mick said, following her gaze. 'Seemed like a good idea at the time. But then so did studying Classics at Cambridge and look where that got me!'

'Mick worked for me in my former . . . career,' said Robert. 'He was the best henchman in the business.'

'Oh, you big charmer!' laughed Mick, slapping Robert playfully on the back and smacking him into the sofa. He picked up a tray of delicate finger sandwiches and placed them on the table before raising his hands to his face. 'Look, I'm actually blushing! And besides, what is "best" anyway? So I've broken more bones than a clumsy butcher – so what? Anyway, I'm retired now. Your father has very kindly given me a new role as his . . . business manager.'

Vi was just wondering if she wanted to know what business, when a low saxophone tune filled the air.

'Well, hello there,' breathed a familiar voice. 'Sorry I'm late. I was waxing.'

Vi grinned. Things always got a little more interesting when Siren was around.

'Well, legs like yours don't achieve perfection without work, my dear,' smiled Robert, rising to kiss his femme fatale companion.

'Who said anything about my legs?' exhaled Siren, blowing a heart from her e-cigarette. 'I was waxing my ears.'

Robert stopped with his face centimetres away from Siren's.

'Jolly good,' he mumbled, sitting down again.

'Hey, kiddo,' Siren winked.

'Hi, Siren,' Vi replied, giving her friend a happy wave.

'*Bonsoir!*' came a high-pitched voice as the creepiest of clowns burst into the room behind Siren.

'Oh. Hey, Auguste,' said Vi, shifting uncomfortably in her chair. She'd known Auguste, another reformed super-villain, for a year now and he still gave her the mega-creeps.

''Ello, *mon petit chou*,' said Auguste. 'I'm afraid to say . . . er, Dave? *Silence, s'il te plaît?*'

Siren's sponsor and saxophonist, Dave, tipped his hat and grabbed a cucumber finger sandwich.

'As I was saying,' Auguste resumed, 'Sandra will not be joining us tonight. She's drowning in work.'

'Overwhelmed, huh?' said Siren.

'*Non* – her Over-Elaborate Death Plan Support Group have 'er locked in a slowly filling tank of mutant piranhas. She sends 'er apologies.'

'Our Ex-Villain Improvement League is shrinking by the minute,' Robert sighed. 'First we lose Dr Doppelganger to that security guard job, then Dimitri to his Vegan Vampire Wilderness Retreat. Soon it'll just be—'

With an almighty bang, the doors blasted open in a fog of smoke and dust. Momentarily stunned, Vi and the band of reformed super-villains took mere seconds to regain their wits. Mick grabbed a cake slice, Auguste cocked his trusty gunbrella, Siren produced a large rifle from somewhere about her person and Robert whipped a pistol from his sock. Vi grabbed her wrist and set her

Eye-Spy watch to eight o'clock: *fire*.

They waited for the smoke to clear to have good sight of their target. Vi didn't know what villainous organization had found them, but they were ready for whoever was coming their way – however huge, terrifying, armed and dangerous they were . . .

But as the dust settled, Vi wasn't the only one to be taken aback by the figure standing in the middle of the room.

Casually slinging a pink, floral bazooka over her shoulders was . . . a little girl. She was wearing a pink dress with pink petticoats, and her blonde hair sat in perfect ringlets around her rosy, white face. Vi guessed the girl was a couple of years younger than her, certainly no older than ten. The child pulled a pink lollipop out of her mouth and smiled sweetly at the group.

'Hello!' she said, waving at everyone. 'I want us to be BFFs for ever. But if we aren't, I'm going to blow you up so hard it would take a jigsaw convention to put you back together again.'

She giggled and popped the lolly back in her mouth.

'Who . . . who are you?' Robert asked in a

daze. The little girl pulled the lolly out again with a big slurp.

'I'm Missy Fit,' she said with a small curtsey. 'Nice to meet you. Suckers.'

CHAPTER 8

'**W**e're so sorry for barging in like this,' said a small, mousy lady, creeping quietly in behind Missy Fit. 'Missy was just so keen to join the EVIL organization and I try to encourage all her extracurricular interests, so—'

'CAN IT, JANET!' Missy screamed at the woman. 'If you wanna keep your job, you'll remember who's boss!'

'You're the boss, Missy,' simpered Janet. 'It's just that, well—'

'WHAT?' Missy roared. 'SPIT IT OUT!'

'It's just,' said Janet more confidently. 'Well . . . I am your mother. And Dr Venkman did say that you needed some boundaries if we're to manage your anger issues . . .'

'WHAT ANGER ISSUES?' Missy screamed at

her mother. 'And I fired Dr Venkman when he said I didn't respect authority figures! So, Janet?'

'Uh-huh?' simpered her mother.

'CAN IT!'

'Yes, Missy dear,' sighed Janet, sitting down in the corner with her handbag on her lap.

'I'm sorry, I'm going to ask again,' said a confused Robert. 'Who are you?'

'I already told you, duh!' said Missy, tossing her lolly and smacking Auguste on the head. 'I'm—'

'Missy Fit,' said Siren admiringly. 'World's youngest super-hacker. Hacked into the Pentagon mainframe aged six using only her Xbox. Threatened to reveal America's greatest secrets unless they offered her free entrance to Disney World for life. Now the founder and CEO of BRAT, global stationery brand that made its first billion before she turned ten. Wanted by every major global detection agency and any parent who's had to spend hard-earned cash on a pencil that smells like a strawberry.'

'Nailed it, Granny,' winked Missy. 'But I wanna go straight. No one invites you to their sleepovers when they keep getting raided by the FBI. The government have promised me a full pardon in return for helping Robert Ford capture Umbra. And if I give all their kids a fluffy pencil case. So here I am!'

'But how did you find him?' asked Vi. 'This is a top-secret safe house – even the government doesn't know where my dad is.'

'Er – I hacked him, duh,' said Missy, producing a pink phone. 'Phone records, bank accounts, internet history – what's with all the interior decor websites, by the way?'

'Guilty!' trilled Mick, raising a hand. 'I'm a sucker for a lovely fabric.'

'Anyway – it wasn't that hard,' said Missy, holding out her skirts and sitting down on the sofa. 'And here I am. So, who is this Umbra moron and how are we going to find him?'

'Well,' said Robert, finally holstering his gun. 'He – or she, or they, no one actually knows – is most likely one of three suspects, currently posing as a SPIDER agent.'

'So why don't you just capture and torture them all until one confesses they are Umbra, duh?' Missy asked. 'I got the Brazilian president to give me free chocolate for life by locking him in my shed and playing "Let It Go" on my recorder for seven hours straight.'

'Tempting, but illegal,' Robert said. 'If I break the law, I will serve out fifty-four consecutive life sentences. I have to do this by the book.'

Vi shuddered. She hadn't known that. Her dad couldn't take any risks. He didn't have a spare fifty-three lives.

'So send someone else, duh,' said Missy, picking up her phone. 'What about Grandma over there? She's supposed to be a cat burglar, right? Although that's one old cat . . .'

'Watch it, sweet cheeks,' Siren shot back. 'I've got an armpit boil ready to burst and it's got your name on it.'

Missy stuck out her tongue.

'Anyway, no can do,' said Siren. 'I'm on my last warning with SPIDER. If I break in there again, I'm going into their Secure Containment Facility. And that's always a one-way ticket.'

'So how do we unmask Umbra?' Vi asked.

Robert flicked on the widescreen TV that nearly covered one of the walls. Labelled pictures of The Cardinal, The Wolf and Honey B popped up.

'All three suspects only joined the organization after Umbra's apparent disappearance ten years ago,' Robert continued. 'Because of the nature of their jobs, personal information is hard to come by. And the government isn't too keen to give a former super-villain security clearance, not that they know much either. Most of what I can find out about The Wolf comes from his parents' military records – he was orphaned as a teenager when both his parents were killed in combat, leaving him to be raised by his older sister.'

'So maybe he has an axe to grind?' said Siren.

'Absolutely,' said Robert. 'Honey B's motives are less clear. We have a little more info for her – she was raised by a single father who struggled for work. Fortunately, an enormous aptitude for science won her a place at grammar school and subsequently Cambridge, where she gained a PhD in just two years. She was immediately recruited by SPIDER for her technical genius.'

'Although maybe ze genius is evil?' Auguste pointed out.

'She'd certainly be a powerful enemy. And Umbra's penchant for technology is well documented, as the Neurotrol showed,' Robert continued. 'But The Cardinal's past is even less clear – he appears just to show up at SPIDER two years ago at a very senior level with no records. This suggests either very high-level security service, or—'

'He's an imposter,' said Vi. 'He's certainly a pain in the bum. Mum says everyone hates him around SPIDER HQ and she can't stand having him as her boss.'

'What?' said Robert. 'Easter is back at SPIDER?'

Vi winced. Turned out she was terrible at keeping secrets too. Must run in the family.

'Well, yes, but—'

'Ha! This is brilliant!' Robert clapped. 'We have someone on the inside.'

'No,' said Vi firmly. 'Mum can't know about Umbra. It's the only thing keeping her safe there.'

'Sure,' said Robert. 'But she'll have all kinds of security clearances that could prove very useful.'

'Yes, but I can't—'

'When's your school trip to SPIDER HQ?' Robert asked.

'Tuesday,' said Vi quietly. 'But I'm really not going to—'

'Excellent,' said Robert. 'It's a golden opportunity. You can report back when I come to your graduation on Friday.'

'Great,' said Vi, inwardly groaning on two counts. Firstly, she was getting caught between her parents. Again. And secondly, unlike bin night, her dad hadn't forgotten about her graduation. Both issues meant choosing a parent. She was going to have to lie to one and disappoint the other. Again.

'Hang on, dummy,' Missy said, chewing on gum. 'Didn't you work for Umbra? You must be able to figure out their next move. Unless you're a total duh-brain, duh.'

'Missy?' said Janet gently. 'Let's be polite to our host, please.'

'CAN IT, JANET!' Missy roared. 'You only have two jobs. One – book my birthday party at EpicBowl – I want bumpers.'

'Yes, dear,' said Janet. 'And what's the second?'

'CAN IT!' screamed Missy. 'Anyway, Robert. You know Umbra. What's the deal?'

'The young lady has a point,' said Robert, changing the screen. 'If we want to catch Umbra, there are two key personnel we need to locate.'

Robert flicked up a black silhouette on the screen.

'Who's that?' Vi asked.

'The Blacksmith,' Robert sighed. 'No one knows much more than that. The Blacksmith, so-called due to his ability to forge anything, created all of Umbra's secret identities. Pound to a penny, he will have forged the credentials that got Umbra the job at SPIDER. If we find The Blacksmith, we can unmask Umbra.'

'So what are we waiting for?' said Auguste. 'Let's go get 'im. I have a bomb in my coat pocket . . .'

'Not that simple, I'm afraid,' Robert grimaced, bringing up a newspaper cutting which showed a handcuffed figure in a black hood being marched into SPIDER HQ by a familiar face. 'The Black-smith was arrested by The Cardinal a couple of years back and, like many security threats, is now held in the SCF – the Secure Containment Facil-ity – at SPIDER HQ. He's a Category A prisoner, so isn't allowed to see anyone or go anywhere – only The Cardinal has access to him. Like Siren says, that place is a fortress. The best way to access it would be if we had someone on the inside with security clearance . . .'

He looked at Vi with a big grin. She didn't grin back.

'Who's the second person we need to find?' she asked.

Robert flicked up a picture of a woman, probably in her thirties. She was pretty – her dark brown eyes shone through her glasses out of her light brown face, which was framed perfectly by black hair that sat on the shoulders of her lab coat.

'This is Dr Charlie Payne,' Robert explained. 'Pioneer in the field of neuroscience. She was the inventor of the original Neurotrol.'

'Where is she now?' Siren asked, exhaling a question mark from her e-cigarette.

'Nobody has seen nor heard from her in months,' said Robert. 'She went underground around the same time Umbra did. It's like she's a ghost.'

'Pffff,' said Missy, tapping into her phone. 'No one's a ghost these days. Everyone leaves a digital fingerprint. Bet I can find her.'

Auguste leant over to Vi.

'Does thees little girl give you the creeps?' he whispered in her ear.

'Sure,' shuddered Vi, moving further along the sofa.

'Bless you, dear,' smiled Robert at Missy. 'But

I've had a year of top-level governmental agents trying to trace her and getting nowhere, so I think it's rather unlikely that you'd be able to—'

'Here she is,' said Missy, thrusting her arm out and smacking Auguste in the face as she did. She turned her phone around to show detailed maps, images and coordinates. 'She's in a cabin in this forest.'

'How on earth did you—'

'I hacked her Deliveroo,' sighed Missy, blowing a gum bubble. 'Doesn't matter who you are or what you're hiding from, no one can go a year without ordering a pizza.'

''Acking is so unethical,' huffed Auguste.

'Unethical?' scoffed Missy. 'What does that even mean?'

'You 'ave no shame . . .' Auguste said uneasily, arming his bomb.

'No, I'm serious – what does it mean?' said Missy. 'I only got to L in my key word spellings before I liquidated my literacy teacher.'

'If Umbra gets to Dr Payne before we do, she could be forced to build another Neurotrol,' said Vi.

'A bigger, better Neurotrol,' Robert agreed.

'Which is why we need to get to her first. We can keep her safe. And maybe use her as bait . . .'

'Speaking of the Neurotrol,' Vi began, before telling the group what she'd learnt from the Silver Service, about the NIDUS space station and what could happen if Umbra got the Neurotrol to it.

'My god,' gasped Robert. 'With the Neurotrol on NIDUS, Umbra could . . . it doesn't bear thinking about. Well, that makes the decision easy . . .'

He tapped some numbers into his remote control, revealing a safe in the wall. He opened it with a fingerprint scanner and took a small, old phone out of it.

'Wow,' said Missy. 'No wonder you're such a dummy, with tech like that . . .'

'The Neurotrol is inside,' Vi explained. 'Duh.'

'I've been wondering what to do with it,' Robert said. 'But given what Valentine's just told us, there is only one option. Mick?'

Robert opened the phone and took what looked just like a SIM card out of it. The Neurotrol. That was all it was — just a little microchip. Vi wondered again how something so small could be so dangerous. Though a quick look at Missy reminded her that both were possible.

Robert placed the Neurotrol on the table and his henchman lumbered towards it with a meat cleaver. Mick brought the cleaver down hard on the Neurotrol, then again – a dozen times.

'I think it's done, Mick,' whispered Robert, pulling his henchman away from the broken smithereens of the Neurotrol. 'Maybe next time, move it off the table first.'

Vi picked up the pieces of the Neurotrol and tossed them into the fire. She watched them melt and burn until they were nothing. The Neurotrol was no more. Mission accomplished. Why wasn't Ms Direction here to grade this one?

'Well, that's the end of that,' said Robert. 'Now to stop Umbra from getting another one. Tomorrow we go on a mission to acquire Dr Payne. Vi – I'm guessing you're in?'

'What?' said Vi. 'You're actually going to let me come? On an actual mission?'

'Of course,' shrugged Robert. 'You're training to be a spy. There's only so much you can get out of textbooks and simulators. You need real experience. In the real world. How else will you really learn?'

Vi grinned appreciatively at Robert. Weekends with her dad were shaping up nicely.

'You know *I'm* in, babe,' winked Siren. 'Just let me reorganize my dental hygienist. My teeth will have to wait. Even if they do look like the porcelain on a public toilet.'

'*Pourquoi pas?*' grinned Auguste. 'I'm in. But where will we find everything we need in twenty-four hours? We need ze transport, ze equipment, ze weapons for killing people—'

'NO KILLING!' Robert, Siren and Vi said simultaneously.

'*Bof,*' said Auguste dismissively, slumping back in his chair.

'I can't come,' said Missy, jumping off the sofa. 'I don't work Sundays – I have a spelling test Monday morning. But you can borrow my private jet if you like. It's got everything you need on board for a successful rescue mission. And it smells like marshmallows.'

'Thank you, Missy,' said Robert. 'That would be a great help. So, I'll see everyone here at 1800 hours tomorrow?'

Siren and Auguste nodded and made for the door. Dave winked and started playing some soft blues as he walked behind them.

'Missy?' said Janet quietly. 'What do you say to Mr Ford for having you?'

'CAN IT, JANET!' Missy shouted. 'Thanks for the sandwiches. See ya, suckers.'

And with that, Robert and Vi were left alone again.

'Well, that was an eventful EVIL meeting,' said Robert, putting the screen away. 'Usually the greatest excitement is stopping Auguste from eliminating his sponsor. Ready for some dinner?'

Vi nodded keenly. She was ready for everything. Because tomorrow, she was going to prove she had what it took to be a spy. Not in some stupid simulator. In the real world on a real mission.

And on this mission, failure was not going to be an option.

CHAPTER 9

'I think I'm gonna puke!' groaned Vi as she stumbled out of Missy's plane and on to the dark forest floor on Sunday evening.

'Yeeesh,' agreed Siren, tottering out after her and holding her nose as Dave gagged on his sax. 'That's the worst thing I've smelt since my gym kit after my last spin class.'

'I must use zees marshmallow scent *dans* my next bomb,' gasped Auguste. 'It is more deadly zan dynamite.'

Robert emerged from the plane, holding a handkerchief to his flushed face.

'I love you, Vi,' he said. 'But if you ever make me buy any of that child's horrendous BRAT stationery, I'm turning back to a life of crime. It's safer.'

Half an hour aboard Missy's scented private jet had been quite enough to convince Vi that she never wanted to shop at BRAT again.

At least, not this week.

'So,' said Robert, pulling out his phone. 'According to Missy's coordinates, the cabin holding Dr Payne should be right about . . .'

'Zere,' said Auguste, pointing to a wooden shack just visible through the trees. 'Ze *petite* crime wave was right. Now I throw a few grenades and we can start ze killing, *non*?'

'NO!' said everyone in the loudest whisper they dared.

'*Les spoily sports*,' pouted Auguste, putting the grenade back in his clown trousers.

'The plane's stealth mode should mean that— David, do you mind?' Robert began.

Dave gave him a small salute and wandered off into the forest playing a jazz version of 'Greensleeves'.

'As I was saying,' Robert continued, 'whoever is in that cabin shouldn't have heard us.'

'They probably smelt us, though,' gagged Vi. 'Somebody shut the door.'

'Vi's right,' said Siren. 'I once blew a robbery I'd

spent six months planning because I forgot to clean my teeth. Now I always gargle before a big mission.'

'Wiz what?' Auguste asked, holding his red nose. 'Manure?'

With lightning speed, Siren karate-kicked Auguste against a nearby tree.

'Oops,' she said insincerely.

'Everyone calm down – we're supposed to be on a covert op here,' chided Robert. 'Now we don't know the situation in that cabin. Dr Payne could be there voluntarily, or she could be someone's prisoner – possibly Umbra's. So we need to go carefully and thoughtfully and – Valentine!'

But whatever her dad had to say, Vi couldn't hear – she was already too far away. She crept towards the shack, keeping her body weight low as she'd been taught at Rimmington Hall – finally all those squats for Mr Repp were paying off. She saw movement in the dimly lit window ahead and stopped. She turned her Eye-Spy watch to four o'clock: *amplify*, so she could hear what was going on inside. Due to the thick forest canopy and the remote location, the signal wasn't great. But she could just about make out the conversation.

'You can't keep me . . . for ever,' a woman's voice, presumably belonging to Dr Payne, urged. 'I want to . . . home.'

So Dr Payne wasn't alone. And it didn't sound like she was there by choice. But who was there with her?

'You h . . . n . . . oice,' came the crackled response. Vi held her watch higher to try to get a clearer signal.

'Valentine!' rasped her father behind her. 'Don't you ever head off like that again – communication is key to any mission and—'

'Shhhhh!' said Vi. 'I can't hear what they're saying.'

'They?' said Robert. 'Who's they?'

Vi shushed her father with her hand and tried to tune back in. The height helped. The signal was slightly clearer.

'I'm telling you,' said Dr Payne, 'I have to leave.'

'Well, you can't,' came the gruff response. 'I won't let you.'

That voice! It was a distinctive one that had growled at Vi a few times now. It was deep and low and a little bit scary—

'The Wolf!' she cried, earning her a giant

115

shushing from her father. 'Sorry – The Wolf is in there with her! He's keeping her captive! The Wolf must be Umbra!'

'We can't leap to conclusions,' Robert cautioned. 'We need to gather more—'

'I know I'm right!' Vi insisted, the scent of success even stronger than Missy's marshmallows. 'We have to go!'

'Who's there?' came The Wolf's voice over her Eye-Spy. 'Whoever you are – don't try anything stupid. I'm armed.'

'Marvellous,' said Robert. 'Now we've lost the element of surprise. I guess we're going to have to—Valentine! Wait!'

But Vi was already running towards the cabin. She wasn't going to let The Wolf get away. She needed to save the world from Umbra. She needed to stop The Wolf before he could force Dr Payne to build a new Neurotrol. She needed to prove to everyone that she *was* a totally brilliant spy . . .

But mainly the first two things.

She pelted across the forest floor – fair play, Mr Repp's sprint runs had also been useful – and reached the cabin door just as The Wolf kicked it open, revealing a stunned Dr Payne inside. Vi stopped dead. The Wolf had a gun. And he was pointing it straight at her.

'Lynx's kid?' he said. 'What are you doing here?'

'Bringing you down, Umbra,' said Vi, setting her watch to one o'clock: *tranquillize*. 'You can come with me voluntarily. Or I'm going to make you.'

'You're a fool, kid,' growled The Wolf, not lowering his gun. 'Stay out of what doesn't concern you.'

'Oh, this concerns me,' said Vi, puffing up. 'This concerns all of us. Now put down your weapon or I'm going to fire this dart in three ...'

'Don't do it, kid,' said The Wolf. 'I will shoot you.'

'Two ...' said Valentine, her heart beating in her ears as the heady rush of fear and adrenaline took hold.

'This is your final warning,' said The Wolf, not budging an inch. 'I really don't want to have to—'

'One!' cried Valentine as she pushed down hard on the button.

What happened in the next few seconds wasn't

entirely clear for some minutes. At the exact second Vi hit the button, a gunshot fired and she was knocked to the ground by a mass of green hair. When she gathered her wits two moments later, she saw that her T-shirt was stained with blood.

But it wasn't hers.

'Auguste!' she cried, checking to see that another gunshot wasn't on the cards. But her shot had been successful too. The Wolf was lying unconscious on the ground.

'Vi!' cried Robert, coming over. 'Are you OK? Are you hurt?'

'I'm fine,' said Vi, looking at the wound on Auguste's shoulder. 'Auguste! Auguste! Can you hear me?'

'*Oui*,' said Auguste groggily. 'So zis is how it feels when you shoot someone, uh? No one ever said it hurt ...'

Vi smiled. Auguste was going to be OK.

'You ... you saved me,' she said as Auguste's big red mouth formed a warm smile. Perhaps he wasn't so creepy after all.

'*Mais oui*,' groaned Auguste as he accepted Robert's handkerchief and pressed it to his shoulder. 'If someone else kills you, 'ow am I going to do it? Zeez is a funny joke, *non*?'

Vi laughed with him. He was only kidding.

Probably.

He pulled himself off the ground and raised a floral hankie to his shoulder.

'If you'll excuse *moi*,' he said, 'I think I will go back to ze plane. The smell should make ze pain easier to bear.'

'We'll be right with you, Auguste,' said Robert, giving the clown a gentle pat on the back. 'And thank you, thank you for—'

'Hold it right there, sister,' came the cool voice of Siren as Vi heard her rifle cock. 'Don't move a muscle.'

Vi turned to see Siren's target as the femme fatale crept out from behind a tree. She recognized the figure holding her hands up from her dad's briefing. It was Dr Charlie Payne.

'Are you Umbra?' Dr Payne said calmly. 'Have you come to kidnap me?'

'No, ma'am. We're here to save you,' said Vi happily. She'd been waiting to use that line too.

'You're what?' said Dr Payne. 'Save me from who?'

'From The Wolf,' said Vi. 'Although you might know him as Umbra.'

Dr Payne rolled her eyes and gave the unconscious Wolf a swift kick.

'I know him as Isaac Payne,' she said forcefully. 'Or Stop Being Such a Payne. Or Payne in the Bum. He's been all of the above. Ever since we were kids.'

'Hold on,' said Vi, rapidly joining the dots. 'Dr Payne . . . Isaac Payne . . . you're The Wolf's . . .'

'Sister,' Dr Payne confirmed. 'Big sister – not that you'd know it from the way he's trying to boss me around. He brought me here to keep me "safe" from Umbra – although I'm also super-suspicious he's still trying to find the first edition *Beano* that he says is his, but our mum gave it to me first and I'm fifteen months older so—'

'Stay on the point, lady,' said Siren. 'I've got nose hairs in-growing faster than this.'

'Isaac thinks that Umbra will want me to build a new Neurotrol,' sighed Dr Payne. 'So he's been hiding me here. The idiot.'

'How do we know you're not working together?' asked Siren. 'Just because you're his sister, doesn't mean he ain't Umbra. You could be in on it too.'

Vi's mind buzzed. Of course – Siren was right! Rod had said to treat everyone like they were guilty. She could take nothing at face value. The Wolf and his sister could be in this together . . .

But before another thought could form, the forest floor was whipped up in a tornado of leaves and twigs, forcing Vi's arms to her face to protect her eyes from the onslaught. The overwhelming combination of a deafening chopper shining a penetrating light assaulted her senses. She spat some forest floor from her mouth.

'If she's Umbra,' came a heavily disguised voice over a loudspeaker, 'then what am I doing here?'

A rope dropped from the chopper and a black figure whizzed down it into the trees beyond.

'Hold your positions,' said Robert. He pointed his pistol into the dark forest.

Vi froze. She knew the voice that was laughing in the darkness. Its owner had nearly killed her several times.

'Umbra,' she said as the figure, swathed in a black cloak and mirrored mask, emerged from the trees, a small device in one hand, a thumb clamped over its button.

'Valentine Day,' said the distorted voice. 'Robert. We meet again.'

Vi looked at The Wolf's unconscious body. Looked like he wasn't Umbra after all.

Oops.

'How did you find us?' said Robert, taking a step forward.

'Uh, Robert?' said Umbra. 'I'd avoid taking another step if I were you. I took the liberty of placing a few landmines around the place when I did my reconnaissance ahead of your arrival. While my finger is on this button, they are perfectly safe. But should you shoot me, should I drop it, or frankly, should I just feel like it, five seconds after I release it, they will detonate.'

'You're bluffing,' said Robert uncertainly.

'There's one sure way to find out,' said Umbra. 'Your daughter is standing on one right now. Move any closer and I'll remove my finger from the button. That should demonstrate my point perfectly.'

Vi stopped the breath that was halfway out of her body. She was standing on a landmine. She'd rushed in and put them all in danger. And the worst outcome here wasn't another F.

'Well, now I have your attention,' Umbra continued. 'Dr Payne, I must ask you to join me.'

'Never,' said Dr Payne, a slight tremble in her voice. 'I'm a scientist. Not a terrorist.'

'You can be both,' said Umbra. 'And you're going to have to be. If you want to survive.'

'My parents died when I was sixteen,' said Dr Payne. 'I've raised my idiotic kid brother alone, got three degrees while working four jobs to feed us, and have risen up through the scientific ranks despite most of my male colleagues thinking a woman is a diagram in a textbook. So kindly don't talk to me about survival.'

'Amen, sister,' said Siren admiringly.

Dr Payne fixed Umbra with a steely stare. Vi was impressed. She had guts.

'Nice speech,' said Umbra. 'Let's see what your brother thought of it.'

Umbra whipped out a gun from the dark cape and fired it straight at The Wolf, missing him by a hair.

'NO!' screamed Dr Payne, dropping to her knees beside her brother.

'That was a warning,' said Umbra, pointing the gun at her. 'There won't be another one. Come with me or I will kill you both.'

'If you kill me, you'll never get your Neurotrol,' said Dr Payne through gritted teeth. 'I'm the only one who knows the tech. I'm the only person in the world who can build it.'

'A skill I insist you share with me,' said Umbra, shifting the gun's focus to The Wolf again. 'And I'm afraid I don't have time to negotiate.'

'Stop!' said Dr Payne, holding up her hand. She looked down at The Wolf. Vi could almost hear the conflict in her brilliant mind.

Vi glanced at her dad. He was standing dead still, with Umbra in his sights. Without even looking at him, Umbra waggled the remote device, by way of a reminder. Robert couldn't shoot Umbra. He couldn't risk the landmines being detonated.

'Tick-tock, Dr Payne,' said Umbra, cocking the gun. 'I'm waiting . . .'

'OK,' said Dr Payne. 'OK. I'll come. Just don't hurt my brother.'

'You have my word,' said Umbra. 'But if you try to deceive me, if you provide me with anything other than a working Neurotrol, I'll be back for him. And next time I won't miss.'

Dr Payne looked at Vi and the EVILs. She leant

down and gave her brother a gentle kiss. Followed by a less gentle punch.

'It'll be OK, Isaac,' she whispered. 'Everything will be OK. You total butthead.'

She got to her feet and walked slowly to Umbra, who grabbed the scientist and walked backwards into the forest with her.

'Get your hands off me,' Dr Payne hissed. 'I have one PhD in neuroscience, another in wedgies. Happy to use both.'

Umbra raised a hand, but continued to retreat slowly into the darkness.

'We're closing in on you, Umbra,' Robert growled. 'It's only a matter of time.'

'Good luck with that,' came the distorted voice as the super-villain and the scientist were winched back into the helicopter. 'And, Robert?'

'What?'

'CATCH!'

Vi watched in horror as the detonator flew through the air towards them.

'VI!' screamed Robert, leaping across the floor and knocking her out of the way, before covering the ground with his own body. 'RUN!'

Vi did as her father asked and sprinted as fast

as she could, feeling Siren next to her.

'You ready, kiddo?'

'For what?' Vi panted.

'To . . . JUMP!' cried Siren, grabbing Vi by the arm and leaping over a massive rock. They lay there, trembling.

'Dad!' cried Vi. 'My dad!'

'Stay down, kiddo,' said Siren, clutching Vi to her. 'Just stay down.'

They waited for the terrible explosion, the one that would blow Robert to smithereens . . .

But it didn't come.

An amplified cackle echoed around the forest as the chopper edged away.

'Gotcha!' laughed Umbra from high above. 'Until next time . . .'

The helicopter swung on to its side and away into the distance.

Robert rolled over and let off a round of bullets towards it. But they were wasted. Umbra had gone.

'You OK, kid?' Siren asked Vi as they both stood up.

'I'm fine,' said Vi, brushing herself down. 'But FYI – you really do need to clean your teeth.'

Siren smiled and gently punched Vi's chin as they made their way back to Robert.

'How?' said Robert, sitting up. 'How did Umbra find us? We swept ourselves for tracking devices – how did Umbra know we were here?'

Vi didn't have the answers. But she did have a question.

'Where is he?'

'Up there,' said Robert, pointing to the sky. 'You just saw him – or her, or them – leave.'

'I don't mean Umbra,' said Vi, looking at the empty space in front of the cabin. 'I meant The Wolf.'

Robert turned around to where The Wolf's unconscious body had been just moments ago. It had disappeared.

'Great,' sighed Robert. 'Another lead lost . . . Come on, Vi. We need to get you home. The car will be coming to pick you up soon for school.'

'Dad . . . I . . .'

Robert looked at her. For the first time, she saw disappointment in his eyes.

'I don't want to discuss it right now,' said Robert. 'Just go back to the plane. Please.'

Vi wanted to explain. But she could see it was

pointless. She trudged towards Missy's plane, letting her sense of smell guide her in the darkness. There was so much she didn't understand.

If The Wolf was innocent, why had he run? Umbra turning up proved they couldn't be the same person. So why wouldn't he stay? And the biggest question of all remained unanswered.

If Isaac Payne wasn't Umbra – who was?

CHAPTER 10

'**N**an . . . Nan – it's a video call, you don't hold it to your ear,' said Vi, wincing at the extreme close-up of her grandmother's ear hole on her screen. Easter had finally relented over her no-phone policy when Vi started Rimmington Hall, and Vi was enjoying her regular Monday morning catch-up with Indy while she waited for her psychology lesson to start.

'Oh, I don't know,' grumbled Nan, flipping the screen around so Vi could see the floor. 'All this new-fangled tech, what's wrong with a normal phone?'

'How are you getting on with finding the NIDUS . . . ground station . . . thingy – Gumfoot?' Vi asked. 'Umbra has Dr Payne. It's only a matter of time until she is forced to build a new Neurotrol

– we have to find Gumfoot and shut NIDUS down, foil Umbra's plan before it starts—'

'I've tried all my old contacts,' came Rod's gruff voice. 'But they're dead ends.'

'None of them knows where it is?' sighed Vi.

'No,' grunted Rod. 'They're all just dead. I'll keep searching. Right up until the end of time. Probably tomorrow ...'

'Listen, I'd better go,' said Vi as Russell plumped down next to her, running a hand through his trendy new haircut. 'My class is about to start – love you, Nan.'

'Love you, gorgeous girl,' said Nan's ear. 'See you soon.'

Vi ended the call, just in time for Russell to pick up the monologue he had been delivering in several instalments all morning.

'... so then we went to the Splashzone, but my mum is really good friends with the guy who owns it, so he let us stay after it closed and we had THE WHOLE place to ourselves and we were riding on all these water slides in the dark and it was totally epic and then ...'

Vi stifled a yawn at her desk. She was partly exhausted from her eventful evening before. But at chapter twenty-five of *The Best Weekend Ever* by Russell Sprout, she was running out of fake enthusiasm.

'So . . . how were Mum and George when you got home?' Vi interrupted as Russell launched into a detailed description of The Best Pizza He'd Ever Eaten at This Great Place His Mum Knew.

'Er, dunno really,' said Russell breezily. 'I only saw them briefly before the car came to get me. Dad was in the shed mostly.'

Vi felt her stomach lurch. George had spent a lot of time in the shed after her dad had ruined her mum's first wedding. It wasn't a great sign that he was back there now.

'But were they angry? Upset? Sad?' Vi prompted.

'Um. Not sure,' said Russell, whose emotional intelligence didn't match his academic one. 'They didn't really speak to each other, so it was hard to say. Anyway, did I tell you about my mum's place? It is The Best Flat Ever, she has—'

'Hey, Tamina!' Vi shouted gratefully as her friend arrived.

'Hey, guys,' said Tamina glumly, offering her friends a bag of roasted sunflower seeds. 'What's new?'

'I took on a super-villain and Russell had pizza,' said Vi, taking a handful of the salty snack.

'Oh, great,' sighed Tamina heavily.

'Is something wrong?' asked Russell.

'Ten out of ten for observation,' Vi said quietly. 'What's up, Tam?'

'Firstly, it's running club this afternoon. I HATE running club,' said Tamina. 'And secondly, it's my dad. He's cancelled all his lectures on Friday to come to this stupid graduation. Apparently I'm getting some kind of special commendation for academic excellence.'

'You poor thing,' said Vi.

'You don't understand,' groaned Tamina. 'He's well proud of me and winning stupid prizes makes it worse ... How can I tell him?'

'Tell him what?' Russell asked.

'That I don't want to be a spy!' Tamina quietly screamed. 'I want to be an environmentalist! What's the point in saving the world if there isn't any world left to save?'

'Have you told him that?' Vi asked.

'I can't,' Tamina grumbled. 'Every time I even mention this place, he's all like "your mother would be so proud, you're living her dreams, she's smiling down on you . . ." How can I disappoint him like that? How can I disappoint her?'

Vi pulled her friend into a hug, largely because she had no idea what to say. Tamina didn't talk about her mum much – she'd died in Iraq when Tamina was a baby. Tamina never said how, and Vi had never asked. But it had something to do with Tamina's dad coming here. And it had something to do with the sad look in Tamina's eyes on the rare occasions she mentioned her mother.

'How could *you* be a disappointment?' Russell chipped in. Tamina blushed to her core. Vi was impressed. That was an unusually emotionally intelligent thing for him to say.

'Thanks,' said Tamina shyly.

'No, I really don't understand,' Russell clarified. 'You win loads of prizes and stuff. Don't all parents like that?'

And . . . normal service was resumed.

'So you took on Umbra, huh?' Tamina asked.

'Yeah . . . well, not exactly,' said Vi, filling Russell and Tam in on her weekend.

'So now Umbra has Dr Payne, Umbra can get another Neurotrol,' Russell said. 'That's really, really bad.'

'Thank you, Professor of the Stupidly Obvious,' Vi grumbled. 'Rod and Nan are working on Gumfoot. But it's even more urgent that we get to The Blacksmith and find out who Umbra really is. If we know their true identity, the authorities can arrest Umbra and we'll all be safe.'

'You need to get to who?' Tam asked.

'The Blacksmith,' Vi explained. 'He forged all Umbra's identities. He knows who Umbra is. And he's in the Secure Containment Facility at SPIDER HQ. Where we are going tomorrow ...'

'Vi,' Russell warned. 'Don't do anything stupid.'

'I didn't say I was going to do anything!' said Vi defensively.

But then again, she hadn't said she wasn't going to either. Last night she'd messed up. Now she needed to prove herself to her dad, as well as to Ms Direction. Tomorrow was her chance to do both.

'Hey, Russ,' Tamina asked, pulling a notepad out of her bag. 'Could I ask your advice on something? I'm trying to design this phone charger that runs on the energy released during photosynthesis. I've got prototypes all round the school, but I just can't get the contact electrification to work.'

She showed Russell the detailed plans in her book and he stared at them admiringly.

'Wow,' he said, hitching his glasses up his nose. 'This is really cool. This could turn any plant into a plug socket, creating clean, green energy. It's brilliant.'

Tamina blushed again. Russell might have had the emotional intelligence of a spoon, but surely even he could see she had a crush on him?

'I think the problem's your sprockets,' he said.

Maybe not.

Vi zoned out as Russell and Tamina had a long conversation in Geek. Her mind drifted back to the cabin in the woods. Even as she sat there, Umbra would be forcing poor Dr Payne to recreate the Neurotrol. Before long, there'd be another Neurotrol in the world – possibly even more powerful than the first. She had to stop Umbra. Dr Payne was out, but there was another chance with The Blacksmith. If Vi could get to the master forger in the Secure Containment Facility, she could find out Umbra's true identity. Tomorrow's school visit to SPIDER was too good an opportunity to waste. That was her chance to prove to everyone that she had what it took to be a spy.

And save the world and stuff. That was important too.

Now if she could just take a little nap on this desk . . .

'Mmmmm – sunflower seeds,' came a saccharine voice, rousing Vi from her sleep. 'Do you eat lots of those where you come from? And what are you doodling?'

Vi looked up groggily to see the unwelcome form of Jenny Stellar looming over their desk. She was carrying all BRAT stationery. That figured.

'For the idiots at the back: I "come" from Enfield,' Tamina sighed. 'I'm British. My father is Kurdish British. You are a moron. My "doodling" – or "schematic drawing" for those of us with a brain – is none of your business. Shall we move on?'

'I just think it's so cute how you techies play with all your geeky little gadgets while we field agents go and do the real work,' said Jenny, wrinkling her nose.

'Those "geeky little gadgets" are what keep us alive in the field,' Vi pointed out. Tamina and

Russell might be mega-geeks. But they were her mega-geeks and she wasn't about to let Jenny Stellar belittle them.

'Sweet,' chimed Jenny again. 'Though I don't think field work is something you'll need to worry about after Friday, is it, Valentine? You'd have to get a score that's . . . well . . . as good as one of mine if you're going to stay here. It'll be such a shame to see you go. You really do give the place such . . . comedy value.'

'I'm not going anywhere,' said Vi with more confidence than she felt.

'Of course you're not,' said Jenny with her wrinkled nose. 'You keep believing that.'

Vi wanted to hold on to Jenny's wrinkled nose and give it a proper tweak, but was interrupted by Tamina.

'Are you still standing here for a reason?' Tamina asked Jenny. 'Because your village called. It wants its idiot back.'

'Oooh – careful, Tammy,' said Jenny, sucking her breath in. 'Rimmington Hall has a zero-tolerance policy for verbal abuse. My mum told me that at her most recent meeting as chair of the board of governors . . .'

'Well, could you ask them to review their policy on verbal diarrhoea?' Tamina shot back. 'Because I have a zero-tolerance policy for that.'

Jenny put on her sweetest smile. It was about as convincing as Russell's emotional intelligence.

'Russy?' she said, turning to her new techie.

'Er . . . hi, Jenny,' said Russell, who had been curiously intrigued by a large textbook during Vi and Tamina's conversation with her. 'What can I do for you?'

'Meet me in the greenhouse after supper tonight?' she said sweetly. 'I just want to go over some things for our assessment. In *private*.'

'Yeah – sure,' said Russell, hitching his glasses up again. 'See you around six?'

'Just what I was going to say,' giggled Jenny. 'You see! We're already a winning team. And there are so few of those around . . .'

'Agent Sprout?' said Mr Poyntment, the office manager, striding into the room. 'I don't appear to have your allocated guest for Friday's graduation. Who shall I put down?'

'Oh – sorry, totally forgot!' Russell laughed nervously. 'Can you please put down my mum,

Genevieve Dupree? That's Genevieve, G–E–N–E–V—'

'Wait – what?' Vi interrupted. 'You're not inviting your dad? Is he OK with that?'

'Er . . . I guess,' said Russell, pushing his glasses up his nose again. 'I didn't really talk to him about it.'

'Well, you probably should,' Vi pointed out to her spoon-like nearly-stepsibling. 'He was so excited about it – did you know that this building—'

'Well, so's my mum,' said Russell defensively. 'And she never gets to come to these things.'

'And whose fault is that?' Vi said quietly. Although according to the look Russell gave her, not quite quietly enough.

'And you, Agent Day – who will be supporting you on Friday?' Mr Poyntment asked.

Vi slumped down in her chair.

'No one,' she said quietly.

'I'm sorry – do you mean you don't require any tickets?' Mr Poyntment checked.

'That's right,' sulked Vi. She sighed deeply. It was going to be easier to upset everyone than pick one. Besides, she didn't really need either parent watching her fail.

'Good morning, class,' said Professor Scott, bustling into the classroom. 'As you'll be able to deduce from my elevated heart rate, the lingering scent of engine oil about my person and the fact that I once watched an Abba tribute band in Inverness in February, I was delayed by car trouble.'

Tamina shot her hand up.

'Yes, Agent Shalli?'

'Can we deduce from the big ketchup stain on your bow tie that your car broke down near the drive-thru burger place on the way?'

Vi tried not to laugh as Professor Scott blushed. He was totally busted.

'See me for detention after school, Agent Shalli,' he said, surreptitiously wiping his tie. 'You will have to miss running club.'

'Yes, sir,' said Tamina with a sly grin, winking at Vi.

'How do you do that?' Vi whispered admiringly.

'Elementary, my dear Valentine,' Tamina whispered back.

CHAPTER 11

As the Rimmington Hall blacked-out minibus pulled up outside SPIDER HQ, Vi felt a tingle of excitement. This was where her mother and her grandmother had proven themselves as top spies – and today, if she got into the Secure Containment Facility and found The Blacksmith, she could do the same. This building housed Vi's destiny. This building was where she belonged. This building was ...

... really hard work to get into.

To access the SPIDER offices, every student had to have full body, fingerprint and retinal scans, followed by a ten-minute interrogation, provide a DNA sample with a lock of hair and recite the unique twenty-six-digit code they'd been sent the day before. No wonder her dad and

Siren couldn't break in here – she barely could and she'd been invited.

Eventually they were ushered through the building towards the demonstration suite where they were to have their tech presentation. The huge open-plan space was full of suited agents, rushing between desks or having conversations in clear booths. For a top-secret agency, there was very little privacy here. But that was probably a good thing. And, Vi smirked to herself, it could be very helpful today.

'First things first, Recruits,' Ms Direction said when everyone was sitting down in the large Perspex box that housed the demonstration suite. 'You are very fortunate today to enjoy a demonstration from one of SPIDER's foremost technicians, Agent Unicorn.'

Honey B took a clumsy bow to the light smattering of applause from the students. Vi's godmother could be Umbra. Vi would be watching her every move. Although as Honey B picked up her coffee and spilt it all down her crumpled suit, Vi wondered how she was masterminding a criminal empire when she couldn't even negotiate a reusable coffee cup.

'I hope I need not remind you that this is a rare privilege and one from which I hope you will sap every advantage,' Ms Direction continued. Vi looked over at Russell who was so excited he looked like he was going to explode. 'I expect you all to conduct yourselves as agents of the highest calibre and pay Agent Unicorn the respect she deserves.'

An inconveniently loud belch escaped Vi's lips. She knew she shouldn't have eaten her packed lunch on the bus. Honey B giggled, hopefully saving Vi from whatever punishment Ms Direction had in store.

'Over to you, Agent Unicorn,' smiled Ms Direction as Honey B took centre stage.

'Thank you, Ms D – and it's my pleasure to welcome you to SPIDER HQ and to introduce you to some of the newest advances we are working on here in our fight against crime. Today I will be showing you our latest line in tracking devices, sensory VR and sonar stunning technology. Let me start with the SonarStun – a device that uses only sound waves to render a suspect totally unconscious . . .'

Vi tried to be interested in the tech but, living

with Russell and Mr Sprout, she had her fill at home. Her mind and gaze started to drift beyond the clear walls of the demonstration suite. She watched the SPIDER agents scurrying about their business around them. Various proud parents were waving at their offspring, who were trying not to wave back, either because of Ms Direction's all-seeing gaze, or pure embarrassment. Vi couldn't see her mum among the agents – perhaps she was so senior she had her own office somewhere else? She looked all the way around the room until her eyes met the disapproving gaze of Ms Direction. She snapped her attention back to Honey B's presentation.

'. . . and that's one of the most exciting, but also most challenging parts of my job – the technology moves faster than we do. Keeping up is difficult sometimes, but in addition to innovating new espionage technology, we are constantly trying to update tried and tested methods. Take this new edible tracking dye that uses a biological enzyme to make it totally untraceable by conventional methods . . .'

Vi felt her attention wander outside the box again as a familiar face rushing past caught her eye. She recognized his sprouty brown hair. She recognized his twitching white face. She recognized his terrible 1980s moustache.

It was The Cardinal.

Vi's spy senses prickled. Umbra could be inside this box, or had just walked past it. She was going to need to keep a close eye on both Honey B and her boss.

'. . . but lightning-speed developments in virtual reality are allowing us to replicate real-life situations with minimum risk to agent safety,' Honey B continued as Vi tried to keep one ear on her and one eye on The Cardinal. He seemed to be looking suspiciously at his colleagues as he hurried through the office, or was that her imagination? Perhaps everyone should start looking more suspiciously at him . . .

'Can I have a volunteer?' Honey B asked. Russell shot his hand up so high, it was a wonder his arm didn't shoot out of his shoulder.

'Russell,' smiled Honey B. 'Would you be my guinea pig?'

Russell got up enthusiastically.

'Careful,' said Vi out of the corner of her mouth. 'She might be Umbra. What if she's trying to do something to you?'

She watched Russell wrestle with the idea for approximately 0.3 seconds before the lure of the new tech won him over.

'Whatever,' he said, rushing to the front of the room.

'Thanks so much, Agent Sprout,' Honey said warmly. 'If you'd like to follow my colleague here, he'll lead you to the VR room, where we can all watch you on this screen. Is that OK?'

Russell nodded like his head was on a spring, and was duly ushered away by another SPIDER agent.

Vi carefully turned her neck so as not to attract attention. She'd lost sight of The Cardinal. Where had he gone?

A buzzing noise redirected her focus to a large, grey metal door at the far corner of the SPIDER office. The Cardinal was standing outside it, still looking around suspiciously, as if everyone were watching him. He took a pass from a lanyard on his belt and swiped it through the scanner. The light above the door changed from red to green and The Cardinal walked through.

Only as the door closed could Vi see what was

written on it.

'*Secure Containment Facility. High-Level Security Only,*' Vi whispered to herself. That's where they were keeping The Blacksmith! That's where she could find Umbra's true identity! She had to get in . . .

'Valentine?' Ms Direction said in a tone that suggested Vi wasn't going to get a commendation any time soon. 'Pay attention.'

Vi nodded quickly and looked to the front, where Russell now appeared on the big screen. He was armed with a laser gun and was fighting off hordes of invading aliens. It looked freakishly real.

'Everything you are seeing here is what Russell is seeing,' Honey B explained. 'You've used similar tech at Rimmington Hall – with the right lighting, it is possible to simulate any visual experience. But this is the next evolution in VR – sensory reality. Within the heightened sensory environment of the VR suite, Russell will not only be able to *see* whatever the program dictates, he will be able to *feel* it as well.'

'Ow!' screamed Russell right on cue, as an alien ray gun fired at his arm. Vi instinctively twitched.

What if Honey B was trying to hurt Russell? What if this was all part of an elaborate plan to take him out? What if—

Russell laughed as one of the aliens offered him an ice cream.

'Mmmm, tastes good,' he grinned, licking the imaginary dessert.

What if Vi was starting to get a teeny bit paranoid?

Yes, there was a chance Honey B was Umbra. But there was a chance she wasn't. She might be suspecting her lovely godmother for nothing when it was The Cardinal who was behaving suspiciously. And she did really like the sherbet lemons . . .

'And so you see,' Honey B concluded, 'the key to the future is utilizing the old and embracing the new. With the right tech at your disposal, you can take on the world. Thanks so much for your attention, good luck with your training!'

A more enthusiastic applause followed as Ms Direction shook Honey B's hand and turned to address the class of Recruits again.

'Thank you, Agent Unicorn, for that scintillating introduction to some of SPIDER's cutting-edge technology,' she smiled. 'Now it is time for you all to go to your assigned mentors for the day.'

Ms Direction gestured to the gaggle of proud parents assembled outside, still determined to embarrass their offspring with a wave. This time, Vi could see Easter – she was hanging back, on the outside of the crowd, looking as if she didn't know what to do with herself.

'Those of you with parents outside, you may join them now,' Ms Direction prompted.

Most of the students rose and went outside to the adult waiting for them. Vi walked past Jenny Stellar and her mother, and wasn't surprised to see the striking family resemblance – both looked totally stuck-up. She made her way through the parents to where Easter was standing awkwardly.

'Hey, you,' said Easter, beaming at the sight of her daughter.

'Hey,' said Vi, giving her mum a big hug. 'How are you? How's George? What happened after—'

'We're fine,' smiled Easter. 'We've got some stuff to figure out, but we're getting there. How was your weekend with Dad?'

'Oh, you know,' said Vi, trying to sound breezy. 'The usual.'

'Glad to hear it,' said Easter, looking relieved.

Vi felt her guts knot. She hated lying to her mum. And if she was going to break into the Secure Containment Facility today, she would have to lie a lot more . . .

'Thank you so much,' Ms Direction announced to the adults, 'for taking the time to share your expertise with our students today. If you are able and happy to have more students shadow you, there are several without a parent here.'

'What are you doing in there, Russ?' Easter laughed. 'Get over here, you big silly!'

'Yes, Agent Sprout,' said Ms Direction. 'What are you still doing here?'

'Oh,' said Russell, hitching his glasses up his nose. 'It's just you said "parents", and Easter – Agent Lynx – isn't actually one of my . . .'

He trailed off, leaving a screaming silence. Vi glanced at Easter, whose hurt was written all over her face.

'You're quite right to challenge my terminology,' said Ms Direction smoothly, easing some of the awkwardness. 'I should have said "families" – not all Recruits have biological ties to their family members within SPIDER. I will choose my words more carefully next time. Go and join your family.'

'Can I come too?' Tamina asked. 'I'm not family, but I'd love to see Agent Lynx's work. She's a real inspiration to me . . .'

Ms Direction smiled.

'Agent Lynx? Would that be all right?'

'Absolutely,' said Easter, regaining her composure. 'Although I hope you'll not be too bored by my—'

'Lynx!' came a shrill voice behind them. 'So this is your family?'

Vi turned around to see Jenny, her mother and all Jenny's sheep standing around simpering.

'Yes, Agent Tarantula,' said Easter in the tone that Vi knew she used for people she didn't like. 'I'm very lucky.'

'You must be such a role model to them,' cooed Vicky Stellar, smiling sweetly. 'Coming back to work after all this time and starting right at the very bottom again. Good for you for not finding that utterly humiliating.'

What did she mean? Vi thought. Easter Day was a top agent. A top agent who looked like she was about to cry.

'There's nothing humiliating about working hard,' Tamina piped up. 'Some people are handed life on a plate. Others cook the meal. And Easter Day is one of life's chefs. So, yes, she's an incredible role model. Glad you realize it.'

Vi had never wanted to hug her friend harder. She just hoped Tamina never had to sample Easter's actual cooking. She looked over to see Ms Direction listening to their conversation. Was that . . . admiration in her eyes?

'Hmmm,' smiled Vicky as she tottered off with her entourage. 'Cute.'

Easter gave Tamina a look that communicated more than speech possibly could. And Tamina's nod suggested she understood every word.

'So let's go,' said Vi, trying to lighten the moment. 'Where's your office, Mum?'

'Well . . . it's not what you might call an office . . . exactly,' Easter stuttered.

'Great,' said Tamina. 'Sounds much better, it's like a greenhouse up here. Show us the way.'

'You coming, Russ?' Easter said quietly.

'Sure,' said Russell, looking all kinds of awkward. Vi hadn't often seen him like this since they started Rimmington Hall. What was going on?

Her thoughts were interrupted as she heard a metal door slam – The Cardinal was exiting the Secure Containment Facility. The Blacksmith had to be in there. What if he was plotting with The Blacksmith even now? What if he knew that Vi and her family were on to him and he was planning to disappear with a whole new identity? Or what if he needed to make sure that The Blacksmith couldn't do anything at all?

Vi didn't have the answers. But she knew they lay behind that door. And one way or another, she was going to get them.

Today.

CHAPTER 12

'So, here it is,' said Easter, flicking the switch in her dim bunker-like office. 'It's not much. But it's . . . no, it's just not much.'

Vi looked at the faded sign on the door.

'Procurement,' she read. 'What does that mean? Sounds important.'

'Ha – it might *sound* important,' said Easter, sitting down at her tiny desk, 'but it's just a fancy way of saying "getting stuff for people". If agents want something, they put in a request with me and I try to source it for them.'

'Sounds important enough to me,' said Tamina, picking up a circuit board from one of the dusty metal shelving units that lined the long, dark room.

'Why are you down here?' Russell asked, with

his emotional-spoon sensitivity. 'Why aren't you . . . up there? With everyone else?'

Vi walked across the room to look at some books on the opposite wall, 'accidentally' treading on Russell's foot on the way past.

'It's . . . it's complicated,' said Easter, looking embarrassed. 'You see, I left SPIDER over ten years ago. It was a different world back then. I'm a VHS in a streaming world!'

'What's a VHS?' Vi asked. She was going to have to learn all these spy abbreviations.

'And . . . there you have it,' said Easter with a strained smile. 'Anyway, while I'm retraining for field work, The Cardinal assigned me down here, just until I get my hand back in.'

'I'm sure it won't take long,' smiled Tamina.

'It might,' said Russell. 'I mean, you've got to learn all the new technology, all the systems that will be totally unrecognizable from a decade ago, not to mention that you're not as young as you were and that's bound to take a toll physically— Ouch!'

'Sorry,' said Vi, after recrossing the room and 'accidentally' standing on his foot again.

'So how does it work?' Tamina asked.

'Well,' sighed Easter. 'The agents come down here and—'

'Knock knock!' came a cheery voice at the door. They all turned around – it was Honey B. Vi watched her mum grin at her bestie. If Honey B were Umbra, Easter certainly had no suspicions. And her mum was a top spy – or used to be. If she wasn't suspicious, should Vi really be? 'Oh – hey, Easter, sorry to interrupt, I'll come back later . . .'

'Not at all,' smiled Easter. 'In fact, you're just in time for me to demonstrate how Procurement works.'

'Oh, well, no . . . that won't be necessary,' Honey blustered, starting to blush. 'The stuff I order is very dull, I'm sure the kids aren't interested. Let's just do it this afternoon.'

'I'm interested,' said Vi quickly, standing next to Honey. She was looking shifty. And any information on any suspect was useful . . .

Vi felt a bag of sherbet lemons press into her palm.

Or maybe she was just a really lovely godmother.

'OK, then,' said Easter brightly. 'So Honey – Agent Unicorn – put in a request a week ago for some parts to be delivered to her house . . .'

'Why her house?' Vi asked innocently. 'I mean, she's got that massive lab here, hasn't she?'

'Oh – I'm afraid it's a sad consequence of having no life,' Honey B sighed. 'I have a work-shop in my basement that I spend all my evenings and weekends tinkering in. I like it. It's peaceful there. And it's got actual walls, unlike this place!'

Sure, Vi thought. *So no one can see what you're doing.*

And then she immediately felt guilty for think-ing it. Vi slipped a sherbet lemon into her mouth and started sucking it into a fang to help her thought process. And because it was cool.

'So it's my job to source all the parts from vari-ous suppliers and get them shipped to her house,' Easter continued. 'I tell you, that VPP gave me the runaround, Hon, but I got there in the end. Everything should be with you tonight.'

There was a crash as Russell dropped the robotic arm he'd been fiddling with.

'What else did you order?' he asked, failing to sound quite as innocent as Vi had. Vi tried not to look at him. Something had clearly caught Russell's attention. She didn't want Honey B to realize it.

'Oh – just some bits and bobs,' said Honey, pushing some hair behind her ear. 'It's just an idea I've had – very early days, I don't want to jinx it . . . Anyway, I should probably—'

'A VCC, a CLK and that pesky VPP,' Easter read from the order. 'I've had all kinds of strange conversations with a supplier in Uzbekistan.'

Vi tried to look at Russell without moving her head. Watching Russell's brain was like watching a computer run a complicated program. And something was downloading.

'Thanks, E,' said Honey, backing out of the room. 'Anyway, I'd better—'

'Agent Unicorn – I've been looking everywhere for you!' barked The Cardinal, who had suddenly appeared in the doorway, making them all jump.

'Sorry, sir, it's been a busy morning, what with the Recruits visiting and—'

'I don't want to hear excuses, I want to hear answers!' The Cardinal interrupted.

Vi could feel her mother tensing. The Cardinal was clearly a lousy boss. But was he also an evil overlord? Was the bad cop a double bluff, designed to hide his true personality? Or was he just a butthead?

'Yes, sir,' said Honey meekly. If Honey was the evil overlord, she was doing a good job of hiding it right now. She just looked very scared. Although that too would be an excellent bluff. Vi's head hurt. Trying to second-guess super-villains was super-tiring. She needed another sherbet lemon.

'I wanted to know if you had those coordinates on Agent Wolf,' The Cardinal snapped. 'He hasn't reported for duty for two days. His tracer was picked up near yours on Sunday evening, shortly before it was deactivated. Do you know where he is?'

'Er, no,' said Honey B. 'I did see him on Sunday – he came to ask if I had any old clothes his sister could have, apparently she lost all her things in a house fire. Sounded awful . . .'

Vi tried to steady her breath. So The Wolf was still missing. He'd run away from SPIDER as well as running away from them in the forest. But why? Surely SPIDER could help him find his sister? This didn't make any sense. Unless Umbra had got to him first.

But as Vi saw The Cardinal's security pass

dangling from his belt, her thoughts were interrupted by another, more urgent matter.

The Blacksmith.

With The Cardinal's pass, Vi could get into the Secure Containment Facility, find the forger and discover Umbra's true identity. But first, she needed that plastic card. She flexed her fingers. It had been a while since Vi had . . . relocated something from someone else's pocket to hers. But it was time for a little bit of putpocketing.

'. . . but after that, I have no idea,' said Honey B. 'Has someone checked his home? Perhaps he's ill.'

'Of course we've checked his home!' The Cardinal roared. 'We are one of the world's foremost intelligence agencies! Don't you think we might have thought of that, Unicorn?'

Vi reached out her arm. The Cardinal was so preoccupied with shouting at Honey B, he wasn't paying attention. His pass was tantalizingly close.

'Yes, of course, sir,' bumbled Honey B, looking like she might start crying. 'I was just—'

'You were *just* being ineffectual and unhelpful!' shouted The Cardinal. 'This is why I denied your promotion request! Promotion? You'll be lucky to have a job here if you continue in this impertinent manner. You are on your last warning, Unicorn! I'm watching your every move and I'm sick and tired of your incompetence!'

Vi reached her fingers out. She could touch the security pass. Now if she could just get it out of the lanyard . . .

'She was only trying to help,' Easter piped up. 'And I have been researching some new surveillance technology that might help us to triangulate Agent Wolf's last known coordinates to give us an insight into his location. If you reinstated my active duty status, I could perhaps—'

The Cardinal whipped around, snatching his pass out of Vi's grasp. She cursed silently. She'd nearly had it. It was half out of the lanyard. If she could just grab it . . .

'I don't recall asking your opinion, Agent Lynx!' he shouted. 'If you ever want to get out of this hovel and back into the field, I'll remind you to listen to authority and stay out of matters that don't concern you!'

'Yes, sir,' said Easter, her bottom lip quaking. She was getting mad. And so was Vi. Umbra or not, she was ready to kick The Cardinal's butt. No one disrespected her mum.

Apart from her, obvs.

'Good,' said The Cardinal. 'Now I'll thank you both to get on with your jobs and let me get on with mine!'

And The Cardinal spun on his heel and stormed out of the room. Vi felt the heavy weight of failure in her chest and cursed rather more loudly. She'd missed her chance. Now she'd never get to The Blacksmith.

'Are you OK?' Easter asked Honey B.

'I'm fine,' said Honey, taking off her glasses and wiping them. 'Nothing I'm not used to.'

'You shouldn't have to get used to it,' said Easter. 'You deserve that promotion. He's a bully.'

'Well, he's our boss,' Honey replied. 'And we'd better do what he says. See you later.'

'See ya,' said Easter, watching her friend leave the room just as the phone rang. 'Procurement, this is Agent Lynx speaking.'

'Tamina,' whispered Russell, his program still clearly downloading. 'Can I ask you something? If I gave you a VCC, a VPP and a CLK what would you make?'

'Well, that's obvious,' scoffed Tamina. 'But are we talking D-plus or D-minus? They're technically optional, but I think these days the USB capability is essential . . .'

'Stop talking in Geek!' Vi hissed. 'What? What would you make with those components?'

Tamina shrugged. 'Isn't it obvious?' she said. 'I'd make a SIM card. Wouldn't everyone?'

'Certainly someone who needed a device capable of controlling every mind on the planet,' said Russell, hitching up his glasses.

Vi gasped as she realized what Russell was implying.

Honey B had ordered the components to build another Neurotrol.

Download complete.

'Well, hello,' said Ms Direction, appearing in the door frame. 'How are we all doing? Have we learnt lots of useful things?'

'Loads,' said Vi, still in shock. The only person in the world who could make a Neurotrol had been kidnapped by Umbra and now Honey B had the components to turn the NIDUS space station into an international mind-control machine. There was only one logical conclusion.

Umbra *was* Honey B.

Vi nearly choked on her sweet as the enormity

of her godmother's deception bore down on her.

'I'm glad to hear it,' said Ms Direction. 'It's time for lunch – thank you for your time, Agent Lynx.'

Easter gave a thumbs up while cradling the phone under her chin. They all left the procurement room. If only Vi had swiped that pass. The Blacksmith could confirm her suspicions and Honey could be under arrest that very day. Now *that* would prove a point to Ms Direction. And to everyone. But Vi had blown it. Again.

'Looking for something?' whispered Tamina, dangling the security pass in front of her.

'How did you get that?' Vi whispered back, grabbing it gratefully.

'I saw you trying to nick it, so I figured it was important,' said Tamina. 'Besides, I don't care if I get kicked out. You do.'

'You're a star,' said Vi, feeling her heart quicken. 'Russ . . . Russ?'

'What?' said Russell as they reached the rest of their class back in the Perspex box.

Vi flashed the security pass. Russell went pale.

'You have to give that back,' he said. 'You'll get us all in massive trouble.'

'Not if we prove for certain that Umbra is

Honey B!' said Vi excitedly. 'We can complete this mission, right here, right now! All I need you to do is create a distraction so I can get into the Secure Containment Facility.'

'No!' Russell whispered loudly. 'It's too risky – we need a proper plan, if this goes wrong—'

'What could possibly go wrong?' said Vi. 'Tam – cover me. I'm going in.'

'OH, NO!' Tamina started screaming, dropping her packed lunch and grabbing her throat. 'My sandwich! It's . . . it's CHEESE!'

Ms Direction came rushing over.

'Whatever's the matter, Agent Shalli?' she said, watching Tamina's reddening face. Vi had to hand it to her friend – she might not want to be a spy, but she would make a great actor.

'I'm allergic!' Tamina gargled.

'What? I have no record of this,' Ms Direction said, looking unusually flustered. 'Why didn't you—'

'It's . . . new,' said Tamina, sinking to the floor and waving Vi away with her hand. 'Just . . . school . . . food. Suggest . . . throwing . . . all . . . away.'

Vi waited a few moments for the drama around Tamina to escalate, before taking her chance and

sneaking out of the box. She knew from experience that the best way to hide doing something
wrong was to look like she was doing something
right. And so, grabbing a file from a desk as she
passed, she strolled through SPIDER HQ like she
owned the place, smiling at agents as she walked
past, paying close attention to the file as she went.

Vi reached the metal door unchallenged. She
didn't dare look behind her for fear of seeming
guilty. But judging from the kerfuffle she could
still hear, Tamina was playing her part to perfection. She held the security pass in her hand. This
was it. This was her moment. She held the card to
the scanner and—

'STOP!'

Her heart nearly leapt out of her chest as a
hand came down hard over hers. She'd been
caught. She was in massive trouble. She was . . .

'I won't let you do this!'

She was staring straight at the angry face of her
nearly-stepbrother.

'Russell, what are you doing here?' she snapped,
now looking deeply suspicious as she glanced
around. 'You're supposed to be causing a scene!'

'You're the one who's going to cause a scene if

you use that pass,' Russell snapped back. 'This isn't a simulation, Vi! This is a top-level spy agency! You're about to trespass in a Secure Containment Facility and you're going to get us arrested – or worse!'

'Some spy you're going to make, with that attitude,' Vi shot back.

'Well, I'm doing better than you so far,' said Russell, his words stinging her heart.

'You think so, huh?' she said. 'Is that why you won't work with me for the assessment? Because you're so much better than me?'

Russell let out a breath through his nose. His mouth was too puckered up to release it.

'No,' he said, hitching up his glasses. 'I won't work with you because you don't know how to work with someone. You're just in this for yourself. You don't know how to be part of a team.'

'Like you're being part of our family's team?' Vi shot back. 'Like you hurt my mum just now? Like you've completely ditched me since we started Rimmington Hall? You know what your problem is? You're selfish.'

'Well, I learnt from the best,' snarled Russell bitterly.

There was a tense stand-off as they stared at each other. Vi could barely speak for the hurt.

'Then I guess this won't surprise you,' said Vi.

And, whipping her arm out of Russell's grasp, she held the card up to the scanner.

The effect was immediate. And very, very loud.

'CODE FOUR SECURITY BREACH! CODE FOUR SECURITY BREACH! STOLEN SECURITY PASS LOCATED IN SECTOR SEVEN! ALL SECTORS IN IMMEDIATE LOCKDOWN! ALL AGENTS TO REMAIN IN SITU OR FACE SEVERE SANCTIONS!'

Vi clamped her hands to her ears as the screeching announcement played over and over to a chorus of lights and alarms. Metal gates dropped from the ceiling, and barriers sprang up from the floor, until Vi and Russell were fully incarcerated behind bars.

'Happy now?' Russell shouted over the deafening noise.

Vi didn't reply.

Because for once, she didn't have anything to say.

CHAPTER 13

'**C**hin up, kid,' said Nan the next day as Rod drove Vi to Robert's house. 'Might never happen.'

'Think it already has,' groaned Vi, her stomach churning as she reflected on the events since her visit to SPIDER HQ. Highlights included:

- Ms Direction's threats of expulsion from Rimmington Hall as The Cardinal marched Russell, Tam and Vi into his office;

- four hours of security checks to make sure they weren't enemy spies – not made any quicker when they discovered the identity of Vi's father;

- the interrogation Easter underwent to ensure she wasn't a double agent, meaning a disciplinary hearing that could cost her job;

• and the silent car journey back to Easter's house as she and Russell were suspended, pending further investigation.

None of it was much fun – despite what Tamina thought.

But the thing that really stuck with Vi was the look on Russell's face. She shifted uncomfortably in the back of the car as the betrayal etched in his eyes came to mind. It wasn't all her fault – if Russell had been more supportive and helped her, maybe things would have gone differently . . . But even as the thought formed, Vi could feel her conscience arguing with her defensiveness. Stupid conscience.

'You did exactly the right thing,' growled Rod. 'I would have done the same. Except better and without getting caught.'

'Don't encourage her,' Nan chided.

'Why not?' Rod replied. 'I have her best interests at heart. Just like I still have your heart . . .'

'You still have a driving licence,' Nan snapped back. 'That's the only reason you're here and don't you forget it.'

Rod snorted. Vi swore she saw the flicker of a smile cross his lips.

'The girl's training to be a field agent,' Rod continued. 'She should take every opportunity. And she's right to suspect everyone and everything.'

'I dunno,' said Vi. 'I think it's making me a bit paranoid.'

'Just because you're paranoid,' said Rod, looking in the rear-view mirror, 'doesn't mean you're wrong.'

'Let's face it, Honey building a SIM card doesn't automatically make her Umbra,' Vi said. 'She's a technician, she must make stuff like that all the time – it could just be a coincidence.'

'Heck of a coincidence, though,' said Nan, and Rod growled in agreement.

'What about The Cardinal?' Vi continued. 'There are any number of reasons he could be going to the Secure Containment Facility – he's one of SPIDER's most senior agents – it might have nothing to do with The Blacksmith. Although if he is Umbra, it would be a great place to hide Dr Payne – urgh! At least we can rule The Wolf out.'

'Why?' said Rod.

'I told you – he was there when Umbra attacked,' Vi said, rolling her eyes. 'He was unconscious.

Umbra kidnapped his sister! He's now missing.'

'So?' shrugged Rod. 'What does that prove? That he's good at deception and double-bluffing? That he can make you think what he wants you to think? That he's just created a watertight alibi to rule himself out? All sounds like Umbra to me . . .'

'Whatever,' sighed Vi. But Rod had a good point. What was to say the whole showdown hadn't been staged for their benefit? What if The Wolf had arranged the whole thing to throw them off the scent? He and Dr Payne could be in it together – they were family after all. And families stick together . . .

Russell's hurt and angry face crossed her mind again, making her feel deeply uncomfortable. She shook it off. She needed to focus.

'So who do you think Umbra is?' she asked.

'I dunno, kid,' said Rod, flicking on the indicator. 'Though in my experience, the most obvious explanation is usually the right one.'

'Rod!' Nan suddenly yelled. 'Watch out for that cyclist, you silly old—'

Before she could finish her insult, she was racked by a violent coughing fit.

'Nan!' Vi said, as Indy struggled for breath. 'Nan! Are you OK?!'

'She's fine,' said Rod, pulling into the car park where they'd arranged to meet Robert. 'Here, Lotus Flower, time for your meds.'

He pulled a bottle of pills out of the glove compartment and gave one to Indy with a water bottle, rubbing her back until the coughing fit passed. Vi sat back in her seat. It was good to see Nan being looked after. But it was worrying to consider why she might need it.

'Nan?' she asked again, once Indy had regained her breath and a normal colour had returned to her cheeks. 'What was that?'

'Seventy-eight years of life, that's all,' said Nan, waving Rod's water bottle away. 'At my age you have to take so many pills you rattle. I'm absolutely fine.'

Vi didn't push Nan any further. Though she wasn't convinced.

Robert's invisible car suddenly appeared in the next parking space.

'Saints preserve us!' Nan said, holding her chest. 'He can materialize from anywhere. Like the devil. Or a cold sore.'

'Indy,' drawled Robert, winding down his window. 'Always a pleasure.'

'Robert,' said Nan stiffly. The passing months had done little to improve Nan's opinion of her father. Although she had stopped swearing every time he came up in conversation, so that was progress.

'Robert Ford!' said Rod admiringly. 'Sir Charge? We met back at that chemical plant in eighty-three. I tried to knock you into the vat of boiling acid?'

'I thought I recognized you!' smiled Robert, getting out of the car. 'I never forget a face. Agent Redback?'

'Once upon a time,' said Rod. 'You still trying to take over the world?'

'You still convinced it's going to end tomorrow?'

The two men laughed and shook hands. Nan turned to Vi.

'Men,' she sighed, shaking her head.

'So how's my little national security threat?' grinned Robert, looking at Vi in the back seat.

'Enough with the dad jokes,' said Vi, rolling her eyes, although she was grateful that at least he was making them again. It had been an uncomfortable flight back to his house on Sunday night after the failed mission to rescue Dr Payne. She and her dad were still getting to know each other. She was worried he might not like her as much after she messed up.

'Come along, then. Let's get you home,' said Robert.

'Easter says she's not to have junk food, TV or late nights,' said Nan strictly. 'She's on suspension, not on holiday.'

'Roger that,' said Robert, performing a small salute as Vi got out of the car. 'I'll have her begging for prison by tomorrow.'

An hour past her bedtime, in front of the TV and over takeaway pizza, Vi and Robert were still discussing what Vi had learnt.

'I have to say, it looks like Honey B is our girl,' sighed Robert. 'The Wolf is a soldier, not a sociopath. And the evidence against The Cardinal is circumstantial at best. If only we could get to The Blacksmith. I know he can shed some light on this. I've got Missy Fit working on a little something for us . . .'

The front doorbell rang. Robert looked at the door cam and fell back on the sofa.

'Oh, no,' he groaned.

'Gary,' smiled Vi as the doorbell rang again. 'Well, don't leave him waiting.'

Robert grunted, but hit the intercom button. 'Evening, Gary,' he sighed. 'To what do I owe the pleasure?'

'Oh, nothing much – just a friendly neighbourhood reminder about bin night tomorrow,' Gary replied. 'You see, we operate an alternate weekly refuse and recycling system here—'

'Yes, thank you, Gary – I've put a reminder on my front door. Goodnight.'

'Just one other quick thing,' Gary said. 'I don't want to be "that guy" but we have an . . . informal understanding here on Nimby Close about lawn maintenance. It's not a rule, exactly, more of . . . an agreement that we all stick to so that no one has to inform the council about it.'

'I see,' said Robert. 'I'll be sure to give it a mow ASAP.'

'Capital,' laughed Gary. 'But not before nine a.m. Here on Nimby Close we operate a quiet zone between the hours of nine p.m. and nine a.m. Stops any unnecessary neighbourhood noise pollution.'

'Not all of it,' muttered Robert.

'Sorry?' said Gary.

'I said, "the gall of it",' Robert added smoothly. 'Honestly, these people who mow their own grass! They should be put in the communal storage area to have rotten fruit thrown at them!'

'I'm so glad you agree!' said Gary enthusiastically. 'Say, you wouldn't be interested in joining our Nimby Close Protection Society, would you? It's a very friendly bunch, the pitchforks are only for show really . . .'

'Bye, Gary,' said Robert, switching the intercom off. He turned to Vi. 'Tell me I'm allowed to vaporize that one?'

''Fraid not,' said Vi, tucking into her fourth slice of pizza.

'Urgh,' sighed Robert. 'Life was so much easier when everything could be solved with a well-aimed laser and some hungry sharks . . . Right, put that down. We've got work to do.'

'You what?' said Vi through a mouthful of margherita. 'What work?'

'If Honey B *is* Umbra, she has both Dr Payne and the delivery of components from SPIDER in her possession,' said Robert. 'So it's only a matter of time before she has a new Neurotrol. She must know something about NIDUS too — we have not a moment to lose.'

'Where are we going?' said Vi, brushing away the pizza crumbs as she struggled off the sofa.

'To Honey B's house, of course,' said Robert. 'You said she has a workshop in her basement?'

'So she said.' Vi shrugged.

'Then that's where we start,' said Robert.

'Er . . . Dad?' said Vi. 'You said you weren't going to break the law? I'm already on suspension and, besides — breaking and entering isn't exactly one of my strong points . . .'

'Well, it is one of mine,' grinned Robert, waggling his eyebrows as he picked up the phone. 'But you're right — we both need to be careful. I'm putting you on lookout while she goes in.'

'She?' Vi asked.

'Oh, yes,' said Robert. 'I know just the woman for the job.'

CHAPTER 14

'Has the target left yet?'

Vi huffed at her father's third enquiry in as many minutes.

'I told you, I will say when I see her!' she said stroppily, going back to her binoculars. The indigestion from that fourth slice of pizza was not helping her mood. She hated to admit it, but Mum was right. Junk food didn't make you feel good. And sleep was actually quite useful.

'Robbie, take a breath,' said Siren, drawing on her e-cigarette and exhaling a rainbow. 'The plan will work. It'll take time and patience. Like treating a verruca.'

They were huddled in the back of Auguste's van, which had been hastily redesigned to look like an electrician's.

'How's Auguste doing?' Vi asked Siren.

'He's good,' Siren smiled. 'He's out of hospital and ... Dave?'

Her saxophonist put his instrument down apologetically, and picked up a book of crossword puzzles.

'. . . and he's recovering at home,' Siren said. 'The doctors thought it was for the best.'

'Oh, yes,' Robert agreed. 'Much better to be in his own bed.'

'No – Auguste kept breaking into the cleaning cupboard to make home-made explosives,' Siren added. 'The hospital's insurers paid his taxi fare themselves. He's going to be out of action for a while. But, for any number of reasons, that's probably no bad thing.'

'Well, I'm glad he's on the mend,' said Robert. 'I owe him a great debt.'

He smiled at Vi, who briefly returned it before turning her attention back to Honey B. She looked through Honey's downstairs window. Honey's house was, rather like its occupant, a bit of a mess. The white exterior had long since lost its freshness and was streaked with the overspill from the overflowing gutters. Like her godmother's hair, the lawn was overgrown and unkempt and the windows needed a good clean, just like her glasses. But even through the slightly grimy windows, Vi could make out her godmother sitting at her desk in her front room, working at her laptop. She looked so . . . normal. Could she really have been an evil overlord all this time? She had always been so kind to Vi. And the sherbet lemons . . .

'Are you sure Missy is up to the job?' Robert asked.

'Keep the faith,' said Siren. 'The kid managed to hack the Ministry of Defence *and* show me how to unlock the digital channels on my TV. She's good.'

A car pulling up next to the van put everyone on alert. Robert grabbed his pistol. Siren cocked a rifle in her thigh-high boots. Dave quietly played some tense jazz. The back door of the van was wrenched open and Vi ducked behind the front seat, awaiting the gunslinging.

'Put your guns down, dummies,' said a familiar voice. 'Or I'll text everyone in your contacts that you have worms.'

'Missy dear,' sighed Robert, holstering his gun.

'Always a pleasure.'

'Can't stay,' said Missy, replacing her trademark lolly. 'I'm being followed.'

'Who's after you, kid?' said Siren, grabbing her rifle again.

'Natalie and her mum, duh,' scoffed Missy. 'We're showing them the way to Brownies.'

'Are you ready, Missy love?' came Janet's voice from outside. 'I'm parked on a double yellow.'

'CAN IT, JANET!' Missy screamed back, making Vi wince at her volume. She took another quick look through Honey's window. Her godmother was still engrossed in her laptop; all was well.

'Aaaaanyway,' said Missy. 'Everything is sorted. I've scheduled an email to tell her that the sprinklers have gone off in her lab at SPIDER. She should receive it any second.'

Vi watched Honey tapping away at her laptop. Then she stopped, stooped in to read something and threw her hands up in exasperation.

Vi smiled. 'I think she's got it.'

'Told you, losers,' smirked Missy. 'I gotta split. Brown Owl is picking the new Sixers today and if she doesn't choose me, I'm going to post pictures of her snogging Akela on the Scouts' Facebook page. I want to lead the Scottish Kelpies. I think they'll make excellent henchmen. See ya, dummies!'

A car horn sounded outside as the van door slammed.

'JANET?' Missy's retreating voice shouted. 'Can't remember if I told you? But . . . CAN IT!'

Vi heard Missy's car drive away and returned to the view from the downstairs window. She saw her godmother check her watch, throw her head back in frustration and rise from the chair, grabbing her coat as she did.

'OK – suspect's on the move,' she reported. 'Are you ready?'

'Kiddo,' smiled Siren, extinguishing her e-cigarette, 'I was born ready.'

The light in the front room went off and everything was still for a few moments.

'There she is!' said Vi as Honey appeared around the corner in her car. 'OK, we don't have long. You need to move it!'

'Roger that,' said Robert, fixing his earpiece. 'I've identified an access point to the basement – it's a ventilation shaft that leads straight inside, circumnavigating any alarms. Siren is the world's greatest cat burglar. She can be in and out within five minutes.'

'Four,' huffed Siren. 'Three when I stole Van Gogh's *Sunflowers* from the National Gallery. I secured the painting, took a selfie with Henry VIII and still had time to stink out the bogs. Are comms up?'

Vi fitted her own earpiece.

'Testing?' Vi asked.

'Receiving,' said Robert. 'We are go!'

Robert opened the back door of the van and allowed Siren to squeeze past him and drop stealthily to the road below. He followed her – rather less gracefully – and Vi watched them scuttle off into the overgrown bushes that surrounded Honey B's house. Vi took a cautious look left and right. If Honey came back and discovered them, their cover would be blown. And if Honey B really was Umbra, that would be the least of their troubles.

Vi tried to focus on her lookout, but found her mind wandering. She hadn't heard from Easter since she'd been at her dad's – was Mum still mad at her? Vi couldn't blame her. She knew how important it was to Easter to earn The Cardinal's respect and Vi had totally blown it. Mum had enough problems with George and Genevieve without Vi making her life any harder. Vi still didn't know if she was even allowed to go back to Rimmington Hall, let alone sit her assessment – hers could be the shortest spy career on record. And then there was Russell – why was he bothering her so much? It wasn't like she cared what he thought or anything . . .

Some whispered communication over the earpiece snapped her back to the moment.

'OK, here it is,' she heard Robert saying. 'You go, I'll keep watch. Any issues at all, pull on the rope.'

'This takes me back,' purred Siren. 'Do you remember that time you paid me to steal the Prime Minister's laptop?'

'How could I forget?' said Robert. 'You were dressed in black, I was wanted in seventeen countries. Our eyes met over the security guard's machine gun . . .'

'Er . . . a little focus maybe?' Vi scolded. 'We're on the clock here, people.'

'Er . . . yes . . . quite right,' Robert blustered.

'Right, Siren – you are go, go, go!'

The talking stopped, but Vi was instead treated to a series of bizarre grunts and groans. She had no idea what was going on.

'Come on, dear,' Robert said impatiently after a while. 'Tick-tock.'

'I . . . I can't,' Siren finally declared.

'What do you mean, you can't?' Robert hissed. 'You're Siren! You got into the vault at Buckingham Palace!'

'Well, that Siren must have been a couple of dress sizes smaller than this one,' Siren snapped. 'I can't fit into this shaft. And I won't be villain-shamed for embracing my natural curves!'

'For goodness' sake – let me have a go,' said Robert. 'Perhaps if I go in backwards . . .'

'Dad!' Vi said. 'That's negative! You are not to break the law, remember?'

'Oh, this isn't breaking the law – just bending it a little bit,' Robert said dismissively. Vi huffed. What was the point in having her there in his earpiece if he wasn't going to listen to a word she said? He'd asked her to keep them safe and now he was just ignoring her advice, this was so . . .

An uncomfortable guilt rumbled in her guts. Vi

chose to ignore it.

Siren's grunts and groans continued to a chorus of criticisms from Robert. Vi rolled her eyes. She'd always assumed that Siren and Robert had retired from villainy because they wanted to be better people. It now occurred to her that perhaps they were just rubbish villains.

'Be my guest,' huffed Siren. 'But don't come crying to me when I have to call the firefighters to get you out.'

Vi held the earpiece closer to her ear as the grunting recommenced. Then she pulled it away quickly as her dad let rip a really big swear.

'This is ridiculous!' he roared. 'There must be a better access point?'

'That would be negative,' Siren said, sounding smug. 'The girl's a tech freak. She has a super-advanced alarm system. This is the only vulnerability. We're going to have to abort mission.'

Vi's heart thumped in her chest. They couldn't abort the mission. They were running out of time. No. Honey B needed be eliminated from their enquiries or unmasked as Umbra. Tonight. Vi threw down her headset and crept out of the van.

She followed the route Robert and Siren had taken through the bushes and quickly found them, Robert half inside the ventilation shaft and Siren trying to pull him out.

'Vi! What are you doing here?' Robert chided as Siren yanked him on to the lawn with a quiet grunt and a much louder fart. 'You're supposed to be keeping watch!'

'And you're supposed to be in Honey B's workshop, so it looks like we're going to have to switch places,' said Vi. 'I'm smaller than you – I can fit in there.'

'No way!' said Robert. 'It's far too dangerous.'

'So's Umbra,' said Vi. 'We have to do this.'

Robert struggled for a response.

'She's right, Robert,' Siren agreed. 'And the kid's got the moves. She can do it.'

Vi accepted Siren's confident smile and turned back to her father.

'OK,' said Robert. 'But we're right here. If anything feels wrong, you pull on the rope and we'll have you out of there between two breaths.'

'Roger that,' grinned Vi, attaching herself to the rope. A proper mission. Take that, Rimmington Hall.

She squatted down and peered into the ventilation shaft. She could see a dim light shining at the other end of it.

'This will take you directly into the basement workshop,' said Siren, securing a head torch to Vi's forehead. 'If you find any evidence of the Neurotrol, NIDUS or Dr Payne, grab it and get the heck out of there, OK?'

'Understood,' said Vi, already making her way into the shaft. She felt a strong hand pull her back.

'Do you really understand?' said Robert. 'This isn't a game, Valentine. You could get seriously hurt.'

'I get it,' said Vi honestly. 'Failure is not an option.'

'Atta girl,' said Robert. 'Now go. We don't have much time.'

Vi didn't need asking twice. She knelt down, put her hands on to the metal surface, and quickly crawled through the short shaft. She was sure to be super-quiet. If someone was in that basement, she didn't want them to know she was—

'WHAT CAN YOU SEE?' Robert's voice bellowed down the ventilation shaft.

'Shush!' Vi snapped back, carefully peering into

the basement room below.

The workshop was precisely what you'd expect from a techie geek. Half-finished devices littered the desk, with tools, plans and books filling the rest. Computer screens lined the walls – Vi did a quick sweep for cameras, but couldn't see any. She pulled herself to the end of the shaft, before she was stopped by the rope. It wasn't long enough to allow her to drop down to the floor below.

'It's too short,' she hissed up the tunnel. 'I need to undo it.'

'No!' said Robert. 'That's the only way we can pull you ba . . .'

Vi didn't hear the rest of his objections as she'd already untied the rope, turned around and dropped into the workshop.

She quietly approached the desk. There was no sign of Dr Payne, nor anywhere she might be imprisoned – the basement had only one door and no cupboards. Vi looked at the bewildering array of devices on the work surface. It suddenly occurred to her that she had no idea what she was looking for. The Neurotrol was a microchip, like a SIM card. There were loads of those lying around. Any of these could be the evidence she needed.

Or all of them could legitimately be things that Honey was working on as a top-grade techie. An uncomfortable truth crossed Vi's mind. If only Russell were here. He'd know what to look for.

Then something caught her eye. It was a geeky gadget drawing, the kind that Russell and Tamina loved to draw. Vi shone her torch on the diagram. She recognized it at once. It looked like a giant, space-age spider's web. And it had a title. She recognized that too.

NIDUS.

It was a diagram of the abandoned space station, the one that Rod had designed! This was it! This was the final proof! What possible reason could Honey B have to need, or even know about NIDUS? There was only one.

Honey B *was* Umbra.

'Vi! Vi!' came Robert's urgent call from outside. 'You need to withdraw! Target approaching in T-minus ninety seconds!'

'What?' said Vi.

'Honey B's back,' Siren clarified. 'Get out of there!'

Vi quickly folded the diagram and stuffed it in her pocket. She ran over to the shaft, but in her haste to get in, hadn't figured how to get out again. The rope and the entrance to the shaft were now two metres beyond her reach. She needed an exit strategy. She needed a techie . . .

'Vi – hurry – she's in the house!' Robert hissed.

Vi urgently scanned the room for anything she could climb up to get back to her only exit route. There was a small swivel chair, but was it high enough? Only one way to find out.

She quickly rolled the chair over to the wall and tried to stand on it. It wasn't ideal – the wheels were moving around on the stone floor and the seat kept trying to swivel, making it hard to find her balance.

'Get out!' cried Robert.

'I'm coming!' Vi hissed, trying to stabilize herself on the chair. OK, she needed to jump. She could do this. She just needed to take a deep breath, and . . .

Several things then happened at once.

Firstly, the lights went on, temporarily blinding Vi as she tried to make the leap. This meant that, secondly, she lost her balance at the crucial moment, meaning that she didn't so much jump as fall to a crumpled heap on the floor. Finally, and most inconveniently, she heard the one voice she didn't want to hear.

'Vi!' cried Honey B. 'Are you OK? What on earth are you doing in here?'

Honey rushed over to pick Vi up off the floor, but Vi pushed her away.

'Don't you touch me!' she snarled, raising her fists. 'I know who you are.'

'Of course you do,' snorted Honey with a bemused smile. 'I'm your favourite godmother.'

'You're Umbra,' said Vi. 'And I've got the proof.'

She pulled the NIDUS diagram out of her pocket, which she quickly realized was a stupid move as she'd now given Honey a chance to take it back. She needed to think through her dramatic spy moments a bit better. Assuming she lived that long . . .

'Oh, gosh – Vi, you've got it all wrong,' bumbled Honey, going pale. 'Yes, I know about NIDUS – the Silver Service aren't the only ones with a dark web – but I'm not Umbra . . . I'm trying to *catch* Umbra.'

'Whatever,' Vi scoffed. 'Tell it to SPIDER. I'm sure they'd love to hear your story.'

'Vi – you heard The Cardinal,' Honey pleaded. 'I'm one mistake away from losing my job. I thought that if I made another Neurotrol, if I could lure Umbra out into the open, I could catch them myself. I realize it looks unbelievably suspicious . . .'

'You've got that right,' said Vi. 'Besides, only Dr Payne knows how to build a Neurotrol.'

'Just because Dr Payne was the first, doesn't mean she's the only,' said Honey, hitching her glasses. 'I studied all Dr Payne's research on the original Neurotrol – it wasn't that hard to figure it out. But you have to trust me. I'm just trying to prove that I can be a good spy. It's all I've ever wanted, since I was your age. I have to show everyone what I'm capable of. I might be going about it the wrong way, but I have the right intentions. You understand that, don't you?'

Vi felt her certainty slip. Yes, she did understand that. Quite a lot, actually.

'I need a win, Vi,' said Honey, her eyes filling with tears. 'I have no partner, no kids and not that many friends. Without my job, I have nothing and no one else. Vi, you have to—'

But suddenly she was cut off, as were the lights

in the room. A red emergency light came on in the ceiling, casting a sinister glow over the dingy room. Vi looked to the door. But with a loud slam, that escape was closed off too.

'What's happening?' stammered Vi, trying to orientate herself in the gloom. 'What are you doing?'

'I'm not doing anything!' Honey insisted, feeling around the wall for the lights. 'I don't know what's—'

'No friends, you say? Yours is a tragic tale, Agent Unicorn,' said a distorted voice from the darkness. 'But if you give me that Neurotrol, I'll be your friend for life – not that it would be a long-term commitment.'

'Umbra!' shouted Honey B. 'Vi – get behind me! Now!'

This time, Vi did as she was told. She ran to the corner of the room behind Honey B, just as Umbra appeared from the shadows, swathed as always in a black cape and mirrored mask. With a ferocious roar, Honey B launched herself at the super-villain. Vi had never seen her godmother fight before – she'd always seen her as a techie geek rather than a field agent. But as Honey high-kicked and karate-punched her way through Umbra's attack, Vi had to give it to her – the girl had moves.

'Give me the Neurotrol and I might let you live!' shouted Umbra, launching a series of vicious punches and kicks at Honey B. Vi expected her godmother to crumple at the force of the attack – but to Honey's credit, she withstood the blows and came back fighting with some of her own.

'Over my dead body!' Honey B shouted back, running up the wall and taking Umbra out with a flying kick.

'That can easily be arranged. I certainly arranged it for Dr Payne when she couldn't make my Neurotrol,' Umbra snapped back, flicking off the ground and back to standing before launching another attack.

Vi's heart lurched. So Dr Payne was dead. Umbra had killed her. Vi winced as Honey B absorbed blow after blow from the super-villain. Honey B was good. But Vi could see that Umbra was better.

'Dad! Siren! We need some back-up in here!' Vi yelled up the ventilation shaft. There was no response. She desperately hoped it was because they were coming to rescue her. And not because Umbra had silenced them.

'You ... can't ... scare ... me,' Honey B panted, starting to look weary as Umbra's unrelenting attack continued. 'I ... won't ... give ... in ...'

'Oh, I think you will,' said Umbra, backflipping across the room. 'Thanks for the help. You're a real *honey*.'

And with lightning speed, Umbra raced across the room and rained a punishing series of blows and kicks down on the exhausted Honey B. Vi watched her godmother's legs collapse beneath her. But even that wouldn't stop Umbra, who continued to beat her on the floor.

'Stop!' Vi yelled. 'Stop!'

But Umbra was merciless and tireless. Vi could feel the tears run down her face as she heard the pained groans of her godmother. She thought the sounds were the worst thing she'd ever heard. But that was before they stopped. The silence was far worse.

Umbra paused and looked down at the motionless agent on the floor. Vi watched as Umbra quickly scanned the work surface and identified a particular SIM card – the Neurotrol –

picked it up and stashed it inside their black cape. The mirrored face turned to Vi.

Vi cowered against the wall – but there was nowhere to go. This was it. Her time was up. Failure was now her only option.

Umbra stalked towards her, then towered over Vi.

She closed her eyes, crouched to the ground and waited for her final moment.

All that came was a mocking laugh.

'You'll keep, Valentine Day,' Umbra scoffed. 'I'm not done with you yet.'

And with a deft leap, Umbra scaled the wall, crawled into the shaft and escaped into the night.

Vi stayed in her corner, stunned by fear and relief. Had Umbra really just . . . let her go? She waited for any sign that the villain was coming back. But there was none. She pulled her head out of her arms and looked cautiously over to Honey B, lying on the floor. She wasn't moving. Was she . . .

Vi got up from the floor shakily, wiping the tears from her eyes. Her godmother was . . . she didn't dare guess.

'Honey?' she said quietly.

There was no response. She moved closer.

'Aunty Honey?'

The lightest of groans confirmed that Honey was still alive. For now.

Vi crawled over to her godmother, but immediately recoiled at the sight. She was ... she was in big trouble. She needed to get to hospital. Now.

'Dad! Siren!' Vi shouted, remembering from her first-aid training at Rimmington Hall not to touch Honey in case she did more harm than good. 'Where are you?'

She looked around for a phone – she could make out little in the gloom, but couldn't see anything she could use to call for help. She scrambled to the door that Honey and Umbra had entered through, found the handle and sprinted upstairs into the house she knew so well from her frequent visits with Easter. Finally, she could hear Robert and Siren banging at the security doors and windows. She yanked open the front door, forcing her father to practically fall inside the house.

'Vi!' he bellowed, grabbing her into a massive hug. 'Thank god – are you OK? Are you hurt?'

'I'm fine,' she said, grabbing his phone and dialling 999 as Siren ran past with her rifle. 'Aunty

Honey protected me. But she's—Yes, ambulance, please. My godmother has been attacked . . . we're at 199 Keyser Road. Hurry! Dad – did you see Umbra? Where did they . . . ?'

'Stay here!' Robert commanded as he followed Siren down to the basement.

Vi did as she was told. She'd never witnessed violence like that. She had no desire to see the state Honey B was in.

The state you put her in, a dark voice inside insisted.

She waited for what seemed like for ever, her mind a tangle of guilt and fear until the ambulance sirens came near. Vi ran out into the road and flagged them down.

'This way – down there,' she instructed the paramedics, leading them towards the basement.

'We'll take it from here,' they said, ushering Robert and Siren back upstairs.

'How is she?' Vi asked her dad.

'Breathing,' said Robert grimly. 'But I can't say much more than that.'

They sat together silently in Honey's living room, until they heard the clanking gurney bringing her upstairs.

'Honey!' said Vi, rushing to her godmother's side. 'Honey? Can you hear me? I'm so, so ...'

Honey B smiled at Vi through her bruised and swollen eyes.

'It's fine,' she groaned, the short words clearly causing her immense pain. 'Find Umbra. Destroy NIDUS. Trust no one ...'

'We need to go,' said the paramedic, pushing Vi aside.

Vi felt two strong arms around her shoulders.

'We've got you, kiddo,' said Siren, giving her a squeeze.

Vi took little comfort. Robert and Siren might have her.

But who was going to take care of Honey B?

CHAPTER 15

'**E**xcuse me, excuse me?' Vi tried to stop the hundredth medical professional who came out of the double doors through which Honey had been taken. 'Can you tell me . . . Is there any news on . . .'

'Let them do their job,' Robert urged, guiding Vi back to her seat. 'When there's news, they'll tell us.'

'How can you stay so calm?' Vi raged. 'Aunty Honey is in there, fighting for her life! Because of us!'

'You don't know that, kid,' said Siren. 'Chances are that Umbra has been watching Honey's every move. If she had what Umbra wanted, it was always going to end this way.'

'But we haven't helped,' growled Vi, sitting

down in her chair with her arms crossed. She'd let her paranoia get the better of her and doubted someone who had been like family to her. If Honey didn't make it . . . No. Vi couldn't think like that. But tonight couldn't have gone any worse.

'VALENTINE DAY!'

Vi winced at the second most terrifying use of her name that day. She took it back. Tonight was about to get a whole lot worse.

'Easter?' Robert asked. 'What are you doing here?'

'I could ask you the same thing!' shouted Easter, storming over. 'I'm Honey's next of kin – the hospital called me! And when they told me— Excuse me? Would you mind knocking the soundtrack on the head, please? This is a hospital, not a jazz club.'

Dave sheepishly took his sax out of his mouth and headed towards the vending machine, his hat tipped over his eyes.

'When they told me that a little girl, her father and a flatulent woman in a catsuit had been at the scene, it didn't take me long to join the dots!'

'Mum – I can explain,' Vi started.

'Oh, and you're going to, young lady, don't you worry,' said Easter. 'Though first, I need to check on my friend. Don't. Move.'

Easter stormed across to the desk, leaving a sheepish Vi and Robert. Siren leant over to them.

'I like that woman more every time I meet her,' she smirked.

'Well, I don't think she's going to like me very much,' said Robert. 'I'd better go and smooth things over.'

Robert waited while Easter talked to the administrator, then intercepted her before she could storm back to Vi. He ushered her outside. Vi watched their animated gestures through the glass. She couldn't hear their conversation. But it didn't look like Robert was smoothing things over.

'This takes me back,' sighed Siren. 'My parents got divorced when I was a kid. It's tough, Vi, but don't sweat it. They'll figure it out. You'll turn out fine.'

'Like you did, you mean?' Vi snapped.

Siren raised a perfectly plucked eyebrow.

'Sorry,' muttered Vi. 'I'm just . . .'

'I know, kiddo,' said Siren, patting her knee. 'I get it.'

They waited an age while Easter and Robert gesticulated outside. After the longest time, Easter stormed back in.

'Valentine, get your things,' she snapped. 'You're coming home with me.'

'But . . . no . . . I need to make sure Honey's OK,' Vi argued.

'I think it's a little late for that,' glowered Easter. 'She's in the operating theatre – we won't be able to see her tonight. They're going to call me first thing with an update. I can't believe you thought your own godmother was Umbra. My best friend . . . What is wrong with you? Now move it.'

'I thought I was staying with Dad,' said Vi quietly. 'For my suspension.'

'Well, now you're staying with me,' said Easter. 'Until your father can behave like a responsible parent, you'll be staying with me a great deal.'

'Mum, you don't understand, it's—' Vi protested.

'Oh, I understand perfectly,' said Easter, with unmasked hurt in her eyes. 'Now get your things. We're going home.'

Vi had already lost one battle tonight. She wasn't ready to fight another.

'Bye, Siren,' she muttered. 'Bye, Dad.'

'Goodbye, darling. See you soon,' said Robert unconvincingly.

Vi tried to smile. She didn't know when she'd next see her dad. But judging by her mum's face, it wouldn't be any time soon.

Breakfast the following morning was a tense affair. Easter and Vi weren't speaking. Vi and Russell weren't speaking. And judging by the amount of time he was spending in the shed, Easter and George weren't speaking very much either.

'Well, this is fun,' sighed Nan, who had come over with Rod.

A big Jamaican breakfast, much beloved by Vi's grandfather, was the one meal that Easter never fused – and therefore, never ruined. But on this occasion, it wasn't the food leaving a bad taste in everyone's mouths.

'Could you pass the johnny cakes, please?' George asked Easter sheepishly.

The basket of fried dumplings was plonked next to him.

'Can I have the cornmeal porridge?' Vi asked Russell.

'Why don't you get it yourself?' Russell shot back, wiping a toast crumb from his new designer T-shirt. 'You usually just do what you want.'

'Whatever,' Vi huffed.

'Change the record,' Russell huffed back.

'Oh, behave, the lot of you!' said Nan, getting uneasily to her feet. 'You're acting like a bunch of kids!'

'We are kids,' Vi grumbled.

'Oi – watch your lip,' said Nan in a tone that Vi didn't want to mess with, however tempting Russell's smirk made it.

'Now my . . . friend has come over to . . . well I have no idea why he's here,' Nan continued, clearing her throat. 'But can you at least do him the courtesy of behaving like civilized humans and let's all HAVE A NICE TIME!'

Nan sat down again with a thud and a small cough. For a moment, no one spoke.

'So, Rod,' said Easter eventually with forced joviality, 'where are your family?'

'Dead,' said Rod, sipping his mango juice.

'They're probably still chattier than this lot,'

mumbled Nan into her tea.

'I see,' said Easter awkwardly. 'I'm sorry.'

'Don't be,' said Rod. 'It's only a matter of time before we all join them. Probably tomorrow.'

'Did you know that fourteen per cent of people think the world will end in their lifetime?' George said feebly.

'Well, the other eighty-six per cent are in for a surprise,' growled Rod. 'I like your garden. Kind of place a man could be buried in. Vi – why don't you show me around?'

'Er, sure,' said Vi, happy for an excuse to leave the table. She opened the back door for Rod and he wheeled outside.

'So – this is the pond,' said Vi, leading him to the bottom of their big garden. 'But don't put your hand in – Mum went through a phase of rehoming mutant piranhas and we haven't fed them yet this morning.'

'Who cares?' said Rod. 'Ponds are only good for garden gnomes and hiding evidence. I've had a breakthrough.'

'With what?' Vi asked.

'Gumfoot – the NIDUS ground station,' he said. 'One of my friends told his son all about it before he died a slow, painful death. The lad didn't know the exact location, but he knows that Gumfoot is buried somewhere in the New Forest.'

'The New Forest?' said Vi. 'But that's huge. And how will we find it if it's buried?'

'We won't,' said Rod. 'We need thermal images of the area, the kind satellites take from space. Gumfoot might be underground, but it will be huge – we'd easily be able to locate it with the right tech. I don't know anyone who can hack a satellite. But I wondered if your father's . . . professional contacts might be able to assist us.'

'Oh, yes,' Vi grinned, feeling a sudden urge for a lollipop. 'Leave it with me.'

'Good work,' said Rod, turning his mobility scooter around. 'And now you need to make peace with your brother.'

'He's not my brother,' Vi grumbled.

'He is in all the ways that count,' Rod insisted as they reached the house. 'He's looking out for you. You might not like it, but he is. And you need him.'

'Please don't give me a lecture on family,' Vi stropped.

'I'm not,' said Rod. 'I'm giving you a lecture on being a spy. Lots of people will try to kill you. Having someone watch your back is vital. Otherwise you'll die. Possibly . . .'

'. . . tomorrow,' said Vi, opening the door. Rod had a point. Umbra knew Vi was on to them. She didn't know how many tomorrows she had.

But Russell was still a butthead.

They went back to the table, where everyone was sitting in stony silence.

'Well, this has been fun,' sighed Nan, rising up from her chair. 'But we'd better get back to Autumn Leaves. They're running a course on weaponizing your false teeth – Deadly Dentures – and I'd hate to miss it.'

'Mum – I'm sorry, it's just . . .' Easter began.

'I get it,' said Nan, following Rod out of the kitchen. 'Families are never straightforward. Especially ours. We'll see ourselves out.'

'Thanks for the meal,' growled Rod. 'It reminded me of my brother's funeral.'

The kitchen returned to awkward silence for a few moments until the ringing phone provided a welcome distraction. Easter sprang up to answer it.

'Hello?' she said urgently. 'Yes, this is she. I

see . . . Is that really necessary? Of course . . . but for how long? Can I come and see her at— No, I understand. Please keep me updated. And . . . thank you. For everything.'

Easter replaced the phone in its cradle.

'Well, Honey's alive,' she said, sitting back at the table and aggressively buttering her hardo bread. 'But they've had to put her in a coma to protect her brain function.'

Vi gasped. That sounded awful.

'She's stable, but critical,' Easter continued. 'She's not allowed any visitors. They're going to call me back later and let me know how she's doing.'

'Well, that's some good news,' said George.

'How do you figure?' Easter snapped.

'She's got a fighting chance,' said George. 'That was all I meant. I was thinking out loud.'

'Well, don't,' said Easter darkly.

George sighed and threw down his toast.

'Russ, do you fancy coming out to the shed?' he asked. 'We could do some system updates on Agadoo – he's been sitting there for weeks!'

'No, thanks,' said Russell. 'I need to prepare for my assessment tomorrow. With Jenny. We're going for a record-breaking score.'

'For what? Biggest butt-kissers?' mumbled Vi. 'We don't even know if we're allowed to sit the test yet.'

'I am,' whispered Russell.

'What do you mean?' snapped Vi, her heart racing. She hadn't heard anything from Rimmington Hall – why were they letting Russell back in and not her? Did this mean she was expelled?

The doorbell rang and Easter slammed her mug down.

'For goodness' sake,' she grumbled, scraping her chair back and storming to the front door. George leant over to Vi.

'Don't worry, Vi – Russell obviously didn't get the chance to tell you,' said George. 'We heard from Ms Direction last night. You've cleared their security checks. They're letting you back for your assessment. So there's some more good news.'

'Right,' said Vi, shooting a smirking Russell a death stare. 'Must have slipped his mind.'

A breezy voice blasting through the hallway pricked everyone's ears.

'What's she doing here?' George muttered, getting up from the table.

'Mum?' said Russell, getting up too. Vi reached

over and grabbed the cornmeal porridge, petulantly filling her bowl to the brim.

'Hey, everyone – hey, Russy!' she heard Genevieve trill from the hallway. 'Can't stay long, only got time for a quick cuppa.'

Vi watched as her mum traipsed back into the kitchen with a face like thunder. Easter put on the kettle like she was firing a gun.

'Sorry to barge in—' Genevieve started.

'So why did you?' George snapped.

'Dad!' Russell reprimanded. 'Let her speak!'

The look on George Sprout's face was heartbreaking. Vi couldn't think of a time she'd ever heard Russell talk back to his dad. And looking at George, neither could he. Who was this Russell? It was one thing to turn his back on Agadoo. But his own dad?

'Aw – thanks, babe,' said Genevieve, chucking Russell under the chin. 'Well, I was just popping over on the off-chance – I got given these two tickets to that new go-karting track – I did their launch, huge success – and I thought Russy and I might head over there.'

'Russell is serving a suspension from school,' George pointed out. 'He has work to do.'

'No, I don't,' said Russell quickly. 'I've finished all my assignments and done some extra-credit work too.'

Vi snorted loudly. Russell was such a swot.

'But you just said . . .' George began, before shaking it out of his head. 'That's not really the point. You're supposed to be taking this time to reflect on your actions, about what you'd do differently next time.'

'Oh, I know what I'd do differently next time,' Russell said, staring daggers at Vi.

'But still—' George insisted.

'It's OK, Russy,' pouted Genevieve. 'If Daddy says no, then I'll have to give the tickets away.'

Russell glared angrily at his father as Genevieve pulled a ringing phone from her handbag. She huffed and rolled her eyes as she answered.

'Lucas, I told you, I can't talk now . . . Mummy is very busy, I'll call you later,' she snapped. 'No, I can't come over today. I have to work.'

'At the go-karting track?' Vi muttered.

'Shush!' Genevieve chided.

Vi waited for her mum to step in. She didn't.

'Yes, I know it's your assembly tomorrow morning, but I can't come, I have to go and see

Russy at his school,' she said, giving Russell a little wink. Russell grinned back. He might be happy. But Vi wondered how Lucas was feeling on the other end of that phone.

'Wh . . . what?' George said, looking at Russell. 'I thought . . . *I* was coming to your graduation ceremony?'

'You were,' said Russell sheepishly, scuffing his shoes. 'It's just . . . it's just that Mum has never seen any of my school stuff and—'

'I wonder why?' said George, unusually bitter. Vi wanted to give him a massive hug. He was clearly gutted.

'For the last time, Lucas!' Genevieve snapped down the phone. 'I will come over when I can! You don't want to make Mummy stressed, do you? Well, then. Be a big boy and I'll see you soon. Yes, I know you do . . . Bye.'

With another eye-roll, Genevieve hung up. Vi whistled to herself. So that's how the other side of those conversations went. She'd heard Russell's often enough.

'OK, then, I'll be off,' said Genevieve.

'No!' said Russell firmly. 'No – I'm coming with you.'

'Russell!' said George. 'I've said no to the go-karting. You're on suspension.'

'I don't care about the go-karting!' Russell shouted. 'I just . . . want to . . . live with Mum for a bit.'

Easter clattered down the teaspoon she'd been using to stir Genevieve's coffee.

'What do you mean?' George asked painfully.

'Well, I . . . I've spent all this time with you and now Mum's got her own place without Dwayne. And it's really cool and she says I can live with her.'

'Is this true?' George asked Genevieve incredulously.

'He's old enough to make up his own mind,' Genevieve said forcefully. 'You've kept him to yourself all these years. A boy needs his mother . . .'

'So where has she been?' muttered Easter.

'Easter,' George warned.

'No, George – I'm not going to stand here and let another parent who has had nothing to do with their child waltz in here and start telling us all—'

'Easter,' Russell said firmly. 'This has nothing to do with you. Stay out of it.'

Easter looked like she'd been shot.

'What . . . what do you mean, Russ?' she said. 'I love you. I want what's best for you. I thought we were friends.'

'We are,' said Russell. 'But . . . you're not my family.'

Forget being shot. Easter now looked like she'd faced a firing squad.

'Russell!' George reprimanded. 'Might I remind you that Easter has welcomed us into her home and *our* family and you have no right to speak to her like that!'

Russell simply stared at his dad.

'Whatever,' he said.

Vi closed her eyes and vowed to use that word more carefully in future. She had no idea how much power it could wield.

'I see,' said George, visibly trembling. 'And this is your final word?'

'I just want to spend time with my mum,' mumbled Russell. 'You always said that was OK.'

'Of course it is,' sighed George. 'I'll call Rimmington Hall and ask them to collect you from your mother's tonight. She can take you home after the graduation tomorrow. I'll see you next weekend for the summer holidays.'

'Actually, Georgie – we were planning on taking a little trip,' Genevieve said. 'I've promised Russell I'll show him the sights of Europe – Paris, Athens, Rome. Won't take more than a month, 'kay?'

Vi looked over at lovely George Sprout. He was a broken man.

'Fine,' said George, looking anything but. 'I'll dig out his suitcase.'

He quickly turned and headed to the shed.

'How's that coffee coming along, Easter?' smiled Genevieve triumphantly.

'I'm just going to pack my things,' Russell muttered.

'Quick as you like, Russy,' said Genevieve, turning up her nose at the coffee Easter handed over and putting it back down on the table. 'Go-karting starts in twenty-five minutes, I'll be waiting in the car. Bye, girls!'

Vi listened to Genevieve's heels totter across the hallway and out of the front door. She turned back to her mother. Easter looked crestfallen.

'Mum?' Vi asked quietly. 'Are you OK?'

She sighed heavily. 'I'm going to work – I'll be late back,' Easter said eventually, straightening up. 'Get on with your schoolwork. I'll see you at graduation tomorrow.'

Vi's heart sank. 'Actually, Mum . . . I haven't booked you a ticket. I didn't know who to—'

Easter looked incredulously at her daughter. 'Of course you didn't,' she said quietly. 'Why would I expect anything else?'

She snatched her keys off the table and stormed out of the house. Vi picked up the juice, then slammed it back on the table. She was watching her family fall apart around her.

And she had absolutely no idea how to fix it.

CHAPTER 16

Later that afternoon, Vi heard the doorbell ring. She ran downstairs, hoping it would be her dad – but was surprised when she heard George Sprout greet the visitor.

'Oh, Tamina!' he said pleasantly. 'I've heard so much about you. Please come in.'

'Hey, Tam!' said Vi, grinning at her friend. 'What are you doing here?'

'I figured we needed to revise for tomorrow,' she said, rolling her eyes. 'I got my dad to drop me round, I hope that's OK?'

Vi looked hopefully at George.

'Well, if you're working towards your assessment,' he smiled, 'I think that counts as schoolwork. Can I get you something to drink, Tamina? A cup of tea, maybe?'

'Wow – you know how to work a kettle?' said Tamina, genuinely surprised. 'The last time my dad tried to make chai, we had to call the fire-fighters . . . but I'm fine, thank you.'

'OK,' said George. 'Well, then, I'll leave you girls to it. Call me if you need anything.'

Vi showed Tamina upstairs to her room and cleared some schoolbooks off her bed for Tamina to sit down.

'So,' Vi began, 'shall we start with rudimentary explosives? I should probably revise my basic firearms too—'

'Stuff that,' said Tamina, pulling her phone out of her bag. 'I'm not really here to revise, I couldn't care less about tomorrow.'

Vi snorted. She wished she shared Tamina's carefree attitude. But in truth, being suspended and the events of the past few days had only reminded her how badly she wanted to be a spy. She had to pass that assessment.

'Check this out,' said Tamina, gesturing for Vi to join her on the bed as she produced a tub of baklava from her rucksack. 'What with every-thing, I only just found this on my phone – but you really need to see, I couldn't believe it, had to play it like fifteen times . . .'

'Slow down,' laughed Vi, putting one of the delicious syrupy pastries in her mouth. 'See what?'

'This,' said Tamina, pulling up a video on her phone. 'It turns out that my plant-based phone charger actually works! I did the stuff that Russell suggested and my phone charged up in the school greenhouse!'

'That's so cool,' said Vi admiringly. 'What's the—'

'So when my phone ran out of charge, I'd been filming my preliminary experiments with micro-bio robotics, like you do,' Tamina began.

'Who doesn't?' nodded Vi sarcastically, earning her a gentle punch from her friend.

'*So* . . . when my phone came back to life, the camera kept on recording. And you won't believe what it captured.'

She passed the phone to Vi, who peered at the screen.

'That's Russell and Jenny,' she said. 'When was this?'

'Monday – the night she wanted him to meet her after supper?' Tamina explained. 'Hit "play".'

Vi did and the film jumped to life.

'I . . . I don't understand,' Russell stammered. 'What do you . . .'

'It's not rocket science,' scoffed Jenny, thrusting an envelope towards him. 'It's the contents of the assessment on Friday. Read it.'

'What?' Vi squealed.

'Uh-huh,' nodded Tamina. 'It gets better. Watch . . .'

'No,' said Russell, recoiling from the envelope like it was made from lava. 'I'm not . . . That's cheating.'

'It's not cheating,' Jenny snapped. 'We want a career in espionage. It's being resourceful.'

'A resourceful cheat,' Vi muttered. 'How did she even get it?'

Tamina nodded at the screen.

'How did you even get it?' Russell asked.

'Dr Scott,' smiled Jenny smugly. 'My family have been paying him for the assessments all year.'

'So that's why you're the top Recruit,' said Russell. 'Because you've been cheating. Not because you're the best.'

'I AM the best,' Jenny hissed. 'I want to be a spy by any means necessary. If you could get access to an enemy's secrets to give you an advantage, you'd do it, right?'

'That's . . . that's not the same,' said Russell. 'That would be to save lives. You're just doing this to cheat the test.'

'Whatever,' Jenny snorted, waving the envelope at him again. 'Are you going to read it or not?'

'No,' said Russell, backing away. 'It's . . . it's not right.'

'Well, that's a shame,' said Jenny.

'I'm sorry,' said Russell, hitching up his glasses.

'Oh, you will be,' trilled Jenny, starting to walk away.

'Wait! What do you mean?'

Jenny stopped and turned slowly around.

'If you're not with me, Russell Sprout, you're against me,' she said. 'And that's not somewhere you want to be.'

'I'm not against you, Jenny – I just don't want to cheat,' Russell insisted.

'And I don't want to plant this envelope some-where Ms Direction is going to find it among your possessions after I tip her off,' said Jenny. 'But that doesn't mean I won't do it.'

'Why would you do that?' Russell said incredulously.

'Because you know too much,' said Jenny. 'And anyone who knows too much needs to be silenced.'

Russell's head looked like it was going to explode. However angry she was with him, Vi felt a twinge of sympathy. For someone with the emotional range of a spoon, this was confusing stuff.

'Of course,' said Jenny quietly, 'you could just take the envelope, we ace the assessment and nothing needs to happen. You keep your place at Rimmington Hall, I keep my place as top Recruit and no one has to know.'

'*I'd* know,' said Russell quietly.

'Well, I don't care,' whispered Jenny. 'Are you going to take it or not?'

'Don't do it, Russell,' Vi urged. 'Don't do it . . .'

Russell looked at the envelope and at Jenny. With a deep sigh, he held out his hand.

'He did it,' said Tamina as Jenny gave him the envelope and walked away.

'Did he read it?' Vi asked, skipping the film ahead.

'Dunno,' shrugged Tamina, taking her phone back. 'He leaves the greenhouse and I don't see what happens after that. But he took it. That's not good.'

'No,' said Vi. 'It really isn't. What should we do?'

'*We're* not going to do anything,' Tamina said. 'He's *your* brother.'

'No, he is not,' Vi corrected. She was still really angry with Russell for the way he'd treated their parents. And because he was a self-righteous idiot.

'Whatever,' sighed Tamina. 'But this has to be your call. I don't care about Rimmington Hall. But you both do. This one's on you, Vi.'

Vi sighed. Great. Another problem. Just what she needed.

'So — what do you want to do?' Tamina asked. 'I've got some great films on my phone. My dad has no idea how to stream TV, so I've got all the channels on here . . .'

'Actually,' said Vi, unable to believe the words forming in her mouth, 'I really need to study for tomorrow. Would you . . . would you help me?'

Tamina gave her a big grin.

'Sure,' she said happily. 'If I'm going to be stuck at Rimmington Hall, I might as well get a decent grade.'

'You still haven't talked to your dad, then?'

'Nah,' said Tamina, picking up a copy of *Fundamental Principles of Laser Beams*. 'It's not worth the fallout. I might as well accept it. I'm just gonna have to be a spy.'

Vi forced a smile as she opened her textbook. Tamina might have resigned herself to her future. But by this time tomorrow, Vi wasn't convinced she was going to have one.

After a long, but super-helpful afternoon of revision, Tamina's dad came to take her home. Easter was working late and George was tinkering in the shed, so Vi made herself a sandwich, changed into her pyjamas and was considering an early night when a light but persistent tapping at her window caught her attention.

Curious, she opened the curtain slightly from one side. She was more than a little surprised to see a familiar figure throwing stones at her window. Vi went downstairs and opened her front door.

'Janet?' she said to Missy's mother. 'What are you doing here?'

'Oh, hello, Valentine dear,' she smiled. 'How nice to see you again. Missy's in the car, she was wondering if she could have a little chat?'

'Er . . . I guess,' said Vi, looking back into the house. There was no sign of George, who must still have been in the shed, so she quietly closed the door and walked down the path to Janet's estate car. She tapped on a back window, which rolled down to reveal Missy in pink sparkly shades.

'Get in,' she instructed, as Janet opened the front passenger door.

'Er – I can't really,' Vi said. 'My mum will be home soon and I'm serving a suspension from school.'

'Yeah – well, I'm on bail in thirty-seven countries and I'm still here, duh,' said Missy. 'Your dad sent me. Get in.'

The now-familiar prickle of adrenaline electrified Vi's skin. With a cautious look around, she got into the car.

'So what do you . . .' she began.

'JANET! FLOOR IT!' Missy roared.

'Does everyone have their seat belt on?' Janet asked, offering Vi a tinned sweet.

'CAN IT, JANET!' Missy screamed. 'GO!'

With a gentle chortle, Janet turned the key in the ignition and screeched away from Vi's house like a Formula One driver.

'What . . . where are we going?' Vi asked as Janet threw her car around a corner.

'SPIDER HQ,' Missy said, slurping on her lolly. 'I've hacked it. I've made you a top-level security pass. You're in. But it has to be tonight. They change their algorithms every day as a security measure – my pass won't work after midnight.'

'Oh,' said Vi, looking down at her pyjamas. She wasn't exactly dressed for a stealth mission to break into one of the world's foremost security agencies.

'I've got everything you could possibly need in this bag,' said Missy, patting a black rucksack. 'Black boiler suit, wetsuit, communication device, post-its in a range of fruit flavours and a pack of marshmallow-scented rubbers – you're covered.'

'Er . . . thanks,' said Vi, trying to get her head around this latest development in her weird world. 'Where's Dad?'

'Meeting us there,' Missy explained. 'He thought he'd better avoid your mother for a while.'

'It's such a shame when parents don't get along,' Janet sighed. 'It's always the children who get caught in the middle. The sweet, innocent, loving children.'

'This is an operation, not *Oprah*! So, Janet?'

'Yes, dear?'

'CAN IT!' Missy hollered again. 'Vi. This is your one chance to locate The Blacksmith and unmask Umbra once and for all. Are you ready?'

Vi took a deep breath and nodded. Yes, she was ready.

And even if she weren't, what choice did she really have?

CHAPTER 17

Janet pulled over in a dark country lane, not far from SPIDER HQ.

'This is the rendezvous point,' Missy explained, handing Vi the rucksack. 'Your dad will meet you here. The access point is through an old sewage pipe – you can see the manhole cover over there. It will lead you directly into a disused staff bathroom on the ground floor of the Secure Containment Facility. The security pass in the front pocket will get you the rest of the way. I downloaded this map from SPIDER's files – it'll tell you which one is The Blacksmith's cell. Get in, get a confession from The Blacksmith of who Umbra really is and get out through the fire exit on the roof. Robert will meet you here to be your techie.'

'And here's something else,' said Janet, handing over a pink box shaped like a unicorn.

'OK, great,' Vi said. 'What's this? Concealed weapon? Explosives? Hidden camera?'

'It's a ham sandwich and some snacks,' said Janet. 'I know how cranky you girls get when you're peckish.'

'CAN IT, JANET!' Missy roared. 'And if you give my salt-and-vinegar squares away again, I'll tell Dad that "school trip" on his credit card was you and Shanice spending three days at the spa! Come on, we're going to be late.'

'Wait – aren't you coming?' Vi asked, taking the lunch box.

'No – duh,' scoffed Missy. 'The extradition treaty that allowed me back here from Brazil means that I cannot be seen to take part in any illegal activity or I risk being returned to a high-security facility in Rio. Plus I've got a bake sale at school tomorrow. We're making butterfly cakes with my friend Lily. I need to split.'

'Lovely to see you again, Valentine,' said Janet kindly, opening the door. 'Perhaps you can come over for a playdate next week?'

'Er . . . hello?' Missy threatened. 'Next week

I'm at that multi-national conference for glitter awareness, duh. Oh, and, Janet?'

'Yes?' smiled Janet.

'CAN IT!' screeched Missy. 'Good luck, Vi. I'll ice a butterfly cake for you.'

'Thanks,' said Vi uncertainly, getting out of the car into the dark, empty lane. 'Er . . . Missy, one other thing? Can you hack satellites?'

Missy removed her lollipop and gave Vi a withering look. 'Can a poodle poop on a pavement?'

'Um, great,' said Vi. 'We need to find something – something big – buried beneath the New Forest. It's the ground station – Gumfoot. We need to get inside so we can force NIDUS to self-destruct.'

'No problemo,' said Missy, returning the lolly to her mouth. 'I'll do it during PE tomorrow. My teacher lets me do whatever I want since I hacked his phone and threatened to put his Morris Dancing photos on the Year Five WhatsApp group.'

'Great – can you send them to my nan? I'll put her number in your phone.'

Missy handed over her pink mobile and Vi input Indy's number.

'Cool,' said Missy. 'See you, dummy.'

'Missy – be nice to your friends,' said Janet gently.

'CAN IT, JANET!' Missy screamed. 'Now let's get out of here before Lily takes all the best sprinkles. MOVE IT!'

Vi slammed the car door shut and watched Janet's car speed off down the lane.

Fortunately it was a warm summer's night – she hadn't even grabbed a coat – but Vi shuddered anyway. It was eerily quiet, the sole sound of the hooting owls doing nothing to relieve the creepy vibe. She heard a twig snap behind her.

'Dad?' she said quickly, spinning around. But there was only a stray badger to answer her. Vi sat on the roadside and opened Janet's packed tea. Her dad would be here soon. She might as well keep her strength up.

But one ham sandwich, two bags of crisps, three chocolate digestives and countless worries about what might happen to her in this deserted country lane later, there was still no sign of Robert. She opened the bag and pulled out the black wetsuit. She may as well get ready. Robert would be there any moment.

But even after figuring out how to squish

herself into the wetsuit, he still hadn't arrived.

She checked her watch. It was 10.37 p.m. Easter would be home by now and going out of her mind – especially as Vi had left her phone in her bedroom, so they had no means of contact. If Vi was going to be grounded for the rest of her life, she might as well make it count. More importantly, the access codes would all change in just over an hour and Missy's hack would no longer work. Where was her dad?

With a frustrated huff, Vi ambled over to the manhole cover Missy had pointed out. It looked heavy and it was – it took all of Vi's strength to yank on the iron ring and shift it enough out of place for her to see inside, leaving it precariously balanced over the open tunnel. A foul stench assaulted her nostrils, making her recoil.

'Spying. Such a glamorous profession,' Vi muttered as she put her hand over her nose and peered into the long dark tunnel. She rummaged around in the bag; she was sure she'd seen . . . yes! A head torch. She attached it to her forehead and switched it on. The long, rusty tunnel stretched ahead of her. Was that a light she could see at the end of it? It was hard to tell from out here.

Perhaps if she just . . .

Putting the backpack on and wriggling through the small gap she'd made for herself, she dropped down in the entrance to the tunnel. The stench was truly unbearable, there was no way she could stay down here without—

Another thought occurred to her.

She rummaged through the bag again and found Missy's scented post-it notes. She stuck one over each nostril. Sickly-sweet bananas might not be her favourite smell, but they beat whatever was down here. Vi peered again along the tunnel – what was that at the end? Was it really a light? Or was it the reflection of her own torch in the bits of water that puddled at the bottom? Maybe she should just—

SLAM!

With a scraping thud, the poorly balanced manhole cover shifted back into place above her.

'No!' said Vi, running the few steps back to the entrance. She pushed and pushed at the heavy iron disc – but it fit perfectly in place. With no handle to grip, and her arms at full stretch, there was just no way to move it. Why hadn't she secured it better? She punched the manhole cover in frustration. She was trapped. When would she learn to wait?

But her spy training quickly took over from the panic. She wasn't trapped. There was an exit strategy. She'd have to go through the Secure Containment Facility. She still had Missy's backpack with her and she'd rather take her chances with The Blacksmith than an abandoned sewage pipe. Dealing with challenges was a vital part of being a spy. Vi just had to deal with this one.

She trudged through the . . . she didn't really want to know what . . . that lined the base of the pipe, and made her way along its dingy confines. She'd been right, there was a faint light at the end of the tunnel – that must be the abandoned bathroom that Missy had mentioned. As she edged nearer, she could see that the light was coming from a rusty grate in the top of the tunnel – a firm shove easily dislodged it with a loud scrape.

Vi looked back to the far end of the tunnel. Was Robert outside it, waiting anxiously for her? Should she go back and shout for him, just in case? She looked at her watch – it was now 11.08 p.m. She didn't have much time. And if Robert were there, wouldn't he be shouting for her? No, the mission parameters had changed. This was her one chance to find The Blacksmith and discover Umbra's true identity. She owed it to herself. She owed it to Honey B. And she owed it to the world.

Pushing the grate aside, Vi jumped up and pulled herself through the hole. OK, so maybe those chin-ups had been useful in PE, she'd never have done that a year ago. She looked around the old, rusty bathroom – there was no one here. She opened the backpack again and was relieved to find Missy's black boiler suit – the wetsuit stank of whatever had been in that pipe and wasn't going to help her sneak around. She zipped herself into it and hooked the gas mask on to her zip. She caught a glance of herself in a broken mirror and smiled. Valentine Day looked like a real spy.

Now it was time for her to act like one.

The door to the bathroom was locked, but her Eye-Spy watch had the answer. She set it to six o'clock: *unlock* – and held it to the ancient lock. The magnetized watch latched on and Vi heard a series of clunks inside the rusty mechanism, but it soon gave way and the door clicked open. Vi turned the watch to reflector mode and checked the corridor beyond. It was empty – she was safe to proceed.

Vi had done many VR assessments at Rimmington Hall and was used to having the reassuring voice of Tamina in her ear telling her where to go and what to do. She really missed it. But Missy's map was detailed and accurate, and she could see The Blacksmith's cell clearly marked in a corridor two floors below. She reached her first security door, removed the pass from the bag and sent up a silent prayer. She held it to the pad, which bleeped three times. Vi winced. Was this about to trigger another massive security alert? She didn't think she'd get away with a suspension this time if so . . .

Access granted.

Vi grinned as the door clicked open. Nice one, Missy. Enjoy those butterfly cakes.

Vi crept into a doorway and quickly surveyed the scene below her. She was in a classic prison block – rows of doors along metal corridors, separated by metal staircases. A lone guard patrolled each level – all the prisoners were presumably inside their heavily secured doors. Vi watched the guards do their rounds – each one had a system. So long as they stuck to that and she timed it right, she could negotiate the stairs without encountering any of them. She waited for the guard to pass on her level, steadied her breath and crept out on to the stairwell below, ducking underneath it before that level's guard could discover her.

She waited, crouched in the darkness, until that one too had passed her by, before dropping down to the level that housed The Blacksmith's cell. She quickly consulted her map. His cell was 112. She looked at the nearest one. 102. Typical – it was right over the other side. She'd need to do more than avoid the guard – she'd need this one out of the way if she was going to get past . . . What to do . . .

Vi grinned as she recalled something else that Missy had left in the bag. She rummaged around inside and smiled when she found what she was looking for. Fitting the gas mask, she opened the pack of rubbers and waited.

It didn't take long.

'Eurgh!' said the guard out loud. 'What in the blazes . . .'

Before the words could come out of her mouth, something more pressing took their place as the overpowering, sickly marshmallow scent polluted the air.

'BLEEEEEEURGH,' vomited the guard, throwing up over the side of the railings. 'That's absolutely disg— BLEEEEEURGH.'

Vi didn't waste a second. With the guard distracted by her own vomiting, Vi crept past and made her way quickly to cell 112. She looked furtively around and held up Missy's security pass, which immediately granted her access. The door opened slightly. Vi felt the rush of adrenaline as she nudged the door open.

This was it. This was The Blacksmith's cell. This cell was where she found out who Umbra really was. This cell was where she proved to everyone she was a top spy. This cell was . . .

This cell was completely empty.

Vi didn't understand. Had they moved him? Had The Blacksmith managed to escape? Had Umbra got to him first?

She stepped inside and looked under the single bed and behind the single bookshelf, even up to the small barred window. But Vi knew.

The Blacksmith wasn't there.

'What the . . .' Vi whispered. This made no sense. Robert had said The Blacksmith was a Category A prisoner – he wasn't allowed to go anywhere or see anyone. Where could he be?

But Vi wasn't alone with her thoughts for long.

Indeed, she wasn't alone.

'You!' came the angry whisper from the door-way. 'What the blazes are you . . .'

It was The Cardinal. And he wasn't exactly pleased to see her.

Vi reached for her Eye-Spy watch to tranquillize him. But before she could, The Cardinal took two massive steps across the room and grabbed her wrist.

'What have you done with him?' she growled. 'Where's The Blacksmith?'

The Cardinal went pale and flustered.

'Shhhh,' he said. 'You'll alert the guards.'

'Well, maybe I *should* alert the guards,' Vi said loudly. 'After all, someone needs to arrest you . . . UMBRA!'

The Cardinal looked around to see if anyone was coming, but the sound of violent retching outside suggested that the guard was still other-wise disposed.

'You leave me no choice,' he said, turning back to Vi.

'About what?' Vi asked, her heart starting to quicken.

'About this,' said The Cardinal, removing a SonarStun from his pocket. Vi heard a low throbbing pulse, suddenly felt overwhelmingly sleepy and then . . . nothing.

CHAPTER 18

The first thought that crossed Vi's mind as she drifted back to consciousness was: what dastardly trap had Umbra – AKA The Cardinal – laid for her? Would she be suspended above mutant piranhas (again)? Aboard an aeroplane set for a mountainside? Cut in half by lasers?

Actually, she was just lying on a bed.

She lifted her head from the pillow and immediately put a hand to it. Wow. That hurt.

As her eyes swam into focus, she could make out a single other figure on a chair. It was The Cardinal. And he was staring straight at her.

'Help!' cried Vi, jumping off the bed in a surge of alertness. 'Someone help me! I'm trapped in here with Umbra!'

She slammed on the door, hoping that the

guard had stopped vomiting sufficiently to hear her. But no matter how hard she banged, no one came.

'They won't hear you,' said The Cardinal. 'That door is designed to contain much louder, much stronger prisoners than you.'

'I knew it – I knew you weren't who you said you were!' shouted Vi accusingly. 'You're Umbra – you've killed The Blacksmith – and Dr Payne – and probably The Wolf too. You attacked Honey B and now you want to take the Neurotrol up to NIDUS to control everyone on the planet! Well, I won't let you . . .'

The Cardinal stood and strode towards Vi. She backed up against the door. This was it. She was trapped in a soundproof room with Umbra. This was the end . . .

'Please take a seat,' said The Cardinal, gesturing to his empty chair. He was less clipped, less brusque, less . . . Cardinally than he usually was. 'I think we need to straighten a few things out.'

Vi tried not to betray her confusion. She knew that super-villains liked to string things out, detail their elaborate plans before making a dramatic exit.

But they weren't often this polite about it.

Vi cautiously walked towards the chair and sat down. Her head was still woozy from the SonarStun. She needed to gather her strength and figure out how she was going to escape.

'Firstly,' said The Cardinal, 'I'm sorry for knocking you out. I would never normally use such force on a child, but I had to stop you from alerting my colleagues.'

'That's nice of you,' said Vi sarcastically, rubbing her head. 'Apology not accepted.'

'Secondly, how did you know about the sewer?' he asked. 'Clearly we have a security breach. I need to make sure that others cannot follow your example. It doesn't reflect well on my leadership if a twelve-year-old child can walk into our Secure Containment Facility.'

'Like I'm gonna tell you!' Vi laughed. 'And I think your job's the least of your problems . . .'

'Thirdly,' said The Cardinal, 'I'm not Umbra.'

'Well, you would say that,' huffed Vi. 'What have you done with The Blacksmith? Let's see if *he* agrees that you're not Umbra – or have you made sure he can't talk?'

'I know The Blacksmith would be delighted to answer any of your questions,' said The Cardinal, sitting down on the bed. 'Fire away.'

Vi was confused. She took a moment to formulate her response.

'You what?' she said. She didn't have a spy comeback for this one.

'I said, you can ask The Blacksmith whatever you like,' said The Cardinal. 'But I can't guarantee he'll be able to give you the answers you seek.'

'Why?' shot Vi. 'Because he's dead?'

'No,' The Cardinal said plainly. 'Because he's me.'

'Well, then, you need to be brought to justice and—' said Vi, standing and pointing at the ceiling before registering exactly what The Cardinal had said. 'Hang on – he's who ... what ... now ... ?'

The Cardinal let out a long sigh.

'I am The Blacksmith,' he said. 'I am the master forger who created some of Umbra's greatest identities. And my own. Although The Cardinal is probably my most daring.'

Vi sat back down.

'So ... you're saying that ... *you*, The Cardinal, are actually ... The Blacksmith?' she asked.

'Yes,' said The ... whoever he was. 'Twice now, in fact. And why don't you call me Walter? It is, after all, my real name. The best forgers tend to hide in plain sight.'

Vi's head was spinning.

'How do I know you're not Umbra?' she said. 'How do I know you are telling the truth?'

'You don't,' said Walter. 'But if I really am Umbra, and you know that and we really are here in this soundproof cell in a top-secret containment facility, do you think you'd still be alive right now?'

Vi paused. He had a point.

'So . . . um . . . what?' she asked. She didn't have a spy comeback for this either.

'Like your father,' Walter sighed, 'I worked for Umbra for many years. And like your father, I reached a point a few years ago where enough was enough. I started to see life . . . differently. I realized I was on the wrong path.'

'What made you change your mind?' said Vi suspiciously. 'My dad had a good reason – me. What was yours?'

'The same as your father's,' smiled Walter. 'Love. Only mine wasn't love for a child. Mine was the love of my wife. When I met her, I knew I wanted to be a better man.'

'You're married?' Vi asked. 'I didn't know that.'

'I was,' said Walter sadly. 'She – Maria – is . . . no longer with us. Umbra . . . Umbra had her eliminated. Because of my defection.'

'Wow. I'm sorry,' said Vi, sitting back down as Walter released an uneven breath.

'Umbra did it to punish me – and to send a warning to anyone else who was thinking of leaving the organization,' he continued. 'And I knew that I was going to be next. So I needed somewhere to hide, somewhere Umbra would never think to come looking . . .'

'I see,' said Vi. 'So, The Cardinal is a fake identity?'

'Yes.'

'And the picture I saw of you "arresting" The Blacksmith?'

'I forged it. It's what I do . . . did.'

'You're not really an uptight butthead?'

'I hope not.'

'But everything I've known about you isn't real?'

'Precisely.'

'Well, that explains the stupid moustache . . . it looks like a dead caterpillar.'

'What do you mean?' said Walter, putting a defensive hand to his moustache. 'It took me ages to grow this.'

Vi shrank back in her seat.

Ooops.

'No one knew who I was,' sighed Walter. 'As a forger I could be whoever I wanted – even Umbra didn't know my true identity. But it was only a matter of time before Umbra found me – especially when I said I wouldn't do the dirty work any more. I thought that would be the end of it. Then there was a fire at my house – and Maria . . .'

He paused, something stuck in his throat. Vi knew how it felt when you really didn't want to cry. She let him take his moment.

'I needed to make amends. I needed to catch Umbra. So I came up with a plan,' he eventually continued. 'Knowing that Umbra was posing as a SPIDER operative, I forged The Cardinal and his top-level security credentials. I walked straight in here. I ordered The Blacksmith's "arrest" and filed all the paperwork – even forged the pictures of it for the papers. One of the helpful things about the secret service is that no one knows what anyone else is doing, so no one questioned it. I designated a cell, made The Blacksmith a Category A prisoner so no one could ever see him, and all I had to do was come down here every day to eat his food and make it look like someone was inside . . . This cell has sat empty and I've been hiding at SPIDER, doing whatever I can to stop Umbra. There's a reason The Cardinal never promotes anyone in his team. No one could have the top-level security clearance to come down here and discover my secret. Why do you think I've kept your mother out of the way in Procurement? She'd sniff me out in a heartbeat. Believe me, no one has better reason to want Umbra behind bars than me.'

'Wow,' said Vi, sitting back in her chair. 'But one thing doesn't make sense.'

'Lots of things don't make sense,' snorted Walter.

'One thing in particular,' said Vi, leaning forward. 'If you're really The Blacksmith . . .'

'And I am,' Walter insisted.

'. . . then why don't you already know who Umbra is?' Vi whispered. 'I mean, it can't be Honey as Umbra put her in hospital. If it's not you, does that mean Umbra is The Wolf? But Umbra attacked him too . . . So is Umbra someone else? Do you even know who Umbra is?'

Walter looked confused.

'Of course I know who Umbra is,' he replied.

Vi left a pause for Walter to fill in the obvious blank. He didn't.

'Well, go on, then!' she exploded. 'Who is it?'

'You have to understand,' Walter began, leaning back again. Vi sighed. Typical spy – why couldn't they ever give a straight answer? 'The problem is – I was too good at my job. When Umbra asked me to create an identity at SPIDER, I created everything – birth certificate, education, medical records, job history – it was flawless. I was the best for a reason.'

'Yes – so Umbra is . . .' Vi prompted.

'. . . as far as the authorities and all their identity documents are concerned, exactly who I created!' Walter laughed, throwing his hands up. 'All my evidence was lost in the fire! So until Umbra makes a move that reveals their true identity, it is just my word against theirs. If I act too soon, no one will arrest Umbra . . .'

'And Umbra will know who you really are,'

said Vi, filling in the blank. 'And will kill you about five seconds later.'

'Exactly,' The Cardinal confirmed. 'I need proof. I need Umbra to do something incriminating. I thought the Neurotrol would force a wrong step, but Umbra slipped through all our fingers at Norton Power Station last year. I hoped Dr Payne's kidnapping would show their hand – who else but Umbra would want another Neurotrol in the world? Then when they started sniffing around NIDUS, I thought I might have enough to build a case . . .'

'OK, SO WHO IS IT?' Vi shouted.

'Some spy you're going to make,' The Cardinal scoffed, a small red light suddenly appearing on his chest. 'Obviously, Umbra is—'

BANG!

The whipping sound of a gunshot filled the air. Vi instinctively ducked under the bed as another shot followed. And another. She curled up, covering her head with her hands to make her body as small as possible, as she'd been taught. It felt as though her whole being was reverberating with her heartbeat. She'd evaded death once tonight. Had her luck run out?

She waited for what seemed hours. As the silence grew, cautiously, she started to unfurl. The shots had stopped. She poked her head out from under the bed. All was clear. She wriggled her body out and crawled over to where Walter lay on the floor.

'Cardinal – Walter – are you OK?' she started, turning him on to his back.

But as she looked at his fixed gaze and the blossoming red stain that was spreading across his chest, it became clear that The Cardinal had been silenced.

For ever.

Vi looked up to the window, where a tiny bullet hole was letting in the midnight air. She had to get out of that cell – she was a sitting target. And Umbra was holding the gun.

Vi ran to the door and hammered on it.

'Let me out! Let me out!' she screamed. But she knew it was no good. No one could hear her.

Vi was trapped.

As she scoured the walls, window, bed, anything that might give her some means of escape, her rising panic was almost immediately interrupted by a deafening alarm – the same one Vi had set off two days earlier. She stumbled backwards with her hands over her ears, just as the door flew open and a vomit-flecked guard appeared in the doorway with a gun to her head. And holding the trigger was a welcome new intruder.

'Siren?' she gasped.

'Hey, kiddo,' said Siren urgently, thumping the guard unconscious on the back of the neck with her elbow. She ran over to Walter and checked for a pulse. She didn't find one. 'Let's get out of here.'

With alarms raging and lights flashing, Vi was grateful for Siren's iron grip dragging her through the metal corridors until they came to where a rope was hanging down from the ceiling. Siren grabbed her close. Vi didn't want to seem ungrateful – but Siren absolutely stank.

'So you had to come through the sewers too, huh?' Vi asked, holding her nose.

'What sewers?' said Siren blankly. 'I blasted in through the roof. Hold on, kid.'

She strapped them both to the rope, then fired a gun at the ceiling, which speedily winched them up to a small bomb-shaped hole. They clambered across the roof and down the long fire escape that Missy had told her was her exit strategy. It was a long climb. Vi had to give it to Mr Repp again. All those ladders were starting to pay off.

They reached the ground and ran into the dark fields beyond. Siren was quick and fit, and Vi struggled to keep pace with her. She was grateful when, some minutes later, the noise of SPIDER HQ behind them, Siren stopped behind a tree.

'Wow – thanks,' Vi panted. 'I can't believe you risked going to prison to save me. You are a real—'

'Kid – I had to come get you,' said Siren, grabbing Vi by the shoulders. 'It's your dad.'

Vi's blood ran cold. She knew there had to be a good reason why Robert hadn't showed. Or a really, really bad one.

'What's happened?' she said, dreading the answer. 'Has Umbra kidnapped him?'

'I wish,' said Siren, a small tear appearing in her perfect blue eyes. 'Kiddo, I don't know how to tell you this but . . . the safe house . . . Robert . . . your dad . . . he—'

'He what?' said Vi, all thoughts on the father she'd only had for one year.

'He's in hospital,' said Siren. 'Someone blew up his safe house. They blew up his safe house – with your father still inside.'

CHAPTER 19

Despite Siren's clear disregard for anything resembling a speed limit, the journey to the hospital was endless. Vi's mind flipped from groundless hope, where she was convinced her father could survive a bomb blast to his house, to dire realism, when she knew there was practically zero chance of that happening. She was grateful that Siren didn't try to placate her with meaningless words. Not least because she needed all her attention on the road at the speed she was driving.

They swung into the hospital car park and Vi practically leapt out of the car and into the reception.

'Robert Ford – my dad – he was brought here,' she garbled. 'I need to see him.'

The receptionist took a long, disapproving look at Vi, but did nothing.

'Please,' said Vi through gritted teeth, her hand reaching for her Eye-Spy before she thought better of it.

The receptionist nodded and started tapping her keyboard. She snorted. Was that good?

'You'll have to wait for the doctor,' she said, not taking her eyes away from the screen. 'Take a seat.'

'You have to tell me – is he alive? He's alive, isn't he?' said Vi eagerly, trying to calm the tears in eyes. 'Or is he dead? You'd tell me if he was dead, wouldn't you?'

The receptionist looked up and peered over her glasses.

'I can't tell you anything,' she said, as Vi's fingers itched around the Eye-Spy again. 'You need to speak to the doctor. And you need to take a seat.'

'But . . . I need to . . . you have to . . .'

Vi felt a gentle arm around her shoulder.

'Come on, kid,' said Siren. 'Let's do as the lady says.'

Vi allowed herself to be guided towards the hard plastic chairs. Siren's arm didn't move.

'How are people like that allowed to work here?' sniffed Vi. 'She was so mean.'

'She'll get hers,' said Siren, producing a set of car keys and dangling them in front of Vi. 'Especially when she wants to drive home tonight.'

Siren elegantly tossed the car keys across the waiting room, landing them perfectly in the bin. Vi tried to laugh. But she couldn't.

After another interminable wait – time must work differently in a hospital waiting room – Vi's name was finally called by a nurse.

'Valentine Day,' she called. 'Please come through. The doctor will see you now.'

Siren and Vi exchanged terrified looks. This was it. Was Robert . . .

'Family only,' said the nurse, stopping Siren at the door.

'She is family,' Vi lied effortlessly. 'She's my . . . mum.'

Siren yanked Vi into a hug. It did not smell good being in her armpit.

The nurse nodded uncertainly and led them through the double doors to a small side room. Vi paused. Good news didn't need privacy. Why were they taking her in there? What had happened to her dad?

A loud laugh from inside stopped her fears in their tracks.

'Dad?' she said, following the laughter into the private room, where her bruised and bloodied father was amusing an armed guard with a story.

'. . . and then I told him, "Call THAT a nuclear warhead?" You should have seen the look on his face!'

'DAD!' Vi shouted, running to her father and throwing her arms around him. 'You're alive!'

'Not for much longer if you squeeze me like that!' groaned Robert painfully. 'Careful with your old man!'

'Hey, Robbie,' breathed Siren, wiping something from her eye. 'I guess you can't keep a good man down.'

'I guess not,' winked Robert. 'Sorry if I gave you a fright, girls.'

'But . . . what happened?' Vi asked. 'Siren said there was an explosion, that the safe house was blown to smithereens.'

'It was,' sighed Robert. 'But fortunately, no one was in it. Mick was at a sourdough baking class and I was outside.'

'Outside?' said Vi. 'What were you doing outside?'

A big grin spread across Robert's face.

'Bin night,' he smiled, waggling his eyebrows. 'Although I think Gary's committee aren't going to be too happy with the state of my lawn right now ...'

Vi gave her dad another, gentler squeeze. Thank goodness he was OK.

'So how did you go?' said Robert eagerly. 'Did you find The Blacksmith?'

'Yes, I did,' sighed Vi, and quickly related the evening's sad events.

'My goodness,' said Robert quietly. 'Poor chap. So that means ... The Wolf is Umbra. He and his sister fooled us. And now he's on the loose with that Neurotrol.'

'I guess so,' sighed Vi, even though it didn't make any sense to her. But then again, what in her life ever did?

'Miss Day?' the nurse asked, coming back into the room. 'There's another woman outside claiming to be your mother. I've told her that you already have one here – her answer has landed her with security. Could you kindly confirm which of these women actually gave birth to you?'

Vi grimaced. Tempting as it was to leave Easter at a safe distance with security, she had to go and face the music.

'I'd better go,' she said to Robert and Siren. 'See you tomorrow?'

'Good luck with your assessment,' said Robert. 'Sorry I won't be there to cheer you on. They're keeping me in overnight.'

'No probs,' smiled Vi. 'By the time Mum's finished with me, I might be in the bed next to you.'

The car ride home had been less a journey, more an interrogation. Easter wanted to know every-thing – and Vi had no choice but to tell her. She filled Easter in on every detail – from the threat to the world if Umbra got to NIDUS, to the shoot-out at the cabin in the woods, which The Wolf must have staged, to The Blacksmith and the death of The Cardinal. As they pulled up outside Easter's house, the blacked-out car that would take Vi back to Rimmington Hall was already waiting outside. Vi was more than a little grateful to see it.

'Poor Walter. So Isaac — The Wolf — is Umbra. I can't believe it . . .' said Easter, echoing Vi's thoughts. She didn't say anything else and Vi had no words left herself.

'Just tell me one thing,' said Easter eventually, not looking Vi in the eye. 'Why didn't you tell me that Umbra might be at SPIDER? That you even suspected my best friend?'

'We thought—' Vi began.

'We?' Easter challenged.

'Well, me and Dad and . . . Nan,' Vi stammered. 'We thought it would keep you safe.'

'You didn't think to let me, a grown woman — your own mother — decide what's safe for me?' said Easter. 'You didn't think that I might need to know that I was working alongside my greatest enemy, one who has a death wish for me?'

'I . . . tried to say that,' Vi insisted. 'I tried to . . .'

'Well, you didn't try hard enough,' said Easter, looking at Vi with eyes full of disappointed hurt. 'I'm still your mum, Vi. I take care of you, not the other way around.'

'I know that, Mum, you're the best, it's just that Dad—'

'Robert,' sighed Easter. 'Of course. Whatever Robert says goes! Robert is wonderful! We know how much you love Robert!'

Vi could feel tears pricking her eyes.

'Don't say that,' she said quietly. 'I love you both.'

Easter let out a deep breath and slammed the steering wheel.

'I know you do, Vi – I shouldn't have said that,' she said more gently, reaching over for Vi's hand. 'It's just . . . before he came, you and I didn't have secrets.'

'Er – yeah, we did,' said Vi. 'Like, you-used-to-be-a-top-spy-and-my-dad-wasn't-dead-but-a-notorious-super-villain-type secrets . . .'

'I mean, not dangerous ones,' said Easter. 'Like, there's-an-arch-enemy-super-villain-working-in-your-office-who-wants-you-dead-type secrets. I just feel like . . . like Robert is taking you away from me.'

Vi looked at her sad mum and squeezed her hand back.

'No one can take me away from you,' said Vi.

'Even if on pickled herring jerk haggis night, I really wish they would.'

Vi and Easter looked at each other and giggled slightly. That was better.

'Go on,' said Easter, gesturing to the Rimmington Hall car. 'Your ride is waiting. Good luck tomorrow – let me know how you get on as soon as you can. I'll be crossing everything for you.'

'Oh,' said Vi. 'Listen, would you like to come? I can try to get you a ticket ...'

'I can't,' Easter grimaced. 'It's my disciplinary hearing tomorrow. And we will need to put everything into catching The Wolf – into catching Umbra. SPIDER protocol will carry on, Walter or no Walter. Sorry, love.'

'Oh,' said Vi again. Suddenly having no parents there to support her didn't seem like such a good idea. 'OK, then.'

'But I'll see you afterwards,' said Easter as Vi opened the car door. 'I think we're all ready for the summer holidays.'

'We sure are,' smiled Vi. 'See you tomorrow. Love you, Mum.'

'Love you, baby,' Easter smiled back. 'Be your best self.'

Vi trudged over to the blacked-out car. She wasn't even sure what her best self was any more. And she wasn't confident her best self would be enough to get her through tomorrow.

CHAPTER 20

Despite collapsing into her bed at Rimmington Hall on Thursday night, Vi was out of it super-early on Friday morning. She crept out of the dorm she shared with the other female Recruits and went to the gym to do a workout before having a big nutritious breakfast – actually, the food at Rimmington Hall wasn't that bad once you got used to it. Even taking her time, she was still in the Great Hall long before all the parents arrived and was so absorbed in *Rudimentary Weapon Selection* that she failed to notice it had nearly filled up.

'You ready?' sighed Tamina, plonking down next to her.

'No,' said Vi honestly, regretting her third helping of protein pancakes as her tummy made an unpleasant squishy noise.

'Too late,' smiled Tam, trying to ignore her father as he came up to them and started taking pictures.

'*Pepkanna*! Smile!' beamed Professor Shalli.

'Jeez, Dad. Knock it off,' said Tamina irritably.

'Hush, *dilum*! Is it a crime to be proud of your child?'

'No,' sighed Tamina. 'But it should be a crime to take a picture with your phone the wrong way around. Give it here.'

Tamina set up the camera and posed for a picture with Vi. This satisfied Professor Shalli, who then tried to grab a selfie with Ms Direction. The head didn't try to stop him once she realized the picture was of the Great Hall ceiling.

'Where are your olds?' Tamina asked, rolling her eyes.

'Couldn't make it,' said Vi, feeling a mixture of sadness and relief that at least they wouldn't be there to see her fail. Because Vi was quite convinced that today, failure was her only option.

She looked over the aisle at Russell, who was sitting very still, staring at his feet. Vi didn't know why he looked so worried – he knew what was going to happen in the assessment, the dirty cheat. She watched as Russell turned around, scanning the audience. No sign of Genevieve yet. What a surprise.

The last of the students and parents filed into the hall. Ms Direction freed herself from Tamina's father and took to the stage.

'Welcome, everyone, to this special day for our Recruits,' she smiled, looking benevolently over the class. 'Today, our first years take this final test to assure their passage to Cadets next year. They are a supremely talented group, and we have high hopes of great things from them and for their bright futures here at Rimmington Hall.'

Vi shifted uncomfortably in her seat. After today she didn't know if she'd have any kind of future at Rimmington Hall.

'So, let's get started,' Ms Direction said, pulling out her clipboard. 'We will assess the students in order of their performance in the mocks. They will be escorted to the VR suite and we can watch their progress on the big screen. Our first pairing is – Agent Stellar and Agent Sprout.'

Jenny stood up, smiled shyly at the audience and headed towards the door. Russell stood up too. But he didn't move.

'Russ?' said Jenny brightly from the door. 'Come along!'

Russell just stood there looking at the floor.

'Russell!' called Jenny, as if she were calling a dog. 'You need to come! Now!'

Russell mumbled something under his breath.

'What was that, Russ?' Jenny said, straining to be sweet. 'I hope you'll be clearer than that in my earpiece!'

'I said,' Russell said quietly, 'I can't.'

Vi craned her neck. Had she heard him correctly?

'Can't what?' said Jenny, the irritation beginning to show on her face.

'I can't do *mmmphmphmph*,' Russell mumbled.

'Oh, do speak up, Russell!' said Jenny through gritted teeth. 'Everyone's waiting.'

'I said,' said Russell, lifting his head and looking directly at Ms Direction, 'I can't do this assessment.'

Ms Direction looked squarely at him.

'Why ever not, Agent Sprout?' she asked. 'Are you unwell?'

Russell bent beneath his seat and pulled out an envelope. It looked like the one Jenny had given him in the greenhouse.

'I've been given the assessment in advance,' said Russell to a sea of gasps. 'It wouldn't be fair to the other Recruits.'

Ms Direction beckoned Russell to the front, where she took the envelope from him.

'It appears to be unopened,' she said. 'Have you read the contents?'

Russell shook his head.

'But that's not the point,' he said. 'Because Jenny has.'

An almighty gasp went up around the room. Jenny switched on a million-watt smile.

'Oh, Russ, you are so funny – gotcha, every-one! Great prank!' she giggled. 'Now let's go.'

'No,' said Russell firmly. 'You wanted me to cheat, but I won't.'

'Wow,' Tamina whispered. 'Check out the sprouts on Russell – the boy's got courage as well as looks. That's so inspiring ...'

Vi couldn't respond. The tongue hanging out of her jaw wouldn't allow it. She looked back at Jenny and then at Ms Direction, who was reading the contents of the envelope with a very stern expression.

'Agent Stellar,' she said briskly. 'These are indeed the transcripts for your assessment. How did you come by them?'

'It was Dr Scott,' squealed Jenny immediately, pointing at their psychology teacher. 'My mum's been paying him!'

'Jenny!' said Vicky Stellar, jumping up in the audience. 'I have done no such thing! No money changed hands. Just a couple of . . . gifts. Can't a parent reward a teacher?'

Vi looked back to Ms Direction. She waited for Dr Scott to get it with both barrels. But instead, Ms Direction gave a small nod. Dr Scott removed his pipe and stepped forward.

'As you know, I have been investigating the Stellar family all year. From the moment I met Mrs Stellar, I detected an antisocial narcissist personality, clear from lingering traces of Italian perfume and the way she tied her left shoe,' Dr Scott began, waving his pipe. 'She was, of course, not a woman to be trusted – you need only refer to the alignment of freckles to the left of her right nostril to know that – but it is plain from the way she parts her hair that she prefers jam to peanut butter, once holidayed in Clacton-on-Sea, and still has a wisdom tooth in her upper-right gum!'

Ms Direction cleared her throat.

'Oh, yes,' muttered Dr Scott. 'And she offered me a Porsche in exchange for the tests.'

'This is an outrage!' Vicky Stellar shouted. 'I will be reporting this to the board of governors!'

'You . . . you framed us!' Jenny Stellar cried.

'You framed yourselves,' said Ms Direction. 'The moment you decided to cheat a Rimmington Hall assessment – and we needed to know if other students were participating in your deception. Fortunately, Agent Sprout has proven he is made of more ethical stuff. But, Agent Tarantula? This will be reported to your superiors at SPIDER HQ, who can decide what action to take. But for now, Agent Stellar is expelled from Rimmington Hall with immediate effect, thus revoking both of your security clearances. I must ask you to leave the premises. Immediately.'

Vicky and Jenny looked at each other, then at the two security guards in black suits who were heading towards them.

'You stupid girl,' hissed Vicky, as she grabbed Jenny and dragged her out of the hall. 'What's the golden rule?'

'Never get caught,' said Jenny glumly. 'But it wasn't my fault, it was—'

'Losers blame others,' said Vicky, marching out of the hall followed by security. 'Winners don't blame anyone because they already won!'

Their voices trailed down the hallway and out of earshot. A scandalized murmur rippled across the room.

'As for you, Agent Sprout,' said Ms Direction, 'I'm disappointed that you took this envelope from Ms Stellar.'

Russell hung his head. Vi couldn't help feeling sorry for him. He didn't deserve to lose his place. He was a really good techie. The best.

'But,' Ms Direction continued, 'it is clear you didn't open it. And your conduct today was courageous and correct. You will not be expelled from Rimmington Hall. But I'm afraid that, without a field agent, nor will you be able to take the assessment. And without the assessment . . .'

'I understand,' said Russell. 'I'll go and pack my things.'

'Wait!' said Tamina, suddenly shooting up from her chair.

'Agent Shalli?' said Ms Direction. 'You have

something to add?'

'Yes, I do,' said Tamina, turning around. 'Dad – I'm sorry. But I don't want to be a spy.'

Professor Shalli stood up awkwardly and smiled at everyone.

'OK ...' he said. 'So, *hayatum*, my life – what do you want to be?'

'I want to be an environmentalist,' said Tamina proudly. 'I want to educate people about the planet and how we can heal the harm if we all commit to real behavioural changes. I understand that you want me to be a spy, but—'

'Wait,' said Professor Shalli, coming towards her. 'I never said anything about you being a spy.'

'Er ... yeah, you did,' said Tamina.

'Name one time,' said her father.

'OK ... just today you told the postman, the taxi driver, the man who served you coffee, you meant to put it on Facebook, but actually ended up texting it to your dentist, you ...'

'Yes, yes, yes,' said her father. 'I am proud of you being a spy. Because I'm proud of everything you do! I always said you'd save the world! And it sounds like that is just what you are going to do!'

'Yes, but the thing is,' Tamina began. 'Hold on.

Did you just say . . . I . . . don't have to be a spy?'

'You don't have to be anything you don't want to be,' shrugged her father. 'You can save the world as an environmentalist too. After all, no one can save the world if there's no world left to save . . .'

'You mean it?' Tamina whispered. 'I don't have to be a spy?'

'Of course not!' beamed her father. 'I've only ever wanted you to be whatever you want to be! You have to live your own life, baby girl! You have to have your own adventures! You have to come home and change the oven clocks twice a year! But this is your story – go and live it! You could be the next Gretal Funberg . . .'

'Ms Direction?' Tamina called to the head teacher.

'Yes, Agent Shalli?' Ms Direction smiled back.

'I QUIT!' shouted Tamina. She ran to her father's outstretched arms and they shared a massive hug. Vi grinned. She was really going to miss Tamina at Rimmington Hall. But she was super-happy for her friend. And all the olm she was going to save.

'So – Vi,' said Tamina. 'You're a field agent

without a techie. Russell is a techie without a field agent. Do you need me to spell out your exit strategy?'

Vi smiled over at Russell, whose smile developed into a grin. He nodded.

'I think we've got this,' beamed Vi. 'See you, Tam. Send my love to the olm.'

'Well, then,' Ms Direction said as Tamina handed over her security pass. 'Shall we proceed? Agent Sprout. Agent Day. Good luck.'

'YES!' cried Vi as she ran out of the VR booth to give Russell a massive high five. 'WE SMASHED IT!'

'That was so cool,' said Russell excitedly, pushing his glasses up his nose. 'I thought we were finished when that assassin jumped out from that lorry – the way you disarmed him with a frisbee was epic ...'

'Only because you gave me the right angle to throw it,' Vi raved. 'And the way you got me out of that underground bunker with just a plastic spoon ... I thought I was done for!'

'You had it under control,' said Russell. 'You were great out there.'

'And you were great in here,' she said, tapping her ear. 'Thanks . . . thanks for having my back, Russ. Turns out this whole "working as a team" thing is kinda awesome.'

'Thanks for getting me my highest score ever,' smiled Russell. 'Turns out we make a pretty awesome team.'

'Whatever,' scoffed Vi with a big grin.

'Whatever,' Russell grinned back as they re-entered the hall to rapturous applause. Ms Direction was smiling on the stage.

'Congratulations, agents, that was a flawless mission,' she beamed. 'I'm delighted to award you both a distinction and look forward to welcoming you to your Cadet year at Rimmington Hall in September. Well done.'

Vi and Russell accepted their handshakes and certificates, as well as the admiring applause from the audience. Vi could see Russell scanning the rows of chairs for his mum. But she wasn't there. She watched him deflate a little.

'Parents,' scoffed Vi, putting her arm around her nearly-stepbrother as they left the stage. 'Can't live with them – except for every other weekend . . .'

Russell smiled. Before they could return to their seats, Vi felt her phone buzz in her pocket. She pulled it out – to see a picture of her nan's feet on the screen. When was Nan going to learn how to take her contact pic?

'Quick,' she said to Russell, creeping out of the hall. 'We need to take this.'

They made their way quickly to the back of the hall and walked outside, where Vi answered the call.

'Hi,' she said.

'Vi – it's your nan,' came Indy's hoarse reply before she cleared her throat. 'Your Missy might be a horrible little madam, but she did it! She found Gumfoot – we know where the NIDUS ground station is buried! I'm sending the coordinates to your Eye-Spy now. We'll meet you there. Robert's discharged himself from hospital and is on his way.'

'And Mum?' asked Vi.

'You want her there?' Indy asked in surprise.

'We need her there,' said Vi. 'Because we need to stop Umbra. And Agent Lynx is the best in the business.'

CHAPTER 21

'**N**an?' whispered Vi in the darkness of the NewForest. 'Nan — are you there?'

Vi tried to pick anything out of the woodland gloom where Nan's coordinates had brought them. With Nan's permission, the Rimmington Hall transport had dropped them at a restaurant in a nearby village for a 'family celebration'. Vi reflected that her family had unusual ways to celebrate. But then again, her family was pretty unusual.

She and Russell had made their way on foot armed with nothing more than a torch.

'Are you sure she's given us the right coordinates?' Russell asked as they walked through the wood. 'You know what Indy's memory is like . . .'

'Good enough to tell everyone about that time

you cried on the ghost train, you cheeky scamp,' whispered Indy behind them, making them both jump.

'Hey, kids,' said Rod, the torchlight revealing that he was on his mobility scooter fiddling with a circuit board and a screwdriver.

'Hello, darling,' said Robert, coming out from the shadow of a nearby tree with Easter. Vi gave him a hug and he groaned slightly. He was battered and bruised – but still had the same wicked smile. 'How did you get on today?'

'Yes, how was it?' said Easter eagerly, giving Vi and Russell a big squeeze.

'We smashed it,' grinned Vi, giving Russell another high five.

''Course you did,' said Nan proudly. 'That's our kids.'

'How was your disciplinary?' Vi asked her mum.

'I've been suspended pending a formal hearing,' Easter replied. 'Until they recruit The Cardinal's replacement, there's no one to make a final decision.'

'I'm so sorry,' said Vi quietly.

'I'm not,' said Easter. 'I'd much rather be here. With you.'

Vi and Easter smiled at each other. Agent Lynx was pretty cool.

'So ... where is it?' said Russell, looking around the desolate woodland.

'Just ... one ... moment,' said Rod as a huge spark came out of the circuit board and it fizzled into life, creating a small puff of smoke. 'That should do it.'

It certainly did something. No sooner had the puff of smoke cleared, than the woodland floor started to tremble violently underneath Vi's feet.

'Vi – careful!' said Easter, snatching Vi out of the way of the growing crevice snaking along the ground.

Vi felt her mum's strong arms around her. It was a good feeling. Unlike the one coming from the ground beneath her as she watched the forest floor literally open up in front of them. The crevice became a crack, the crack became a crater and the crater became a canyon. Whatever was down there, it was big.

'Er – found it!' yelled Rod as a huge satellite dish the size of a tennis court emerged from the ground, rising up above them on a long grey column, like someone opening a giant umbrella.

Beneath it, a vast circular grey building surged up from the massive hole, like a concrete plant emerging from the soil, shaking the very earth as it grew to its full vast height. Vi was transfixed as the NIDUS ground station loomed taller before her eyes, eventually shuddering to a halt in the darkness.

'Gumfoot,' said Russell, surveying the building, from its black domed ceiling, down its mossy grey walls to the rusting metal entrance in front of them.

'Damn it,' said Rod, peering at the number pad in front of him. 'Passcode. Old school. Tough to crack. So many potential codes . . .'

'Pah – you reckon?' said Indy. 'When you've worked in cryptology as long as I have, you know that you don't just have to crack the code, you have to crack the person. And that spies are spectacularly unimaginative when it comes to passcodes. Who was commander when this was built?'

'David Horne, AKA Agent Funnel,' Rod replied.

''Course it was,' said Nan. 'Remember him well. Nice bloke. Bald as a coot. And if I remember rightly, he got married on Christmas Eve, so let's try . . .'

Nan pressed 2412 on the keypad. Nothing happened.

'Alrighty,' she said, thinking hard. 'His wife's birthday – 1208.'

She punched in the numbers: nothing again.

'How do you remember this stuff?' Russell asked admiringly.

'Cryptologists never forget a number,' said Nan, tapping the side of her head. 'I can tell you what my plumber's phone number was fifty years ago. Can't tell you what I had for breakfast yesterday. That's ageing for you. Right . . . David Horne, David Horne . . . Ah! Got it.'

Indy punched in another four-digit code. There was a tense wait. Then a loud buzz.

The doors opened up.

'Nice one, Nan,' said Vi, giving her Nan a high five. 'What was it?'

'David Horne had an incredible mind but a terrible memory,' smiled Nan. 'It was 1234.'

'Wow,' said Vi as Robert turned on a torch. 'Spies.'

Easter's phone suddenly rang out through the

forest, making the whole group jump.

'Do you think you could possibly put your social life on hold while we save the world, dear?' said Robert sarcastically.

'It's the hospital,' Easter snarled back. 'They'll be calling about Honey. You know, my best friend? The one you wrongly thought was Umbra? The one you nearly got killed? The one still lying in a coma?'

Vi watched her dad bite his lip. There wasn't a comeback for that.

'Hello,' Easter said briskly, answering the call. 'Yes, this is she. That's great news, but . . . oh my days, that's awful. Was anyone . . . OK. OK. Thanks for letting me know.'

She hung up the phone. This wasn't good.

'Honey regained consciousness today,' said Easter slowly.

'That's great,' said Vi, confused by her mum's scared face. 'That *is* good news.'

'But she was kidnapped from the hospital an hour ago,' Easter said grimly.

'No'!' gasped Vi.

'No one was hurt, but no one knows where she is,' Easter continued. 'All they know is that her kidnapper was heavily armed, highly trained and wore a black suit with a mirrored mask.'

'Umbra,' said Vi, as if they all didn't already know. 'The Wolf has kidnapped her. But why?'

'Umbra needs someone to control this thing,' said Indy. 'He needs—'

'A techie,' said Russell. 'Umbra knows that Honey studied the plans for NIDUS – she could launch the rocket from down here in Gumfoot.'

'We have to find her,' said Easter, starting to stride away.

'We have to focus on the mission,' said Robert, blocking her path. 'If we destroy NIDUS, Umbra has no plan.'

'No!' cried Easter. 'I have to go. I have to save my friend . . .'

'Negative,' growled Rod, rolling up some wire. 'She's an agent. She knows the score. Greatest good of the greatest number. If we succeed, we save the world. If we save Honey, we might all die.'

'But . . .' Vi watched her mum try to come up with a defence. But there wasn't one. They had to destroy NIDUS before Umbra could get to it. That was their mission priority. They could save Honey later. Hopefully.

Easter nodded grimly.

'Let's get on with it,' she said, as Rod unfurled a big map.

'This is a floor plan of Gumfoot,' Rod explained. 'It's a big site, we'll need to split up. The control panel is located here, right at the heart of the circle.' He turned to Russell. 'Young man?'

'Me?' Russell replied.

'You,' Rod confirmed. 'Seems you're a bit of a whizz with the old tech. Your job is to get into the system and initiate NIDUS's self-destruct system. Activate the Doomsday Protocol. Here are my old security details. I designed this system. This should get you in.'

'1911,' Nan said, reading over Russell's shoulder. 'Nineteenth of November. Our wedding day.'

'The day my world ended, Lotus Flower,' said Rod, kissing Indy's hand. 'At least until it actually ends. Probably tomorrow . . . Vi, you go with Russell and make sure nothing and no one distracts him.'

'But . . .' Vi began.

'THAT'S AN ORDER!' commanded Rod firmly. Vi didn't dare to disagree.

'Lotus Flower – you stay out here and keep

watch,' said Rod. 'I'm going to lay charges around this station to blow the whole thing to bits. My scooter will help me cover the most ground. Easter and Robert – you're on security patrol. I've put a couple of . . . accessories in my shopping basket. Anyone tries to interrupt us – you know what to do.'

Both Easter and Robert nodded and pulled the large guns from Rod's mobility scooter. Vi didn't really want to know what they were agreeing to. But she didn't get the impression her parents were going to be sending anyone to their room.

'Easter – did you bring the comms?'

'Oh – yes,' said Easter, pulling her rucksack off her back. 'Working in Procurement has its advantages.'

Easter pulled out six headsets, like the ones Vi and Russell used at Rimmington Hall, and handed them around the family.

'Testing, testing,' said Rod, talking into his mic. 'Are we all receiving?'

'Loud and clear,' the group repeated.

'OK,' said Rod. 'The charges will be set to detonate at 2200 hours. That gives us a little under thirty minutes to get in, do our jobs and get out again. Is everyone clear?'

Everyone nodded vaguely.

'I said, is everyone clear?!' Rod asked more forcefully.

'Yes, sir!' they chanted simultaneously.

'Good,' said Rod. 'We rendezvous back at that oak tree at 2155 hours. Good luck. And in case I don't make it . . .'

Without any warning, Rod grabbed Indy on to his lap, leant her backwards and gave her a great big kiss.

'Oooh – watch me hip,' squealed Nan, blushing as she was returned to standing.

'Lotus Flower, I should never have left you at the altar,' said Rod. 'If we survive this, I'm gonna do what I should have done sixty-two years ago.'

'You're going to marry her?' Easter gasped.

'I was thinking of building us a double nuclear bunker to survive the apocalypse together,' said Rod. 'But marriage works too.'

'Go on – get on with you,' said Nan, looking slightly flustered as she patted her hair. 'And don't get dead.'

'I'll be fine,' said Rod. 'Until tomorrow . . .'

'Now you listen to me,' said Easter, grabbing

Vi tightly by her arms. 'You stay safe. Any sign of danger, you call and I'll—'

'We'll,' Robert corrected.

'*We'll* come running,' Easter said. 'Don't be a hero, Valentine. Be alive.'

'Whatever,' said Vi quietly. She wasn't ruling out anything at this stage. She'd just aced her assessment. There was nothing she couldn't do.

'Synchronize watches,' said Rod, adjusting his own Eye-Spy. 'And . . . GO, GO, GO!'

They all ran into Gumfoot, Easter unsheathing her gun and heading down a left corridor, Robert clicking his and heading down the right.

'This way,' said Russell, clearly doing a much better job of remembering Rod's map than Vi. 'The control centre is just up here.'

They ran down a long, dark hallway, their footsteps clanking on the grated metal floor beneath them, the rusting metallic walls reflecting blurred versions of themselves back at them. Vi looked back to the dim light behind them. She hoped this wasn't a one-way journey.

They wove their way around circular corridors, all of which looked the same – how did Russell remember this stuff? – until the control centre door rose up ahead. They stopped outside and Russell tried the heavy metal handle.

'Locked,' he said. 'Of course.'

'No stress,' said Vi, setting her Eye-Spy to six o'clock: *unlock*. She held it to the rusting lock, which gave immediately, swinging the metal door open. Vi took a big step inside, but felt Russell's hand on her shoulder.

'Wait,' he said, holding up his torch. 'Surveillance, then action.'

Vi rolled her eyes. Just because he was right didn't mean that she had to let him know.

Russell shone the beam around the abandoned room. There were five rows of desks in semi-circles, each with ancient computers pointing towards a giant screen. NIDUS was clearly designed to be a big deal – this room could easily have held two hundred people. And Vi could quickly see they didn't need to worry about anyone being there. Judging by the thick layers of dust and cobwebs over every ancient console, no one had been there for decades.

'Clear,' said Russell. 'Let's shut this thing down.'

They walked quickly inside and Russell picked a workstation in the centre of the room. He wiped the dusty console down with his sleeve and pulled out Rod's login credentials. He typed in the code, which popped up as green type on the black screen, and the system slowly whirred into life. Vi looked nervously around. She wasn't feeling especially heroic right now. She was feeling pretty scared.

'This is Agent Redback requesting situation report,' came Rod's gruff shout in her ears, making her jump. 'Number off. Zero. All clear.'

'One,' came Nan's response. 'All clear.'

'Two,' came Easter's. 'All clear.'

'Three,' said Russell in turn, still focusing on the computer.

'Four,' said Vi. 'All clear. For both of us.'

'Five,' said Robert. 'All clear.'

'As you were,' said Rod. 'Out.'

Vi looked to the door again. The sooner they shut down the space station and got out of this creepy place, the better.

'How are you doing?' she asked Russell, trying to keep the urgency from her voice.

'I'm in!' said Russell. 'I just need to find this Doomsday Protocol and— Got it! And . . . activated! In a few minutes, NIDUS should explode harmlessly in space. Umbra will have nowhere to go.'

'Nice one!' said Vi, offering a proud high five. 'Well, that wasn't too hard as missions go. Let's get out of—'

'This is Agent Redback requesting sit rep,' came Rod's gruff voice again. 'Number off. Zero. All clear.'

'Oh, for goodness' sake,' said Vi, heading for the door. 'We only just—'

'Agent Labyrinth? Come in, Agent Labyrinth?' came Rod's more insistent voice. 'Sit rep required. Zero . . .'

Vi and Russell both pushed their earpieces to their ears.

'Come on, Nan,' said Vi under her breath. 'Check in.'

'Indy?' said Rod again. 'Lotus Flower?'

'Already on it,' puffed Easter, sounding as if she were running. 'Will file sit rep ASAP.'

Vi and Russell looked at each other.

'Nan!' said Vi, starting for the door. But once again, she felt Russell's firm grip on her arm.

'No,' he said, getting up calmly from the console. 'Gumfoot might have been compromised. We stay here until we receive further instruction.'

He walked over to the heavy control centre door, shut it firmly and lifted the handle to lock it.

'We are unarmed and have no exit strategy,' he said. 'Here we have comms and can request back-up if necessary. I'm sure all is fine. But we stay here.'

'But my nan . . .' Vi started to protest.

'. . . has three highly trained professionals checking on her,' said Russell. 'You heard your mum. This is a time for heads, not heroism.'

Vi grumbled. Again, no need to point out Russell was right.

'Agent Labyrinth? Agent Lynx?' Rod broad-cast. 'Requesting urgent sit rep. Immediately.'

His tone was that of a man who wasn't to be messed with. And yet still no answer came.

'I don't like this,' said Robert, sounding breath-less. 'Kids, secure your positions. Confirm you are safe and the door is locked.'

'Roger that,' said Russell and Vi simultaneously.

'I'll report back immediately,' said Robert, signing off.

Vi looked towards the door again.

'No,' said Russell firmly. 'We stay.'

'This is my family!' Vi insisted.

'Mine too,' said Russell. 'It's my job to analyse the data and make a call. We stay.'

They sat in silence, Vi willing Rod's, her dad's, anyone's voice to come in over the earpiece.

But there was nothing.

'This is Agent Sprout,' said Russell after what felt like an hour. 'Requesting immediate sit rep. I repeat, this is an all-agent alert for an immediate situation report, over.'

'Come on, come on,' urged Vi almost silently. 'Someone . . . anyone . . .'

'I repeat,' Russell said again. 'This is an all-agent alert. If you are receiving, please respond, over.'

But no one answered.

They were all alone.

'Right, that's it,' said Vi, throwing off her head-set. 'We're getting out of here.'

'Vi – no!' cried Russell. 'That's not our mission. We stay here until we receive further instruction.'

'From who?' Vi yelled. 'No one is responding! They're all hurt, or kidnapped, or . . .'

She couldn't say what else they might be. She didn't dare think about what might have happened to them all.

'What if Rod has set the explosives? What if this place is going to blow at 2200 hours?'

'It won't,' said Russell, shaking his head uncertainly.

'Can you be sure?' Vi asked.

There was a long pause.

'Let me see what I can do with this,' said Russell, turning to the keyboard again. 'I can try to contact SPIDER on the emergency frequency.'

'SPIDER is ages away!' Vi shouted. 'My family need us now!'

'*Our* family need us alive!' Russell shouted back. 'You need to stay here!'

'What if it was your mum?' Vi shot at him. 'Would you be sitting there then?'

Russell paused as if the words were stuck in his mouth.

'Yes,' he said, less surely.

'Well, I won't,' said Vi, pushing the handle down to unlock the door. 'Are you coming?'

Russell hesitated. She knew he'd do the right thing. They couldn't sit there and do nothing.

'No,' he said. 'The mission parameters have changed. The best thing I can do for everyone is call for back-up.'

Vi looked murderously at him. She couldn't believe he was abandoning her. Again.

'Whatever,' she said, yanking open the door and storming out into the corridor.

It took her only a few steps to start wondering if she'd done the right thing. Her loud footsteps on the metal flooring below were a dead give-away and she was totally unarmed. If she was to have any hope, she needed to stay quiet. She quickly removed her shoes and was satisfied that her socked feet were far less revealing.

Vi crept along the corridor, her mind whirring with adrenaline and questions. Was she doing the right thing? Should she have stayed with Russell and waited for back-up? Was it too late to go back to the control room and . . .

No. This was her family. Saving them was now her only mission.

She forged on and soon reached the entrance hall where she and the adults had split up. The main door was shut – hadn't they left it open? She pushed it gently.

'Nan?' she whispered into the darkness. 'Nan? Are you there?'

But there was no reply. Had someone taken

her? Or was someone else inside Gumfoot too? Should Vi run for help? The nearest village was a twenty-minute walk away – even if she ran, she'd not be back before ten p.m. when Gumfoot might just blow. With her family inside.

She had to stay.

Vi tried to remember the map – if only she had Russell's memory. She was pretty sure that the rocket launch pad was to the left. If Umbra – The Wolf – were here, that's where he'd go.

She took the left corridor and was only a few steps along when her torch started to flicker, moments before dying altogether. She smacked it a few times, as if that ever worked with any torch ever, before throwing it down in a temper. Gumfoot was dark – really dark. She turned her Eye-Spy to nine o'clock: *torch*. There was only so much light a small watch face could emit, but it was probably enough to make sure she could see where she was—

'AAAAAARGH!'

Vi screamed as she tripped over something large and soft on the floor. Taking a moment to check her body was still in one piece, she quickly turned around and shone the light on whatever had tripped her.

'Rod!' she exclaimed, looking at the unconscious pensioner, slumped next to his mobility scooter. 'Rod!'

She shook him in a vain attempt to revive him. She checked – he had a pulse. But he was out cold.

Vi felt her heartbeat quicken. Someone *was* in here. They *were* under attack. And she *was* alone, unarmed and locked inside a dark, remote building with their attacker. An attacker who was probably Umbra. But that wasn't even the worst thing.

Russell was right.

The control centre was a long, dark walk back and Vi had no idea where her attacker was. Perhaps if she carried on, at least she could find somewhere safer to hide?

'I'll be back, I promise,' she whispered to Rod, giving him a squeeze as she got to her feet again. She crept further along the corridor, trying every door she came to. All were locked with keypads – and her Eye-Spy could do nothing to open them. She was trying not to panic when another dark shape caught her attention on the floor ahead.

'DAD!' she gasped, recognizing Robert's outline. She ran to him and turned him over, slapping his face a few times. He too was out cold. She sat back on the floor.

Now she was panicking.

Vi looked around her father's sprawled form to try to find the gun he'd been carrying when he entered the control centre. She couldn't see it — but then a memory flickered across her mind.

'Socks,' she said to herself, feeling down her dad's left ankle. There was nothing there. 'Come on, Dad, please have remembered your . . .'

A relieved smile crossed her lips as she felt a heavy shape in her father's right sock.

'Gotcha,' she said, pulling the pistol from his ankle. She checked the chamber — it was loaded. She'd only done basic firearms training at Rimmington Hall, and only then on simulators. But just having it with her made her feel less vulnerable. If not less scared.

She carried on down the corridor, checking her three, nine and twelve o'clock like she'd been taught. There must be somewhere to hide, there just had to be . . .

Suddenly, a thin beam of light sprang out of the

darkness up ahead. It was coming from beneath a door a little further along the corridor. Vi's heartbeat quickened again. Was that where her attacker was hiding?

'Help!' came a familiar voice, accompanied by banging on the door. 'Someone! Please help me!'

'Honey?' said Vi, lowering her gun. 'Honey, is that you?'

'Vi?' Honey called back. 'Vi, please come here! Please help me!'

The tiniest alarm rang in the back of Vi's head. She remembered Rod's advice about everything being a trap. But Honey had been kidnapped from hospital earlier that night, where she'd been for days. This wasn't a trap. This was a rescue mission.

She raised her gun again and crept towards the light. A mouldy sign on the door informed her that this was the caretaker's closet – she tried the handle, but it was locked. Was this too easy?

Whatever else Vi's head had to ask, her body had already made its own decision. She set her Eye-Spy to *unlock*, picked up her right leg and kicked open the door, bursting into the room and sweeping it with her gun.

'Everybody – FREEZE!' she yelled, mentally ticking off another phrase she'd been dying to use.

'Vi!' came Honey's relieved voice. 'Thank goodness!'

Vi's head snapped around to her godmother's voice.

'Aunty Honey!' she shrieked, giving her godmother a hug. 'Are you OK? What are you doing here?'

She looked to the centre of the room to where Dr Charlie Payne – still very much alive – and The Wolf were tied up with chains on chairs in the centre of the room. There was one further chair, with chains discarded around the base. The Paynes were both gagged, but The Wolf's gag had some bite marks in the fabric. He looked terrifyingly angry.

Vi was confused. Did this mean that . . .

'Thank god you're here,' said Honey, hugging her as a small tear of relief ran down her face. 'It was Isaac all along! Umbra is The Wolf! He and his sister are in it together! They SonarStunned your family! He brought me here to launch the rocket to NIDUS, then was going to leave me to die in Rod's explosion. Fortunately I overpowered him and was able to detain him – but I've been locked in here and I couldn't find the key. I thought I was going to die . . .'

Vi watched Charlie and Isaac Payne wrestling against their restraints, muffled cries coming from their mouths.

'Quick – give me your gun,' said Honey, gesturing to the pistol. 'I'll hold them here. You go for help.'

'Sure,' said Vi, handing over the gun and breathing a sigh of relief. They were going to be OK. Umbra was caught. Everyone was safe. She watched as The Wolf struggled and gnashed at his gag. She walked over to him. She was feeling a lot braver now.

'So you were Umbra all along,' she sneered. 'You nearly had us fooled with that little performance in the forest. But you don't mess with my family. Because we're taking you down. Aren't we, Aunty Honey? Aunty Honey?'

'STOP!' roared The Wolf, finally freeing himself from his gag. 'It's a trap!'

'Whatever,' laughed Vi, as Dr Payne spat her gag out too. 'You're not going to fool me again. I know who to trust now . . .'

'Valentine,' said Charlie Payne with a tremor in her voice, staring fixedly at the door. 'Think about it. If Isaac is Umbra, who locked us all in here? It doesn't make any sense. And you need to slowly and calmly raise your hands. Please.'

'Why should I do what you say?' she said stroppily. 'You and your brother are going to prison for a really, really long time, aren't they, Aunty H?'

'Do as she says, Valentine,' came Aunty Honey's voice from the doorway, accompanied by the sound of a gun being cocked. They were under attack. But from whom? Umbra was right in front of her, there was no one left to—

Vi felt the blood drain from her heart as she realized exactly what was going on. The double bluff. She'd fallen for it again. Umbra *was* right in front of her. But Umbra wasn't The Wolf.

'It's you,' she said, turning around to face her attacker, who was aiming both a killer smile and a lethal weapon at her. 'Of course it's you.'

'Umbra, at your service,' said the super-villain, taking a small bow. 'Although you can still call me Aunty Honey.'

CHAPTER 22

'**Y**ou absolute and utter . . .' Vi raged, launching herself towards her godmother. 'What have you done to my—'

'Uh, uh, uh,' Honey warned, waving the gun at Vi. 'No sweeties today, Vi. Please don't think for a moment I won't shoot you where you stand.'

'Why don't you, then?' said Vi, for reasons that weren't at all clear to her.

'Where's the fun in that?' shrugged Honey. 'I mean . . . I *am* going to kill you. This whole place is rigged to blow in just under twenty minutes and you'll be locked in here and tied to a chair when it does. But I wouldn't be doing my job right if I didn't make you suffer a bit first. Sit down. Now.'

Vi stood her ground, putting her arms behind

her back. Through the fug of her betrayal, confusion, anger – and disappointment about the sweets – she reached for her left wrist. If she could just set her Eye-Spy to stun . . .

But within a split second, Honey had flipped across the room, grabbed Vi's wrist and slammed the butt of the gun on to the Eye-Spy, smashing it to pieces.

'I don't think so,' she said, forcing Vi into the chair behind The Wolf and binding her hands with the chains. Vi winced as the links brought her wrists tightly together, but she refused to make a noise. She wasn't going to give Honey – Umbra – the satisfaction.

'There,' said Umbra, securing the padlock and patting Vi's head. 'All done.'

Vi fixed her godmother with a steely stare as she tried to untangle the angry thoughts in her head. Honey was Umbra all along. All this time she'd been pretending to be her mum's best friend, while secretly plotting to kill her. The treachery . . . the lies . . . the deceit.

The giant sherbet lemons had been nice, though.

'You won't get away with this,' The Wolf growled. 'SPIDER will be on to you – The

Cardinal already suspects you . . .'

'Oh, silly me,' said Honey, twirling her gun around. 'I forgot to tell you. The Cardinal is dead. I shot him myself. Didn't I, Valentine?'

Vi looked around at The Wolf and nodded grimly.

'You see,' said Honey proudly, producing a small tablet with locator dots flashing all over it, 'that edible tracking dye has been a handy little invention. I can see and hear everything you've all been doing! A few drops in the SPIDER canteen and I can track any agent. A few in a wedding buffet . . .'

Vi inwardly groaned. The wedding. That's why she'd showed up – to put her edible tracking dye in her mum's wedding buffet, knowing the whole family would be forced to eat it. That's how Umbra had found Dr Payne – she and Robert had led her straight to the cabin. That's how Umbra knew where Robert lived. That's how she killed The Cardinal – Vi being there gave her the right cell to aim for. And that's how she'd found Gumfoot . . .

'You took me straight to everyone and every-thing I needed,' Honey giggled. 'And it wasn't like I didn't give you fair warning. I showed you how I was going to do it all when you came to SPIDER HQ. The edible tracking dye. The SonarStun. The VR that makes you see and feel something that isn't happening . . .'

'Your basement,' groaned Vi, closing her eyes as the truth smacked her around the head. 'It's a VR simulator . . .'

'Now you're getting it,' grinned Umbra. 'Once you were in there, I controlled everything you saw. My time as a stuntwoman taught me how to fake a fight. When you left the room, you kindly gave me enough time to apply the stage make-up I needed to complete the illusion for the benefit of you and your father.'

'But the paramedics, the doctors?' Vi asked. 'They must have known there was nothing wrong with you . . .'

'By then Dr Payne had already built me a brand new Neurotrol,' trilled Honey B. 'The one you saw in my workshop was a fake, the whole thing was fake – I only ordered those parts from your mother because I knew they'd lure you to my house. I already had a Neurotrol. I controlled the medics from the moment they picked me up. I could tell the doctors what to say, who to phone – all the while giving me the perfect alibi to follow you, right up until you led me to The Blacksmith, the only person who knew who I really was. The Blacksmith had to be eliminated. And you couldn't have been more helpful.'

Vi's mind was a whirr as she pieced it all together. How could she have been so stupid?

'I must say, when The Blacksmith – naughty Cardinal, I'll admit that was clever – invented mousy little Honey B, I thought she was just too obvious for words,' Umbra laughed. 'But then I clearly overestimated your family, Valentine. Not you, though. I never thought you were anything special. Rimmington Hall seems to agree . . .'

'Whatever,' snorted Vi, trying to ignore the dagger in her guts.

'But we must move forward,' said Umbra decisively. 'I have everything I need – largely thanks to you, Valentine – to take over the world. I have a Neurotrol to hold the world to ransom and – amazing what you can learn online these days – all I need to know to launch the rocket to take me up to NIDUS and control the Earth's population. I've won. Go, me.'

'Good luck with that,' spat Vi. 'Russell has already initiated the Doomsday Protocol. NIDUS is going to blow up any minute.'

Vi stopped, wishing she could suck the words back into her mouth. There were some things it was better Umbra didn't know. She'd just put Russell in huge danger. Surveillance, then action. She was an idiot.

'Thank you, Vi,' said Honey sincerely. 'Looks like I need to pay Russell a little visit.'

'Where are my mum and nan?' Vi asked. She hadn't seen them in the corridors. And Umbra had made no secret of her vendetta.

'So glad you asked,' said Umbra, switching on a screen on the wall. Vi tried not to gasp at the picture. There, lying bound and gagged in some kind of deep metal trench, were Easter and Indy.

'Where are they? What have you done to them?' Vi shouted.

'What any good friend would do!' Umbra laughed. 'Given them front row seats to my launch! In fact, you couldn't get much closer. They're right beneath the rocket boosters.'

'You're a maniac!' cried Dr Payne. 'Those boosters reach temperatures of five thousand degrees Fahrenheit! No one could survive that!'

'And no one is going to,' smiled Umbra. 'There should be just enough time for you to watch it before this place is blown sky-high. The bad news is, it won't make pretty viewing. But on the brighter side, the traumatic effects shouldn't be very long-term. Now if you'll excuse me, I have a launch to prepare for.'

'We will stop you,' Vi swore. 'This isn't the end.'

'Oh, but it really, really is,' said Umbra, running her gun down Vi's face. 'Game, set and match to Honey B. See you in the next life, sweetie. Better luck then. And, here ...'

She walked over and forced a giant sherbet lemon into Vi's mouth. Vi thought about spitting it back in her face.

But a sweet was still a sweet. No point wasting it.

'For old time's sake. Bye-bye, Vi Spy.'

And with a villainous giggle, Umbra slammed the door to the cleaning cupboard shut. Vi heard the lock turn and then sprinting footsteps towards the control room.

'I'm not going to say "I told you so",' said Dr Payne. 'But I told you so.'

'Be quiet, Charlie,' The Wolf growled.

'You be quiet,' Dr Payne mocked.

'You be quiet,' The Wolf mocked back.

'Can you both be quiet?!' Vi tried to shout over the huge sweet in her mouth. 'We have a few things to figure out . . .'

'Are you OK?' The Wolf growled at Vi. 'Did she hurt you?'

'I'm fine,' said Vi, struggling against her restraints. 'But we need to get out of here.'

'Roger that,' said The Wolf. 'Do you have anything on you? Anything at all that we can use to pick these locks?'

Vi thought of the knife in her Eye-Spy watch – that would work. But now it was smashed beyond repair.

'Urgh!' she raged, shaking against her restraints in frustration. She could feel the fear growing in her stomach. Was this it? For her family? For the world? She couldn't let that happen. She just couldn't . . .

Vi gritted her teeth in frustration, shattering the giant sherbet lemon in her mouth and spiking her tongue with its jagged edge.

'Ow!' she cried as a shard dug into her cheek.

She thought of the long fangs Honey had taught her to make with the boiled sweet. Oh, what she'd like to do with one of them now.

'Wait!' she said, an idea flashing into her mind.

She started to slurp loudly on her sweet.

'What are you doing?' The Wolf asked. 'This is no time for sweet treats!'

Vi smiled as she felt the plan form in her mouth.

'That was the sound of "anything at all",' she said, producing the large spike between her lips. 'I need to spit this into your hand and then you need to pass it to me.'

'That's absolutely disgusting,' said The Wolf.

'Probably better than the sight of your own innards splattered around this room!' Dr Payne shouted. 'Stop being such a baby and do what she says.'

'You do it,' snapped The Wolf. 'I have a . . . thing about other people's spit.'

'You're closer,' Dr Payne shot back.

'I am so glad I'm an only child,' Vi sighed. 'Are you ready?'

She felt The Wolf nod. Vi turned her neck as far over her shoulder as she could, tried to position herself right over The Wolf's cupped hands . . . and spat the shard of hard sugar towards his open palms.

'NOOOOOO!' The Wolf shouted almost immediately.

'What?' cried Dr Payne.

'What?' Vi echoed. 'Did you drop it?'

'No,' grunted The Wolf. 'It's just really sticky and . . . spitty.'

'Give it here,' said Vi, stretching her fingers towards his. She felt the sharp point transfer from his grip to hers.

'Got it!' she said triumphantly as she got to work on her padlock.

'Can you do it?' Dr Payne asked urgently.

'Are you kidding me?' said Vi, jaggling the sharp sweet inside the familiar lock mechanism. 'When you've lost the key to your school locker as many times as I have, you learn to pick a lock with anything. Last week I rescued my History of Espionage assignment using a hair grip and a toothpick. I've got this.'

'How do we get out of here?' said The Wolf. 'That door is locked from the outside.'

'Leave that to me,' said Dr Payne, surveying the

contents of the cleaning cupboard. 'There are sufficient ingredients in here to make a small explosive. If you get me free, I'll blast that door open. How we doing, Vi?'

'I'm fine – I'm nearly—'

'THIS IS AN ALL-STATIONS ALERT!' an automated voice suddenly rang out through the control centre. 'LAUNCH WILL COMMENCE IN T-MINUS TEN MINUTES! ALL NON-ESSENTIAL PERSONNEL TO LEAVE THE FACILITY IMMEDIATELY!'

'You heard the woman,' said The Wolf. 'We have ten minutes. Are you—'

'I'm free!' said Vi, as the padlock succumbed to her makeshift key. She looked for the padlock on The Wolf's chains.

'Charlie first,' The Wolf insisted. 'Her skills are mission critical.'

'About time you realized it.'

'Shut up, Charlie.'

Vi nodded – The Wolf was right. They needed Dr Payne's explosive to get out of the room. She worked quickly and nimbly on the doctor's padlock, which she picked in a matter of seconds. Once freed, Dr Payne didn't waste a heartbeat, running to the chemicals that lined the floor of the room. Vi immediately set to work on The Wolf's chains.

'Hey,' she said quietly. 'I'm sorry I doubted you.'

The Wolf let out a snort.

'And I'm sorry I doubted you,' he said. 'And I'm sorry we've lost Walter. He was a good man.'

'He was,' Vi agreed, releasing the chains that bound him. 'But we can finish what he started.'

'No,' growled The Wolf, standing up, making Vi shrink back. He was still quite intimidating, even if he wasn't Umbra. 'We WILL finish what he started . . . How you doing, Charlie?'

'Nearly there,' said Dr Payne, pouring one cleaning product into another. 'We're going to need a blast shield. With no way to measure quantities precisely, I can't accurately predict the strength of the explosion.'

The Wolf looked over to a large metal cabinet in the corner. He walked towards it and, with a single yank, pulled the whole thing over, spilling the contents on to the floor with a deafening crash.

'That do?' he asked.

'Subtle as ever, brother dearest,' sighed Charlie Payne. 'Grab me those matches.'

Vi helped The Wolf position the cabinet in the corner of the room, creating a small shelter behind it. She looked up at the screen, where a digital time count told her they had just eight minutes and twenty-four seconds left.

'Charlie?' said The Wolf urgently. 'Status update?'

'Don't get your knickers in a twist. We . . . are . . . done,' Dr Payne confirmed, shaking her makeshift bomb in a plastic container. 'Get into positions.'

The Wolf ushered Vi behind the cabinet, as Dr Payne ran a trail of her chemical along the floor, eventually positioning the bottle by the locked door. She picked up the matches and ran to join Vi and her brother.

'So,' she said nervously, pulling a match out of the box. 'When I light that trail, this is going to go quickly. Like I say, I don't know how powerful it will be – but as soon as this is lit, we duck, OK?'

Vi nodded. This was no time for chit-chat. They had under eight minutes to save her family.

'OK,' said Dr Payne, striking the match. 'Here goes. You ready?'

Vi and The Wolf nodded again.

'And . . . DUCK!' said Charlie Payne, dropping the lit match on to the floor in front of them and immediately crouching down. Vi felt The Wolf's strong arms pull her to the ground and his strong body cover her own. Charlie Payne's fingers wrapped around hers as she waited with a racing heart to see what would happen . . .

Which was nothing.

'Er — isn't it working?' she whispered.

'It should,' Dr Payne whispered back. 'I put enough chemical in there to blow up a—'

KERBOOOOOOOOOOOOM!

A massive explosion ripped through the room, making The Wolf hold Vi tighter to the ground. The noise was so immense that for a few moments Vi was totally disorientated. She opened her eyes and tried to shake off her ringing ears but the dust and debris from the explosion made it impossible to see.

'Everyone OK?' The Wolf spluttered, releasing his iron grip. Vi went to sit up.

'Careful!' Dr Payne cried as Vi tried to straighten. She allowed the Paynes to guide her to standing — and only fully appreciated their care once she was upright.

Because there, embedded deep into the wall, were the twisted and smouldering remains of the metal door.

'I guess it worked,' she said, running towards the large hole where the door had been moments ago.

'Charlie – you get out of here,' The Wolf commanded as they ran into the corridor. 'Go and get some help.'

'The heck I will,' said Dr Payne defiantly. 'Vi just saved both our lives. I'm not going to sit around while her family is in danger. Put me to work.'

'Negative,' said The Wolf. 'I am in command and I will give *you* the orders.'

'Hush up,' said Dr Payne. 'I am your older sister and I will give *you* a wedgie.'

'We don't have time, people!' Vi cried. 'We need to save my family . . . Dr Payne – your brother is right. We need help. Please will you go?'

'Affirmative,' smiled Dr Payne, running out of the room. 'You be careful, Isaac.'

'You too, sis,' The Wolf called after her, looking at Vi. 'I suppose there's no point in telling you to wait outside.'

'Now you're getting it,' said Vi, taking off towards the launch pad. 'We have to hurry! Let's go!'

CHAPTER 23

They sprinted in urgent silence around the circular corridors. The Wolf apparently had studied the map and it was only moments before they reached a set of opaque glass doors. She thought about Russell in the control room. But he'd be safe there. Wouldn't he?

'How are we going to—' Vi began.

SMASH!

Vi winced as the pieces of broken glass shattered across the metal floor, courtesy of The Wolf's left foot.

'OK. That works,' said Vi as they burst through the gap. 'Whoa!'

She stopped as the enormity of the sight that greeted her came into focus. In front of her was a real-life, actual rocket. It was huge. It looked like an aeroplane that was standing upright, sitting on a giant bullet with two enormous pencils either side. The rocket itself was white with a black nose and wing tips, the bullet and the pencils decorated the same way. Right down the middle, in big black capitals, was the rocket's name: *SPINNERET*.

'LAUNCH COMMENCES IN T-MINUS FIVE MINUTES,' the voice boomed through the station – as if they needed reminding.

'There they are!' cried Vi, seeing Easter and Indy tied at the bottom of the deep well beneath the rocket.

'I'm going down,' said The Wolf, heading towards the long ladder that would take him to them.

'No,' said Vi, holding his arm. 'I need you to bring them back up, I'm not strong enough. Go and find a rope, anything that we can use to pull them up again. I'm going down.'

The Wolf looked like he wanted to argue – but they both knew Vi was right. He nodded his agreement and Vi ran to the ladder. She looked at the bullet and pencils – which were in fact the vast boosters that would power the rocket – and tried to slow her heart. Those engines would roast them like marshmallows in seconds. She had to get them all out of there.

Trying to clear her mind of anything but her mission objective, Vi hurried down the ladder. She could see Mum and Nan were starting to regain consciousness.

'Mum!' she shouted. 'Mum! Don't panic! We're going to get you out of here.'

She watched her mum's groggy eyes take in the deep pit, the rocket boosters over her head, the ropes around her hands, her semi-conscious mother lying next to her . . .

'HELP!' Easter screamed. 'We have to get out of here!'

Vi jumped down the last rungs of the ladder and raced to her mum's side.

'Nan,' she said, trying to rouse Indy. 'Nan! Wake up!'

'What the . . .' Indy said, starting to come to and assess the situation herself. 'HELP! We have to get out of here!'

'Glad we all agree,' said Vi. 'Come on – we don't have long, we need to climb up the ladder.'

'You're joking, aren't you?' said Indy in between the coughs that accompanied her return to consciousness. 'I'll never make it up there. You girls go, leave me . . .'

'Not a chance,' said Easter, grabbing her mum's arm. 'There has to be another way out of—'

'Vi! Catch!' A voice came from the top of the pit as a coil of thick rope snaked down towards them.

'Got it!' said Easter, wrapping the rope under Indy's arms and tying it securely. 'Isaac! We're ready. Wait? Aren't you Umbra?'

'No,' grunted The Wolf.

Easter looked at Vi, who nodded her agreement.

'Oh,' said Easter. 'Good . . . pull her up!'

Vi watched the rope tighten and her nan slowly lift off the ground in jerky increments. She looked at the huge distance she had to cover in just a few minutes. This wasn't fast enough.

'You girls get up there!' Nan commanded as she rose. 'No time to stand around. I'll be . . .'

'Lotus Flower!' came an impassioned growl from the top of the pit. 'Hang on.'

'Not like I've got a lot of choice, you fool!' said Nan, now suspended several metres in the air.

'We're hooking you on to my scooter!' Rod called down. 'We'll have you out of there faster than a nuclear apocalypse!'

'LAUNCH PROTOCOL COMMENCES IN T-MINUS FOUR MINUTES!' the voice announced.

'I won't tell you again,' Nan chided as she started to rise far more smoothly and quickly as Rod's mobility scooter went into turbo mode. 'Get up that ladder!'

Vi and Easter didn't need to be told again. Gesturing to her daughter to go first, Easter followed Vi swiftly up the ladder, Vi sending another silent thanks to Mr Repp. Indy was nearing the top of the pit.

'Rod – get Mum out of here!' Easter ordered. 'You two are slower. And make sure you stop that explosion!'

'That's affirmative on objective one,' said Rod as The Wolf helped Indy over the edge and they zoomed away on his mobility scooter. 'But negative on objective two. The program cannot be uninitiated. Device set to blow in ten minutes! We're on our way . . .'

'Wonderful,' sighed Easter, her footsteps speeding up behind Vi's. They carried on clambering up the ladder as quickly as they could for endless seconds, when Russell flashed again in Vi's mind.

'Wolf? You need to go to the control room and get Russell out,' Vi shouted up. 'Wolf? Isaac? Can you hear me?'

'Valentine!' Robert's voice boomed back. 'Are you OK?'

'I'm fine,' Vi called. 'Where's The Wolf?'

'He's out cold on the floor,' Robert cried down. 'I've taken him out.'

Vi groaned. *Parents*.

'He's not Umbra,' she cried. 'You both need to know that Umbra is actually—'

'Hello, everyone,' came Umbra's sickly-sweet voice as Robert let out a pained groan above them. 'How lovely to see the whole family together!'

'Honey!' cried Easter. 'Thank god you're here – you have to help us . . .'

'Mum!' Vi hissed. 'Stop! She's not going to help us. She's Umbra!'

'Not this again,' Easter huffed. 'My best friend is NOT Umbra.'

The sound of a large punch reverberated around the room.

'Er, yes,' groaned Robert. 'Yes, she is.'

'No,' whispered Easter. 'You can't be, it's not possible, the hospital . . .'

'I'll let Valentine explain!' shouted Umbra, the sounds of her and Robert fighting echoing around the pit. 'But I'm boarding that rocket.'

'Over my dead body!' Robert called back, the grunts and groans of physical combat punctuating his words. Vi quickened her pace up the ladder. They had to get out of here. They had to stop Umbra.

'Happy to oblige,' cried Honey, emitting a mighty roar.

'DAD!' screamed Vi as Robert suddenly appeared flying over the edge of the pit, his body hurtling down to certain death. 'Noooooooo!'

Vi closed her eyes and waited for the awful sound of her father's body landing at the bottom of the well . . .

But it didn't come.

'Wow,' came her mother's strained voice instead. 'Robert? What have you been eating?'

Vi looked down behind her. Easter was hanging backwards from the ladder by her knees. And hanging from her left arm – was Robert.

Vi grinned. Easter Day still had it.

'Mum – Dad – are you OK?' she cried.

'LAUNCH PROTOCOL INITIATED IN T-MINUS THREE MINUTES.'

'See ya!' cried Umbra, running off to the rocket waiting on the launch pad beyond.

'This isn't over, Honey!' Easter roared after her. 'I will hunt you down! There's nowhere you can hide!'

'Whatever!' cried Umbra.

Easter swung Robert back on to the ladder, before crunching herself the right way up again.

'I could have done that,' Robert grumbled as they continued their speedy ascent of the ladder.

'Sure you could,' Easter replied, barely out of breath. 'Twenty years ago.'

'Not now!' Vi warned her parents as the top of the ladder finally came into sight. She pulled herself over the top and panted for a moment as Easter – and with a rather greater struggle, Robert – appeared over the top as well.

'We need to get out of here,' Robert panted. 'We do not want to be in this room when that rocket launches . . .'

'But Honey – Umbra – we have to stop her!' Vi objected.

'And we will,' said Easter, taking Vi's hand. 'But we need to live if we're to fight another day. This isn't the time for heroics. Come on.'

The rumble of the engine thrusters warned them to get moving. They ran out of the launch area and back into the corridor.

'Russell!' said Vi. 'We have to get him out, he could be locked in there or hurt or − follow me!'

'Robert − you get Isaac out of here,' Easter commanded. 'We'll get Russ.'

Robert nodded. 'Be careful,' he said, picking Isaac up and slinging him around his shoulders. 'Both of you. We don't have long.'

'We've got this,' Easter promised. 'This is what we've been trained for.'

Vi smiled gratefully at her mum. It felt good to be on the same side as Agent Lynx.

They ran back through the corridors that led to the control centre. The door was ajar and Vi could hear Russell's agitated voice from inside.

'There must be something!' she heard him mutter.

Thank goodness − he was still alive. They ran into the dusty room, where the previously neat rows of computers were now riddled with bullet holes. Russell was on his feet, frantically typing into each one, before moving in frustration to the next.

'Russ!' cried Easter, running over and holding Russell's face to reveal a cut above his left eye. 'What did she do to you?'

'I'm fine,' said Russell quietly. 'I hid under a desk – the cut's from some broken glass. But Honey undid the Doomsday Protocol. NIDUS isn't going to self-destruct. I have to stop this launch.'

'Honey . . . Umbra is a highly skilled technician,' Easter insisted. 'She will have thought of everything. We need to get out of here.'

'No!' Russell cried, his fingers hammering at the next keyboard. 'There has to be a way – there just has to . . .'

'Russ, it's time to go,' Easter said calmly, but firmly. 'This whole place is rigged to blow in minutes.'

'No!' Russell cried again. 'I can stop this. I know I can. I just need more time . . .'

'We're all out of time,' said Easter more urgently. 'We have to go, Russell. I need to get you out of here. I need to get you back to your parents.'

'I can stop this!' Russell cried. 'I know I can!'

Vi walked over and put her hands gently over his.

'You were right,' she said. 'This is a time for heads, not heroism. Please, Russell. This is a battle, not the war. And we can't do anything if we're dead. We need an exit strategy. We need you.'

Russell looked up at Vi, who smiled back at him.

'Come on,' she said. 'Let's get out of here.'

With a heavy sigh, Russell stood up from the console.

'LAUNCHING!' the automated voice announced as the whole station started to tremble. 'LAUNCHING!'

The screen suddenly lit up with the roar of the rocket boosters. Vi clung to a nearby desk as the ground shook beneath them. They all watched as the rocket rose majestically from the pad and out through the open roof into the dark night sky. Umbra had done it. She'd got away. She was on her way to NIDUS and now there was no way of stopping her.

Vi shook her head. Failure was the world's only option. Umbra had won.

'This way,' said Easter, ushering them through the door. 'Hurry!'

They raced back along the narrow corridor and towards the entrance, where the cool night air promised safety.

'Over here!' cried Robert's voice from a distance as they raced out of Gumfoot.

Vi, Easter and Russell started sprinting towards Robert and the paramedics Charlie Payne had clearly summoned. They were nearly there, they were nearly safe, they were nearly—

'Aaaaaargh!' cried Russell as he tripped and went flying along the woodland floor. Vi turned to see him sprawled on the ground, feeling around for his glasses.

'Russell!' she cried, running back for him.

'You go!' he said, desperately trying to find the glasses without which he could barely see. 'I'll be fine.'

'*We'll* be fine,' said Vi, picking him up off the ground. 'Turns out we make a pretty awesome team.'

She put Russell's arm around her shoulder and dragged him towards the safety of the trees beyond. They were so nearly there . . .

'Vi!' screamed Easter from several metres ahead, where her long strides had already taken her. 'Russ! Look out – Gumfoot is going to—'

But whatever her mum was warning was lost to the almighty blast of the explosion behind them.

'WHOOOOOOOOAAAAAAA!' Vi screamed as she was propelled through the air by the force of the blast, before hitting something far too hard, far too fast.

The world went a little dark for a moment. Was she dead? She guessed it wouldn't hurt this much if she were. A searing pain in her forehead threw her back to consciousness, as a strong pair of arms picked her up off the ground.

'Valentine!' she heard her father's voice shout. 'Vi – are you OK?'

'Ouch,' Vi groaned, raising a hand to her head. 'That hurt. Did you feel that, Russell? That was . . . Russell? Russ?'

'It's OK,' said Robert unconvincingly. 'You just stay there.'

'That was a very brave thing you did,' said Indy, taking her hand as Rod scooted over. 'But you've taken a nasty knock to the head. Stay down.'

'Russell?' Vi cried, pulling herself up to her

elbows, despite her head making the whole world spin. 'Russ?!'

She looked over to where Easter, Isaac and a paramedic were huddled around a very still, very small body on the floor.

'RUSS!' she screamed, getting unsteadily to her feet and running over to Russell's lifeless form.

'Don't move him!' the paramedic warned as Vi approached. 'Just— don't move him. We need to get him to hospital. Now.'

'How?' Easter cried. 'We're in the middle of nowhere – the nearest hospital is over an hour away, how are we ever going to—'

Suddenly, the sky was filled with light and noise as a flock of helicopters filled the night sky.

'THIS IS SPIDER!' a voice cried over a mega-phone. 'PLEASE RAISE YOUR HANDS AND IDENTIFY YOURSELVES IMMEDIATELY!'

'SPIDER?' Easter said. 'How did they find—'

'Russell,' said Vi, trying to keep the tears out of her voice. 'He said he was going to call for back-up on SPIDER's emergency frequency. He must have done it.'

'Brilliant boy,' said Easter, tenderly stroking his face as Isaac stood up.

'This is Agent Wolf, operative number 7985784,' he barked. 'Agent down, seriously wounded. Request immediate transfer to nearest medical facility. Agent Lynx, operative number 79985748 in attendance.'

There was a brief silence.

'IDENTITY CONFIRMED,' the voice boomed back. 'Medical assistance being dispatched.'

A series of ropes dropped out of the nearest helicopters, with SPIDER operatives dropping deftly down them. They ran to Russell's side as he emitted a gentle groan.

'Russ?' Easter said frantically. 'He's coming to! Russ? Can you hear us?'

'Agent Sprout?' the medic said. 'I'm Agent Weaver, SPIDER's field medic. Where are you hurt?'

'Everywhere,' Russell panted. 'I can't . . . I can't breathe properly . . .'

'We're going to take care of you,' Agent Weaver replied. She turned to Easter. 'Where are his parents? We'll need their permission to operate.'

'They're not here,' Easter flustered. 'I live with his father, but I'll need to contact him . . .'

Russell's hand reached out and held Easter's.

'She is my parent,' he gasped to Agent Weaver. 'Easter is my stepmum.'

Easter clung to his hand as the tears started to roll down her face. Russell slipped into unconsciousness again.

'We can help him, but we have to hurry,' said Agent Weaver. 'I think he's punctured a lung. Please, everyone stand back.'

They all did as they were told, allowing the medics to work their efficient magic as Russell was loaded carefully on to a stretcher and winched up into the helicopter.

'Who's coming with him?' Agent Weaver asked.

'I am,' said Easter and Vi together.

'We'll follow on behind,' said Robert. 'I'll make sure your mother gets home safely.'

'You? You're a complete idiot,' said Indy, shrugging off the blanket the paramedic had put around her shoulders.

'You're welcome,' smiled Robert.

Vi felt expert hands fit her harness, then attach the winch that would transport her up to the chopper. It was a long way up. Her stomach lurched as Easter's hand found hers.

'Is Russell going to be OK?' Vi asked Agent Weaver.

'If I have anything to do with it,' smiled the SPIDER agent. 'You ready?'

'She was born ready,' Easter smiled back, squeezing Vi's hand. The signal was given and with a huge jolt, Vi felt her body shoot up into the night sky.

'WHOOOOOOAAAAAAAA!' Vi screamed, the adrenaline flooding her body as she was carried higher into the darkness. 'It's like flying!'

'Then fly, baby,' Easter grinned as they zoomed through the starlit night. 'You just fly . . .'

CHAPTER 24

The wedding day came around in a flash. It was a beautiful day and welcomed by all after the tumultuous recent past. The ceremony passed without incident and Vi shed a few happy tears. It was great having something so joyful for her family to celebrate. And she hadn't had to wear a stupid bridesmaid's dress.

'I wish I'd had time to do the food myself,' Easter said anxiously, watching the caterers tend to the select group of guests at the reception. 'It's so impersonal . . .'

'Better than so inedible,' quipped Indy, stealing a canapé from a passing waiter. 'Besides, there wasn't time to faff about with only two days to plan.'

'And whose fault was that?' Easter chided. 'You're the one who was in a great big hurry. I couldn't see the rush, personally.'

'You wouldn't,' Indy muttered. A distracted Easter didn't hear her, but Vi did. What did her nan mean?

'So how's my beautiful wife?' came the groom's voice behind them.

'She's starving,' came the reply as the newly-weds shared a gross, but quite sweet, little kiss. Vi smiled at the happy couple. Nan and Rod were going to be really great together.

'Congratulations, you two,' said Easter, raising her glass. 'And, Rod, welcome to our patchwork family. Thanks so much for hosting the reception in your lovely home.'

Vi looked around the splendour of Rod's grand mansion. For someone who'd spent most of his life thinking the world was going to end, he'd certainly invested in some nice property.

'Happy to have you all here,' said Rod. 'After all, tomorrow . . .'

'. . . will probably be the end of the world. We know, you old misery,' Nan chided.

'I was going to say, "is the start of the rest of my life",' Rod replied. 'But do you know something I don't—'

Vi giggled as Nan swatted her new husband

with her bridal bouquet. Rod was going to fit in just fine.

A nearby waiter with their back to them suddenly whispered out loud.

'Are we secure?' he asked. 'Urgent briefing requested.'

Vi rolled her eyes. *Spies*.

'Don't you ever take a day off?' Easter sighed. 'What can I do for you, Isaac?'

The Wolf turned to check no one was listening.

'Forgive me for infiltrating your day, but I bring important comms,' he began.

'You didn't have to infiltrate it, you prune!' Nan cried. 'I sent you a bloomin' invite. But congrats on the promotion. You'll be a fantastic head of SPIDER.'

'Thank you, Agent Labyrinth,' growled The Wolf. 'But this isn't a social call. I am assembling an elite team to help us defeat Umbra. I'd like you all to be a part of it.'

'Count me in,' growled Rod. 'It would be my pleasure to die in the line of duty.'

'Thank you, Agent Redback,' The Wolf nodded. 'Your expertise and knowledge of NIDUS will be invaluable. Yours too, Agent Labyrinth. SPIDER has dismissed our retired agents for too long. You possess a wealth of expertise we've been foolish not to utilize. I would greatly value your input going forward – and will of course ensure you are fully compensated for your time.'

'Good lad,' said Indy approvingly. 'That'll help down the bingo.'

'We are accelerating our efforts to pursue Umbra,' said The Wolf. 'A special team is being fast-tracked for space travel and we are in advanced negotiations to secure a suitable shuttle. With our space programme shut down many years ago, we simply aren't equipped for this eventuality. But we're working on it. We're trying to remain positive and proactive. And all of you will be vital to our success.'

Vi tried to smile and share The Wolf's confidence. Umbra had been in space for two days. She had a massive head start – SPIDER didn't even have a spacecraft yet. How were they ever going to catch her before she could reach NIDUS and use the Neurotrol to hold the world to ransom?

'I'm afraid I can't help you,' said Easter sadly. 'I'm still on suspension – I'm not cleared for active duty.'

'Negative,' said The Wolf, looking suspiciously at a nearby wedding guest. 'Your suspension has been revoked with immediate effect. Plus you are returned to your former rank of commander.'

'But . . . what about Procurement?' Easter asked. 'I can't just leave it, it's a vital cog in the machine.'

The Wolf snorted.

'You will be relieved by Agent Tarantula,' he said, something resembling a smile crossing his lips.

'What? Jenny's mum?' Vi exclaimed. 'Vicky Stellar's going into the cupboard?'

'Agent Tarantula will be undergoing some . . . professional development for the foreseeable future,' The Wolf replied. 'If you'd be kind enough to show her the ropes on Monday?'

'Oh, it will be my absolute pleasure,' said Easter, a big grin spreading across her face. 'George! George! I'm back in the field!'

'Great,' said George uncertainly, pushing Russell over in his wheelchair. 'But you all need to be careful. I don't want to be collecting anyone else from hospital.'

'Dad, I'm fine,' Russell sighed, pushing his glasses up his nose. 'It's just a couple of cracked ribs. You heard what the doctor said – I'll make a full recovery. Just . . . chill.'

Russell looked at Vi and winked. He started to laugh – but stopped and clutched his ribs with a painful gasp.

'You see?' said George. 'This is what I mean. There's no way you can go on this trip with your mother now – you're just not up to it . . .'

'George,' said Easter, putting her arms around his shoulders. 'I think our kids have proven beyond a shadow of a doubt that they can take care of themselves. Let him go. It'll be good for him.'

George Sprout looked far from convinced. But before he could say anything, his phone rang.

'Sorry, everyone,' he said. 'Thought I'd switched it off . . . Hello . . . Oh, hi. Yes, he's here. I'll put him on.'

George handed the phone over to Russell with a forced smile.

'It's your mum,' he said, as Easter gave Russell a gentle kiss on his head.

'Hi, Mum,' said Russell brightly. 'Can't wait to see you – I'm all packed and I'll be ready for you at— Oh.'

George and Easter dropped their heads.

Another 'Oh'. Vi watched Russell's face start to crumble. Surely Genevieve wouldn't let him down again? Surely she'd learnt her lesson? Surely . . .

'So you're back with Dwayne?' Russell said, his whole body starting to slump. 'Of course I'm happy for you, that's great. It's just . . . no, honestly, I'm fine, the doctor said that I'll be able to . . . I'm sure Lucas has missed you, but so do . . . No. No, I'm not trying to be selfish. I understand, I do. But perhaps, when you've spent your quality time together we could . . . oh. OK. Yeah, we'll speak then. Mum? OK. Bye, then . . .'

Russell's arm dropped to his lap, the phone still in his hand. Vi could see the tears building in his eyes. A murderous George took the phone and put his hand on Russell's shoulder as Easter gave Russell a big hug. Russell's hand instinctively went to his ribs. But Vi knew that wasn't where he was hurting the most.

'Russell,' said Rod, 'there's something I've been meaning to show you. Something I'd like to show you all . . .'

'Hello, everyone,' said Robert, grabbing a glass of champagne from a passing waiter. 'Sorry I'm late to get you, Vi. I was meeting my new neighbour.'

'New neighbour?' Vi asked. 'What about Gary?'

'Oh, I'm afraid the residents' committee evicted him after they received an anonymous tip-off that he didn't have the correct planning permission for his conservatory,' said Robert with a wicked twinkle in his eye.

'Anonymous, huh?' Vi grinned.

'Absolutely,' winked Robert.

'Robert, why don't you tag along as well?' said Rod. 'I think you'll be interested.'

The group exchanged shrugs as Rod scooted away down his wood-panelled hallway ahead of Robert. Vi, Russell, Easter, Indy, George and The Wolf followed behind curiously.

They came to a large library. Rod drove over to a shelf of encyclopedias.

'It might surprise you to know,' he said, 'that I have been concerned for some time about an extinction-level event hitting Planet Earth and destroying everyone and everything on it.'

'You kept that quiet,' said Indy sarcastically.

'When SPIDER let me go, they paid me a vast

sum of money for my silence,' he said. 'It's how I bought this house. It's how I've lived these past forty years. But there was more money than I knew what to do with. So I decided to put it to good use. I decided to prepare for the end of the world.'

'Saints preserve us,' said Nan, throwing back the last of her champagne. 'So what did you chuck it all away on? A nuclear bunker? Fifty years' worth of beans? A thousand pairs of elasticated leather trousers?'

'Only some of it, Lotus Flower,' Rod replied. 'I joined SPIDER to realize a dream of going into space. And if the world is going to end, I want a decent seat.'

'Oh, my,' said George excitedly. 'Have you got a Celestron Nexstar 8SE Telescope? Its single fork arm mount is nothing short of revolutionary.'

'I have several,' growled Rod. 'Useful for stargazing. And watching out for asteroids that could destroy all life. But I don't want to watch the end of the world from down here. I want to watch it . . . from up there.'

'The upstairs loo?' Nan said, following his pointed finger. 'I'm not sure you'll get the best view of the apocalypse from the bog, love.'

'Not there, Lotus Flower,' Rod said, kissing Indy's hand. 'From space.'

Nan snorted like a horse.

'You silly old coot!' she said. 'To watch it from space, you'd need a—'

'Space shuttle,' said The Wolf, staring intently at Rod. 'Agent Redback, you were the foremost space technician of your age. You were integral to designing the *Spinneret* for NIDUS. Very few people alive know as much about the mechanics of space travel as you. Indeed, you are one of very few people alive who would have the knowledge to build a spacecraft. All you'd need is . . .'

'A huge amount of money,' Rod smiled. 'And a fair bit of spare time. It's amazing how much of it passes when you're waiting for the end of the world.'

'Hang on,' said Vi, her brain trying to fit the pieces together. 'Are you trying to tell us that you've spent all of these years building . . . a spaceship?'

'A space shuttle,' smiled Rod, pulling one of the encyclopedias out of the wall. 'But you get the idea.'

As the heavy book clicked back into place, the whole side of the vast library wall split down the middle and opened up to reveal a vast space very much like one Vi had recently seen. It was huge, metallic, and had a domed glass ceiling showing the glittering starlit evening above them.

And sitting in the middle of it was an enormous aeroplane, standing on its butt with a giant bullet and two massive pencils.

'Ladies and gentlemen,' grinned Rod, 'may I introduce . . . the *Moonbreaker*!'

He flicked a switch and the launch pad lit up, to reveal a fully operational control centre beyond the screens.

'So,' said Rod, sitting back in his mobility scooter. 'Anyone wanna go get Umbra?'

'YES!' came the roaring reply from everyone in the room as they all erupted in hugs and cheers.

Vi looked around the happy group and felt her heart swell with pride. Umbra wasn't getting away with anything.

Because this family was awesome.

And this family was going to save the world.

Whatever.

END OF MISSION 2

MISSION REPORT 2

Hey there, Vi's Spies!

Another mission comes to an end – and with only one more left, who knows what's in store for Vi and her family . . . ? It's been an uncertain time for us all, hasn't it? But I'm so grateful that I've had these fun adventures to write and so many lovely people to help me on the way. My thanks, as always, must first go to Chicken House and all who cluck in her, especially my Super Ed Rachel Leyshon and my publicist Jazz Bartlett Love who somehow managed to get *Vi Spy: Licence to Chill* to my wonderful readers in the midst of a gloomy winter lockdown – now that was quite the mission. My enormous thanks to Jez Tuya, too, for creating his wonderful artwork and bringing Vi to life so perfectly with Helen Crawford-White and Steve Wells' brilliant designs. I sincerely hope my books will be judged by your brilliant covers.

I have the best techies in my ear at all times and must thank my agent Veronique for always helping me to define my mission parameters. My gorgeous family are forever beside me to equip me with everything I need for my missions and I love you all to NIDUS and back. This book is dedicated to the man who is my fiancé at the time of writing and will hopefully be my husband by the time of reading. But even if we continue to have more dates for our wedding than Rod has for the end of the world, Johnny B, you will forever be my love. And a fantastic source of random general knowledge. I really should use that in a book one day . . . I am also indebted to Dilly, my youngest Recruit, whose brilliant imagination developed Missy Fit. A cute 10-year-old girl who is secretly an evil mastermind? I have no idea where you get your ideas, baby girl. But I love them. And you. Even more than chocolate toast.

I so hope you've enjoyed Vi's second mission and will be with her for her third and final one soon. Thank you, thank you for all your love and support for this new series during these testing times — I have the best readers in the world, FACT.

Love, and . . . whatever,

Maz

xxx

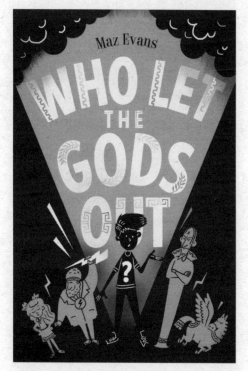

WHO LET THE GODS OUT?

When Elliot wished upon a star, he didn't expect a constellation to crash into his dung heap. Virgo thinks she's perfect. Elliot doesn't. Together they release Thanatos, evil Daemon of Death. Epic fail.

The need the King of the Gods and his noble steed. They get a chubby Zeus and his high horse Pegasus.

Are the Gods really ready to save the world? And is the world really ready for the Gods?

> . . . lashings of adventure, the Olympic gods
> as you've never seen them before and a
> wonderfully British sense of humour.
> FIONA NOBLE, THE BOOKSELLER

Paperback, ISBN 978-1-910655-41-2, £6.99 • ebook, ISBN 978-1-910655-64-1, £6.99

SPACE ODDITY by CHRISTOPHER EDGE
Illustrated by Ben Mantle

You might think that this story is going to be an inter-galactic adventure filled with UFOs, black holes, killer robots and some very foul-smelling aliens. And you'd be right. But it's mostly about a boy called Jake, his embarrassing dad, and the mind-boggling question . . . are we really alone in the universe?

. . . a bright, brainy book.
THE TIMES

Paperback, ISBN 978-1-912626-86-1, £6.99 • ebook, ISBN 978-1-913322-50-2, £6.99

BEETLE BOY by M. G. LEONARD

Darkus can't believe his eyes when a huge insect drops out of the trouser leg of his horrible new neighbour. It's a giant beetle – and it seems to want to communicate.

But how can a boy be friends with a beetle? And what does a beetle have to do with the disappearance of his dad and the arrival of Lucretia Cutter, with her taste for creepy jewellery?

A darkly funny Dahl-esque adventure.
KATHERINE WOODFINE

A wonderful book, full to the brim
with very cool beetles!
THE GUARDIAN

Paperback, ISBN 978-1-910002-70-4, £6.99 • ebook, ISBN 978-1-910002-98-8, £6.99